WOOED BY THE WALLFLOWER

Perks of Being an Heiress, Book 4

By Jillian Eaton

Dragonblade Publishing, Inc. is an imprint of Kathryn Le Veque Novels, Inc.
P.O. Box 7968
La Verne CA 91750
ceo@dragonbladepublishing.com

Produced in the United States of America

First Edition February 2022
Print Edition

ARE YOU SIGNED UP FOR DRAGONBLADE'S BLOG?

You'll get the latest news and information on exclusive giveaways, exclusive excerpts, coming releases, sales, free books, cover reveals and more.

Check out our complete list of authors, too!

No spam, no junk. That's a promise!

Sign Up Here

www.dragonbladepublishing.com

Dearest Reader;

Thank you for your support of a small press. At Dragonblade Publishing, we strive to bring you the highest quality Historical Romance from the some of the best authors in the business. Without your support, there is no 'us', so we sincerely hope you adore these stories and find some new favorite authors along the way.

Happy Reading!

CEO, Dragonblade Publishing

Additional Dragonblade books by Author Jillian Eaton

The Perks of Being an Heiress Series
Bewitched by the Bluestocking
Entranced by the Earl
Seduced by the Scot
Wooed by the Wallflower

PROLOGUE

"**N**OTTINGHAM, GET UP! It's urgent."

Grumbling and groaning, Sterling untangled himself from his sheets and the slender limbs of three gorgeous women–actresses all that he'd coaxed back to his bed after a smashing rendition of Shakespeare's *A Midsummer's Night Dream*–to sit up and glower at Lord Fieldstone.

"London better bloody well be on fire," he growled, "if you're waking me at this godforsaken hour." Squinting, he rubbed his bloodshot eyes and peered through the thin gossamer curtains lining the windows of his opulently appointed Mayfair townhouse. He'd another, larger home in Grosvenor Square, but this was closer to the theater and besides, his sister was visiting.

As a general rule, Sterling did not abide by any rules.

He drank to excess.

He slept with whomever he pleased.

He caroused all hours of the night and stayed in bed all day.

But a few of the multitude of benefits that came from being the second son of a duke, a title that now belonged to his older–and much less fun–brother, Sebastian.

Some might have bemoaned their lot at having been born the spare, and thus denied the opportunity to inherit a dukedom. But not Sterling. He liked his life. In fact, he damned well loved it. There were no responsibilities. No high expectations. No expectations at all, really.

However, there was *one* rule that he tried to follow amidst all the debauchery. And that was no orgies at the house when his little sister was present. Thus, when he'd stumbled out of the theater with Titania, Hermia, and Helena, he came to Mayfair to protect Sarah's delicate sensibilities.

Which explained what *he* was doing here.

But not Lord Fieldstone.

"Did you leave something in the carriage?" he asked, scratching his unshaven jaw where he'd allowed five–or was it six?–days of stubble to grow, much to the dismay of his personal valet who insisted on clinging to the vain hope that one day Sterling would wake up and decide to make a gentleman of himself.

"No, no. I mean I might have, but–" Fieldstone cut himself short and raked an agitated hand through his short blond hair. "It's Sebastian."

Sterling grimaced. "Is he downstairs? Damnit, I thought he was at Hanover Park until tomorrow. Does he have that glint in his eyes? The judgmental one." He sighed. "I hate that glint."

Fieldstone stared at him. "Your brother is in London. We spoke with him last night after we left the theater. You insisted on it."

"Did I?" Now he frowned. "That doesn't sound like me."

"I told you it wasn't a good idea, that it should wait until morning, but you were adamant. Wouldn't take no for an answer. Jumped right out of the carriage when you saw him walking by."

"That *does* sound like me." He started to grin, winced when the inside of his skull gave an answering throb. "Did you bring any scotch with you, per chance?"

"Sterling, this is *serious.*"

"Only if you didn't bring any scotch. Whiskey? Gin?" he said hopefully when Fieldstone gave a curt shake of his head. "You mean to tell me you've come knocking on my door at–what time is it, anyway?"

"Half past five. Sterling–"

"At half past five in the morning to talk about my perfect older brother, and you didn't bring so much as a bottle of cheap gin? For shame, Fieldstone. For *shame.*"

Titania sat up, her delightful breasts on full display and her mouth curved in a pout. "Come back to bed," she implored, patting the mattress. Her gaze slid to Fieldstone and turned coy. "You too, handsome."

"Another time," Fieldstone said distractedly.

"Are you feeling all right?" Sterling asked his friend with great concern. "Should I call a doctor?"

"Yes, yes you should call a doctor! Have him sent immediately to Wimbledon Common."

The throbbing in Sterling's head abruptly ceased as everything inside of him went very still and very cold. Comprised of a thousand acres, Wimbledon Common dwarfed Hyde Park in both size and notoriety. While not a popular destination for flaunting a new curricle or a mistress, it *was* renowned for one thing: dueling.

Such an act had been outlawed in England for longer than Sterling had been alive. But a recent, highly publicized duel between Colonel James Boswell and the Earl of Grenville over a dispute involving a horse had brought it into favor again.

Dueling was still against the law.

Very much so.

But when had that ever stopped the nobility from doing anything?

"Sebastian is due to arrive there at any minute," Fairfield went on. "He's challenged the Marquess of Aston to pistols at dawn. Lord Henwick is standing in as his second. It's all been arranged, and word has already gotten out. The papers are getting ready to print as we speak."

"*Why?*" Sterling managed through the tightness in his throat.

"Because *you* told him to. Last night. Don't you remember?" Fairfield gave an exasperated shake of his head. "You were goading Sebastian into winning Lady Beatrice back after she chose Aston over him."

Vaguely, through the thick curtain of a whiskey-soaked night that had involved a quick dip into an opium den, Sterling recalled teasing his brother about losing Lady Beatrice to Lord Aston. Sebastian had been sweet on the curvaceous little brunette for *years*, but he'd been too focused on his duties as duke to do anything about it. Which was probably why the poor chit had finally given up waiting on Sebastian's proposal and had accepted Lord Aston's.

As it was one of the rare–if only–times that Sterling's perfect brother had failed at something, *of course* he had given him grief over it. That's what siblings were for. But he'd never actually thought that Sebastian would call for a duel, of all things! Good God, his brother never drove his carriage on the wrong side of the road for fear of setting a bad example. Now he was calling for pistols at dawn?

"How fast can we get to Wimbledon Common?" he said grimly.

"I've two horses waiting outside. But Sterling–"

"What?" he snapped over his shoulder as he strode towards the door.

"You're naked."

He glanced down.

So he was.

"Here," Titania called, holding up his shirt from the night before.

"You'll need these," added Helena, brandishing his breeches.

"And these," Hermia said, holding up his boots.

Sterling threw on his clothes and sprinted out of the house with Fieldstone right behind. They mounted their horses and tore off down the quiet lane as if the devil himself was at their heels, which he very well could have been.

Sterling's tongue was dry. His stomach was in knots. He felt as if he were going to be sick, and, for once, it wasn't because of pure overindulgence. He and Sebastian may not have always seen eye to eye, but they were brothers first and foremost. Bonded by blood, and the mutual loss of their parents in a boating accident five years prior.

If he lost Sebastian as well…

No.

He couldn't even think it.

They would get there in time to stop the duel. They *had* to.

And they almost did.

Almost.

The sound of the pistols exploding caused Sterling's horse to sit back on its haunches and rear. He grappled for control, then gave it up completely as he sprang from the saddle. With a toss of its head, the horse galloped away. He paid it no heed, his gaze locked with slowly dawning horror on his brother wrapped in a plume of dark smoke.

His brother, falling to his knees.

His brother, keeling over onto his side.

His brother, lying motionless, one hand still clinging to his pistol as an uneven red circle began to spread across his chest.

For several precious seconds, Sterling could only stare. He was too stunned to move. Too shocked to fully comprehend what had just happened. His brother, his mentor, his hero…fallen. Then he was shouting, and running, and sliding onto grass already slicked red with blood.

"I'm sorry," Lord Aston gasped as he came stumbling over, completely unharmed. "I–I meant to hit his arm. I swear it. I–"

"*Go*," Sterling snarled, as savage as any feral creature that had ever lived. "Get out of my sight before I beat you to death with my bare hands, you bastard. Go!" Then he bent over Sebastian, whose eyes were already beginning to glaze over. Eyes that were blue, like their mother's had been.

Trembling, shaking, he cradled his brother's head on his lap, stroking his hair, lightly tapping his pale cheek. "It's all right," he said hoarsely. "It's all right. The doctor is on his way, and he'll fix you right up. Do you hear me? Right up. You'll be on your feet and pestering me about honoring the family name in no time at all."

"Sterling," Sebastian rasped. "Is that you?"

"Yes." Hope flared, bright and brilliant and blinding. "Yes, it's me."

"I…" Blood gurgled in Sebastian's throat, then spilled out the side of his mouth in a trickle of crimson. "I…"

"Don't speak," Sterling ordered. "You need your strength for when the doctor arrives. He'll be here any minute." He looked helplessly at Fieldstone, who stood off to the side, his face as white as the clouds passing lazily overhead. "Where is the damned doctor?"

Fieldstone hesitated, then gave a slight shake of his head. "I don't know. Sterling…Sterling, even if he gets here–"

"Don't say it. By God, don't you say it!"

His brother, dead?

It was unfathomable.

Sebastian was…Sebastian was invincible.

Except he didn't feel invincible in Sterling's arms. He felt cold, and stiff, and *heavy*.

Like a corpse.

More blood spurted onto the ground.

It was everywhere.

Who knew a body had so much?

Still, he clung to his brother with the desperate determination of a sailor hanging on to a sinking ship. Waiting for a miracle that was never going to come. Waiting for help that was never going to arrive. Because somewhere in the tortured fragments of his grief, Sterling knew that Fieldstone was right. Even if a doctor did come, it would be too late. His brother was dying. There was nothing anyone could do. Nothing *he* could do but hold on. So that when Sebastian did pass from this world into the next, he wasn't alone.

Sterling didn't want him to be alone.

"I'm sorry," he said raggedly. "I'm so damned sorry, Bastian. For so many things."

Sebastian made a wet, choking sound. "Look–look after S-Sarah."

"I will. I swear it. She'll want for nothing."

"And H-Hanover Park. You are the duke now, S-Sterling." The ghost of a smile touched Sebastian's bloodstained lips. "Whatever you do, d-don't gamble her away."

"I won't. I–Bastian? *Sebastian!*" he cried when his brother's eyes closed and his breathing quickened.

A last, shuddering gasp…then he was gone.

And Sterling was the one left alone.

CHAPTER ONE

Six years later
Hawkridge Manor

I T WAS A truth universally acknowledged that a single woman in possession of a pet squirrel was not soon to be in possession of a husband.

And that suited Miss Rosemary Stanhope just fine.

Sir Reginald may not have had a title, or wealth, or even opposable thumbs, but he made for an excellent companion. The little red squirrel that she'd rescued as a baby when he'd fallen from his nest had never pestered her to dance, did not judge her when she snuck a second piece of cake (as long as she shared it with him), and never made her feel foolish or awkward. Which was why, during the past six weeks she'd spent as a guest at Hawkridge Manor, she had missed his presence terribly.

The decision to leave him behind at the London townhouse that she shared with her grandmother, Lady Dorothea Ellinwood, had been a difficult, but necessary one. Sir Reginald did not care for long carriage trips and, besides, Rosemary was only going to be away for a short while.

But then her grandmother's gout had flared up, and what was meant to be a brief house party had turned into something much longer. Long enough for the party to end, the guests to depart, and Rosemary and her grandmother to become semi-permanent residents. At least, that was what it felt like.

With the Earl of Hawkridge and his sister, Lady Brynne, in London, the massive country estate—ten thousand acres in all—was nearly vacant. It was just them, the staff...and the deplorable Duke of Hanover, whom she'd have gladly traded for Sir Reginald if the opportunity ever happened to present itself.

It continued to baffle Rosemary that in a residence of this size, the duke would continue to cross her path with alarming regularity. The first few times they found themselves in the same room, she'd chalked it up to sheer coincidence. Maybe he really *had* wanted to eat an early dinner, and the rear terrace *was* a lovely place to sit as the sun was setting.

But that had all changed yesterday, when he'd found her in the library reading...and what had begun as a more or less pleasant exchange of words between two people trapped in the same house together had ended—quite unexpectedly—with a kiss.

Sterling Nottingham, Duke of Hanover, had kissed *her*.

Miss Rosemary Stanhope, Squirrel Keeper Extraordinaire.

It went without saying that it had been her very first kiss. While her peers had escaped their chaperones and flitted out to the gardens to indulge in moonlight trysts with handsome suitors, Rosemary had remained behind in her corner of the ballroom, Sir Reginald peeking out of her reticule and a book firmly placed upon her lap.

Other matrons envied Lady Ellinwood her obedient charge, but the truth was that Rosemary wasn't so much a rule follower as she was a reader. And how was one supposed to read if they were being kissed in the moonlight?

Or in the library.

Her cheeks burned as she recalled the weight of Sterling's mouth on hers. The hot, damp slide of his tongue between her lips which had parted not so much in passion as surprise. The tingling in her belly…and down lower, between her thighs, where she'd never dared explore.

His fingers gliding through her hair before anchoring at the nape of her neck, thumbs resting just beneath her earlobes, and who knew such a tiny, inconspicuous piece of her body was capable of such sensation?

He'd yanked her against him, causing her breasts to press against his hard chest. It was not, she'd noted with a spark of curiosity, the only part of his body that was hard.

The kiss had deepened.

The hand at her nape had tightened.

One of them–she was fairly certain it was her–had moaned.

Another–definitely him–had cursed.

Then he'd drawn back, his gray eyes as dark as a brooding storm cloud, and swiped a hand across his mouth, as if to erase the taste of her lips.

Which had, Rosemary could admit now, hurt her feelings.

But not quite as much as what he'd said next.

"That was a bloody mistake."

He wasn't wrong.

Obviously, a duke had no business kissing a wallflower.

But did he have to say it out loud?

"*You* kissed *me*," she reminded him, lest he'd forgotten that this certainly wasn't her idea. She had been happy reading her book in peace and quiet, thank you very much. He was the one who had walked in on her. And he was the one who had put his tongue *in her mouth*. Heaven knew she hadn't even known such a thing was possible!

Although now that she did, she rather liked it.

She rather liked it quite a bit.

"A mistake," he'd repeated before he raked a hand through his glossy mane of black, gave her one last, searing glare, and then quit the room, slamming the door shut behind him.

That was the last Rosemary had seen of Sterling. He hadn't appeared at dinner that night, nor breakfast the next morning. He wasn't in the parlor passed out on the sofa where she'd found him thrice before. Nor was he in the library, or the music room, or the gazebo.

"Not that I am looking for him," she told Posy, a young pet lamb that belonged to her American cousin, Evie Thorncroft, as they went on their daily walk around the pond. Evie had attended the house party, too, but had left abruptly for London, leaving Posy in Rosemary's care. A duty that she'd gladly taken on as she really *did* miss Sir Reginald, and it gave her someone to talk to. Never mind that Posy didn't talk back. At least, not in so many words.

"It's just that it would be nice if he offered me an apology. That is what a gentleman would do."

Snatching a bite of yellow buttercups from a clump of wildflowers growing in the marshy wet beside the pond, Posy tossed her head and quickly spat them back out.

"I know, I know," she said with a sigh. "I'm sure the word isn't even in his vocabulary. And Sterling may be a duke, but I doubt very much that anyone would ever mistake him for a gentleman."

It was probably a passing fly, but Rosemary could have sworn the lamb bobbed her head in agreement.

"I simply imagined my first kiss being different, that's all. And at the end of it, the man did not call it a *mistake*." She nibbled her bottom lip, a nervous habit from childhood that she'd never been able to quell no matter how many times her grandmother had slapped a thin birch rod across her knuckles whenever she'd caught her granddaughter doing it. "Sterling took something from me. An experience–a moment of note–that I'll never get back. The least he could do is tell me that he's sorry for ruining it. But I suppose I won't endeavor to hold my breath." Another sigh, this one more forlorn than the last. She patted the lamb between her floppy ears. "Come along, Posy. Let's get you home."

But no sooner had she turned onto a winding stone path that would lead them back to the manor than Sterling came sauntering out from behind an oak tree, arms linked behind his back and a dark brow arched in curious amusement.

Comprised of a myriad of walking trails, towering shrubbery, and sculpted gardens with a mixture of native trees, some of them as old as the estate itself, the grounds surrounding Hawkridge Manor provided ample opportunity for one person to sneak up on another. Which was why, when her heart pitched inside of her chest, Rosemary told herself it was due to the shock of Sterling's sudden appearance.

It definitely–absolutely–had nothing to do with how rakishly handsome he appeared in his linen shirt with the sleeves rolled up to reveal a dusting of ebony hair on his forearms and his long, muscular legs encased in a pair of breeches that were so snug she doubted he'd ever be able to successfully bend his knee to mount a horse.

"Who the devil are you speaking to?" he drawled, his head canting to the side as he raked his gaze across her dress. "And why are you so…dirty?"

Defensively grabbing a handful of her skirts, which were rumpled and grass-stained from frolicking in the fields with Posy, she ducked her chin and muttered, "Nobody. I was…I was talking to nobody."

When she was a young girl, Rosemary hadn't understood why the other children had laughed at her and poked fun when she told them she could understand what animals said. Of course, she hadn't meant *literally*. She'd been an odd child, not a daft one. But she had known, more often than not, what they were thinking. To her it was obvious what a horse was trying to say when its ears turned in a certain direction, or that a dog needed quiet reassurance when its tail slipped between its legs. An animal may not have been able to form words, but there were so many ways to communicate beyond language.

As she had grown older and somewhat wiser to the barbed cruelty that her peers were capable of, Rosemary took to keeping such knowledge to herself. What seemed utterly natural to her–if a cat jumped on your lap, why *wouldn't* you ask it how its day was going?– was derided by others as foolish at best and lunacy at worst.

After a particularly humiliating event at a garden party that had left her in tears, she'd learned that some things were best hidden. It was bad enough that everyone knew she had a pet squirrel. If they realized she and Sir Reginald had conversations on a regular basis...well, maybe they *would* lock her in Bedlam. Then who would take care of her grandmother?

"You were talking to *somebody*," Sterling insisted, those devilishly gray eyes of his watching her with an uncomfortable intensity that brought a rosy flush to her cheeks. "I could hear you chattering away like a magpie from all the way inside the house. Woke me up from my nap."

"Your nap?" she exclaimed, incredulous. "It's half-past ten in the morning!"

"I had trouble sleeping." For an instant, his gaze flicked to her mouth. A muscle ticked in his jaw. "If we are going to share the same quarters, it would behoove you to be more considerate."

Her, more considerate?

Even Posy snorted.

"I thought you'd returned to London."

He grimaced. "Go back to that bloody gossip pot? Not likely. I've run out of gin and need to go into town to procure some more. Can you drive a phaeton?"

Her lips parted. "I..."

"I'd drive it myself, naturally. But I've a splitting headache and would probably end up in a ditch somewhere. You don't want me to end up in a ditch somewhere, do you, Rebecca?"

"My name is Rosemary." Didn't he know by now? She'd only told him half a dozen times. He had no problem remembering her cousins, Evie and Joanna. But then they were far prettier, and thus more memorable. Except–to the best of her knowledge–he hadn't kissed either of *them*. "I've other things to do," she said sourly, even though she didn't. "Why don't you have a footman take you?"

Or better yet, not drink yourself into a stupor every night.

She'd heard whispers about the Duke of Hanover. As an outsider looking in, she wasn't privy to very much of the gossip circulating through the *ton*, but she would have to be deaf and blind not to have heard the rumors about Sterling.

Rumors that he'd come into his dukedom by nefarious means.

Rumors that he'd redefined the meaning of debauchery.

Rumors that he'd murdered his mistress.

The second, she could easily believe. Sterling was as much of a scoundrel as any she'd ever met. Not to say she'd met very many. Strictly speaking, he was her first.

Her first rogue…and her first kiss. Surely not a coincidence, and the reason her grandmother had shielded her from men like Sterling since her debut. But even though he was most certainly a rake and a ne'er-do-well (amongst other less polite terms), she had difficulty picturing him as a *murderer*. Or someone who had cheated his way into a title. Mostly because he didn't seem to enjoy being a duke all that much.

"A footman?" he said dryly. "Now why didn't I think of that? Oh, that's right. Because Brynne, interfering busybody that she is, banned them from driving me into the village lest I go there to purchase more spirits and launch myself into a despairing pit of my own making." He gave a vague wave of his hand. "Or something like that."

"If Lady Brynne didn't want you going into town, I don't think I should take you," Rosemary said uncertainly. "She's been very generous in letting me remain at Hawkridge until my grandmother's health improves, and I wouldn't want to upset her."

"Brynne isn't even here," he pointed out. "What she doesn't know won't hurt her."

"But I'll see her once I return to London. What would you have me do?" Rosemary's brows jutted together in bemusement. "Lie?"

Sterling blinked. "Yes. Of course. What else would you do?"

"Tell the truth?" she ventured.

"The truth." For some reason, that caused him to laugh. "By God, Renee. You really *are* as innocent and naïve as you seem, aren't you? What a quaint little mouse you are. Destined for spinsterhood already, I'd gather."

"It's Rosemary," she said through gritted teeth. "And I'm not that innocent."

Once again, his gaze dropped to her mouth where it lingered long enough to cause her to face to heat all over again. "Aren't you?" he said in a rough, husky voice that did strange things to her belly.

"No." In a rare fit of rebellion, she lifted her chin. "To prove it, I will take you into the village. And I won't tell Lady Brynne about it."

Probably, she added silently.

I probably won't. But then, I most likely will.

Sterling clucked his tongue. "Well, well, well." A glint of approval shone in his eyes. Approval...and something else. Something darker. Something that even Rosemary, in all of her innocence and sexual naiveté, recognized as sensuous. "In that case, I'll have the phaeton brought round."

IF STERLING HAD an honorable bone left in his miserable body, he'd have steered miles clear of Miss Rosemary Stanhope. Sweet and good and kind, she wasn't for the likes of him. He was a blackguard of the first order. A depraved sinner who, on his best day, wasn't fit to lick her shoe. And even though the rumors surrounding his mistress' disappearance were wildly exaggerated (he hadn't accidentally strangled Eloise to death while they were making love, nor had he chopped up her body in a fit of passionate rage and tossed the pieces of it into the Thames), he was still a killer. Sebastian's death was proof of that.

An excellent reason why he never should have given in to impulse and kissed Rosemary in the library. And he most *definitely* shouldn't have been sitting within inches of her in a tiny little racing carriage on their way into town. Just the two of them. With nary a proper chaperone in sight. But having sunk this far into depravity, there was nowhere for him to go but further down in the hope that eventually he'd hit the bottom.

If Sebastian could see him now...

Sterling's hands clenched into fists, nails biting forcefully into the palms of his leather gloves as he cut the thought short. His brother couldn't see him because his brother couldn't see anything on account of being dead. Shot in a duel that he'd been goaded into by his own brother. Betrayed by his own blood. And if Sterling found himself trapped in a hell's cape of misery and darkness, it was no less than what he deserved for what he'd done.

"Why do you need more gin?" asked Rosemary, slanting him a quick sideways peek before her gaze returned promptly to the dirt lane in front of them. Lined with trees, it required a steady hand to navigate the various twists and turns. Especially in a curricle, wheeled convey-ances notorious for tipping over if they took a corner at a high rate of speed. But despite those two impediments, Rosemary handled the buggy with ease, enough so that Sterling–who was never impressed by anyone or anything–found himself secretly admiring her from his side of the velvet seat cushion that they both shared.

What a strange little bird Evie Thorncroft's cousin was.

At first glance, he'd likened the chit to a common brown sparrow. Plain, boring, and ordinary. But upon closer inspection, he'd discov-ered that she was more like a hawfinch. Still somewhat plain, but with sufficient variation in the feathers to catch the eye.

His mother had loved birds. She used to leave seed for them on the nursery windowsill and point out the different types to him as they flitted in and out in a swirl of changing colors.

"There's a robin," she'd say, looping her arms around his scrawny torso and resting her chin on the top of his dark head. "You can tell by the red on its breast. And that one there, that's a goldfinch. Do you see how yellow it is?"

At seven, Sterling hadn't had much interest in birds. He'd liked ships and soldiers the best. But he'd loved his mother, and in those quiet times, when it was only the two of them, he had leaned against her and drank in every word with the instinctive knowledge that there'd come a time—fairly soon—when young boys had to grow up and leave the innocence of childhood behind.

If only he'd known how horribly fast that day would arrive.

"What's that one?" he'd asked once, frowning at an unfamiliar bird with a dusky golden cap on its head and blue on its wings. "It's different from the others."

"Well done, Sterling!" his mother had said excitedly, kissing his cheek. "That's a hawfinch. They usually prefer the countryside, and even then it can be hard to spot them in the dense underbrush. I don't know if I've ever seen one this far south, and never in the city. They were my favorite to look for when I was a girl because they are so difficult to find. Do you see its curved beak? It uses that to crack open cherry stones."

"Cherry stones! But they're so hard and the hawfinch is so small."

"Small things can be strong, too, Sterling. It's the size of the heart that matters most. Remember that, my darling boy."

"I will, Mama," he'd vowed, and as he stared at Rosemary, he realized that some part of him really *had* remembered.

How wretchedly maudlin.

"Why do I want more gin?" he said brusquely. "So that I can drink it, obviously."

Another peek in his direction, this one even more fleeting than the last.

She bit her lip.

He rolled his eyes.

"Out with it, Regina."

"I wasn't going to say anything. And it's Rosemary. Rose. Mary." She gave an agitated toss of her head that sent the hideously ugly bonnet she'd jammed over her hair before they'd departed Hawkridge Manor sliding forward onto her face. A muffled squeal, a startled pull on the left rein, and the curricle would have sailed off into the ditch had Sterling not covered her hands with his and straightened them out at the last possible second.

"*Oh,*" she gasped, hauling the buggy to a shuddering halt right in the middle of the lane. "Oh, I'm terribly sorry. How frightening! I didn't mean–"

"I blame this potato sack on your head," he interrupted before he grabbed the bonnet and threw it unceremoniously in the bushes.

"That was mine!" she cried. "My grandmother had it made for my birthday."

"Trust me. I did you a favor." He paused. "I take it your grand-mother selects all of your clothes?"

"Not *all* of them."

"The dress you wore to breakfast on the last day of the house party. The pale blue with the violet ribbon. It wasn't completely awful," he allowed.

"I borrowed that gown from Evie."

He nodded sagely. "That explains it, then."

"My clothes...my clothes should be none of your concern, Your Grace."

"I have to look at them, don't I?" Absently, he glanced down to see that his hand was still wrapped around hers in an intimate grip that was no longer necessary given that they were stopped. Scowling, he withdrew his arm and draped it across the back of the seat instead, fingers idly drumming on the wood trim.

It was the lack of gin, he decided. The bloody stuff had gone to his head and without it…without it he had started to do all sorts of crazed things, like kissing Rosemary in the library and holding her hand and recalling the exact dress she'd worn nearly a fortnight ago. If he didn't get liquor into his bloodstream soon, he'd do something truly out of character, like telling her that in the dappled sunlight her hair held glimmers of gold amidst all the silky tendrils of brown and her eyes were the color of a soft fog rolling in over the field right before sunrise.

"We need to go," he said abruptly.

"But my bonnet—"

"Leave it. I'm sure the forest animals will give it the proper funeral that it deserves."

She pressed her lips together as she adjusted her grip on the reins. "Has anyone told you that just because you *can* say anything you want and not suffer repercussions due to your rank doesn't mean that you *should?*"

"No," he said after he thought about it for a moment. "Never."

"That explains it, then."

Tipping his head back, he closed his eyes. "Just drive, Rosalie. And do try to keep us out of the ditch."

CHAPTER TWO

A S ROSEMARY WAITED impatiently for Sterling to come out from
the pub, she gave serious consideration to returning to
Hawkridge Manor without him. Walking the eight or so miles back to
the estate would serve him right after the way he'd treated her. Poking
fun at her bonnet (even though it was, admittedly, quite hideous),
repeatedly calling her by the wrong name, and–worst of all, in her
opinion–going on as if their kiss had never happened.

He hadn't made a single mention of it. Not one! If she didn't know
any better, she might be tempted to believe she'd fallen asleep while
she was reading and dreamed the entire thing. Except that reading
never made her tired. If anything, she had the opposite problem. And
she hadn't imagined that kiss. She knew she hadn't! Which meant that
either it was of such minor insignificance to Sterling that he'd already
forgotten about it, or he was purposefully choosing to pretend it had
never happened.

Neither scenario made her feel very good, and both were an excellent reminder of why she preferred the company of Sir Reginald, who
liked her clothes if only because there was plenty of extra space for
him to dash up her sleeve in case one of her grandmother's yappy dogs
came searching for a tasty, squirrel-sized snack.

What she wouldn't do to be back in London with her beloved pet
tucked cozily on her lap and not a single surly duke in sight. Speaking

of which…where *was* Sterling?

By her estimation she'd already been waiting for the better part of twenty minutes. Without her bonnet to provide shade, the sun was beating mercilessly down on her head, causing a trickle of sweat to drip between her shoulder blades. The duke had left her–quite literally–to bake in the early afternoon heat without a thought to her comfort or that of the poor horse who had brought them here.

The carriage rocked from side to side as Rosemary dismounted. Waving down a young lad with a gray felt cap tugged low over his mess of blond hair, she dug around in her reticule and gave him a shilling to bring the horse a cool bucket of water and then keep watch over the gelding while she went to track down Sterling.

It wasn't difficult to locate him. Once her eyes had adjusted to the pub's dimly lit interior, she spotted the duke immediately. Aside from the barman, he was apparently the only other person who saw fit to frequent a drinking establishment before noon.

She pinched her bottom lip between her teeth as she hovered indecisively in the open doorway. Maybe it would be best to return to the carriage and wait. Except Sterling didn't seem to be in any rush to leave. Sitting on a stool at the bar, he had his chin in one hand and a metal tankard in the other. Half-cast in shadow, his countenance was unreadable. His posture was somehow both stiff and weary at the same time, as if he'd traveled a great distance to get here. Except *she'd* done the driving, hadn't she? He had just sat there like a bump on a log. An ill-mannered bump, at that.

Her mind made up, Rosemary squared her shoulders. A floorboard creaked beneath her foot as she walked briskly into the pub, causing Sterling's head to lift and his eyes to narrow.

"You can't be in here," he said.

"*You're* here," she pointed out.

"That's because I'm a man and you're…"

"I'm…?"

"You." He lifted the tankard to his mouth. "I'll be out in a minute."

"I have already waited twenty."

He shrugged. "Then you won't mind another five."

Oh!

Maybe it was because she was sheltered. Or maybe she'd just never really paid attention before. But Rosemary was fairly certain that she'd never, *ever* met someone as infuriatingly disagreeable as the Duke of Hanover!

All things considered, she wouldn't be surprised to discover that he *had* killed his mistress. But not by use of brute force. The poor woman had probably expired due to explicit rudeness.

"What is so good about that drink that you couldn't wait until we were back at the estate?" she demanded. When Sterling was not forthcoming with an answer, she decided to figure it out for herself. Before he could stop her, she marched up to his stool, plucked the tankard right out of his hand, and took a big swill of whatever was inside.

"Rosemary," he said with some alarm. "I wouldn't–*devil take it!*" Cursing when she choked and gagged and blindly thrust the fire–for surely it was fire–onto the bar, he sprang from his seat and wrapped a supporting arm around her waist as she doubled over, tears streaming down her cheeks while the flames shot from her throat into her belly.

"That's–that's vile!" she cried. "The worst thing I've ever tasted. And I once ate a boiled pig's tongue by accident!"

"How on earth did you eat a–never mind. Take deep breaths. That's it." He began to rub her back in large, soothing circles. "That's better."

When the worst of it had passed and her tongue had regained some feeling, his hand fell away and she lifted her head to find him grinning crookedly at her, a glint of amusement shining in those wolfish gray eyes. His smile–the first genuine one she'd seen from him–stripped years of hard, polished veneer from his countenance, giving her a rare glimpse at the man beneath.

"This is not humorous in the least," she said primly, pretending not to notice the lick of heat under her skin that had nothing to do with whatever terrible concoction she'd drank and everything to do with the duke standing in front of her.

Rosemary wasn't–couldn't be–attracted to Sterling.

He was everything she detested in a person.

Obnoxious, unpleasant, and belligerent.

Not to mention discourteous.

But then, she'd always been drawn to the hurt and the vulnerable. The baby bird that had fallen from its nest. The orphaned squirrel without a home to return to. The carriage horse in need of a comforting hand upon its shoulder and a fresh bucket of water to quench its thirst.

Sterling wasn't a wounded animal. That much was clear. But there was hurt there just the same, hiding behind the sharp-edged charm that he used like a sword to keep everyone at arm's length. Everyone, it seemed, except for her.

"It's a *little* humorous." He propped his elbow on the edge of the bar. "I take it from your reaction that you've never had gin before?"

"*That's* gin? *That's* what you drink every night?" she said, eyeing the tankard in disbelief. Having sipped the occasional glass of wine and champagne at her grandmother's dinner parties, she had naturally assumed that was what Sterling was drinking whenever he took a nip from the silver flask he carried with him. Not some foul-tasting brew that had most likely burned a hole in the bottom of her stomach! "But...it's so terrible. How do you do it? *Why* do you do it?"

"Because it's better than the alternative," he said with a careless shrug.

"What's the alternative? Lye?"

"Feeling."

"Feeling what?" she asked, confused.

His grin faded. "Everything."

He'd said something similar to her before, but now having sampled gin herself she was loath to imagine what kind of demons would be worth such daily abuse.

"Maybe...maybe you could try a nice tea with lemon instead?" she suggested.

Picking up the tankard, he drank what was left, slammed it down onto the bar, and swiped a hand across his mouth. His eyes, when they met hers, were as dark and bitter as a cloudy sky brewing above a tempestuous sea. "Maybe you can mind your own damned business." With that, he grabbed a brown glass jug presumably filled with more gin and stalked out of the tavern, leaving Rosemary to trail behind him, her expression troubled.

It would have been simpler if the duke had sustained his illusion of a careless rogue. But having seen his pain, she couldn't make herself *unsee* it. Some might come across a stray dog in the street and turn the other way when it showed its teeth and growled. But she preferred to take a different approach. An animal with its hackles up was an animal that was either afraid or injured. Often both. Such a creature needed gentleness and understanding, not condemnation and judgment.

It was in Rosemary's nature to be a healer. A helper. A nurturer of all things broken.

And it appeared as though she'd just found her next stray dog.

A DOCTOR CAME the next day to examine Rosemary's grandmother. At eighty-two years of age, Lady Ellinwood, who'd reverted back to her maiden name after the death of her husband, had also outlived her sister, her daughter-in-law, and her child. She was a stern woman with an iron constitution. A battle class naval ship in a sea of wooden schooners.

Rosemary had learned at an early age not to cross her. Where her grandmother was concerned, obedience was the best way to preserve calm waters. No doubt her American cousins would have chaffed and rebelled against such an arrangement, but Rosemary was content to do what was asked of her if it meant being left alone to do what she wanted. She was also aware–more so now than when she'd been a young girl still reeling from the sudden death of her parents–that her grandmother was her best means by which to keep a roof over her head and clothes on her back and food in her belly…lest she exchange what independence she had for a wedding ring and marriage to a husband who would most likely expect unfavorable things of her, such as hosting dinner parties and–horror of all horrors–releasing Sir Reginald back into the wild.

It made Lady Ellinwood's lingering illness all the more concerning. Of course, Rosemary was worried for her grandmother's sake. But she was also worried about what would happen to *her* if something happened to her grandmother.

Lady Ellinwood had battled flare-ups of her gout before. A painful condition that affected the joints, particularly those in the ankles and feet, it rendered her completely bedridden. Their family physician, a man even older than Lady Ellinwood, had come up with a plethora of treatments over the years, from applying a slab of raw steak to the afflicted area to draining the diseased blood with leeches. In Rosemary's opinion, blood was better served *in* the body than out of it, but she also understood that when faced with an incurable disease doing something was often better than doing nothing.

The Earl of Hawkridge's doctor, however, hadn't brought in dead hunks of cow flesh *or* sucker worms. Instead, he'd ordered Lady Ellinwood's personal maid to maintain a strict regime of hot compresses followed by cold, and a tonic with anti-inflammatory properties to be taken thrice daily.

To Rosemary's enormous relief, the unconventional treatment had actually worked and her grandmother's gout had never looked better. But for some reason, Lady Ellinwood continued to insist that her legs were too painful to get out of bed, thus preventing their departure from the manor and causing Rosemary to call upon the doctor once more to see if there was anything he had missed during his previous examination.

"Her joints are swollen," he told Rosemary in the privacy of the hallway once they'd left Lady Ellinwood's chambers in order to let her rest. "But then, that is to be expected given her age and natural degradation of the joints from her prior episodes of gout."

Rosemary knotted her hands together behind her back. "Then she *can* walk?"

"Not just that, but she must. Staying in bed is doing no favors to your grandmother's circulation." The doctor, a tall man with brown hair that was beginning to gray at the temple, studied Rosemary with calm, intelligent blue eyes. "I prescribe to the theory that as a person ages, their muscles and bones begin to lose mass and strength. This process is only increased by lack of exercise and movement. To put it bluntly, the longer Lady Ellinwood chooses to remain bedridden the longer she shall *have* to remain bedridden."

"Then what you are saying, if I understand correctly, is that there is no medical reason why my grandmother is not on her feet," Rosemary summarized, her brow creasing.

The doctor nodded. "Precisely. If there is no improvement over the next two days, let me know and I shall refer you to a specialist from the Belclaire Institution."

"But that's...that's an asylum," she said, taken aback.

"Part of it, yes. However, there is a growing constituency of doctors and philosophers, led by Dr. Wilhelm Wundt, who believe that a person's mind is just as important, if not more so, in the healing process as what ails them physically. Have you ever the opportunity to attend one of Dr. Wundt's lectures, I highly recommend it. If you are fluent in German, his most recent publication, *Handbuch der Medicinischen Physik*, is an excellent read. It is my understanding that they are working on an English translation." He adjusted his grip on his black leather medical bag. "If there is nothing else, Miss Stanhope, I've a newborn with croup to attend."

She wished the doctor luck and then waited until he'd gone downstairs and she heard the front door open and close before she quietly slipped back into her grandmother's room. The curtains were closed and the room was dark; her grandmother a small lump under the covers in the middle of the bed. The size of the mattress dwarfed her, making her appear frail in stature. But while Lady Ellinwood was many things–autocratic, strict, and officious, to name a few–frail was *not* an adjective that Rosemary would ever use to describe the elder matriarch.

"Grandmother," she called softly. "Are you awake?"

"Yes," came the feeble reply. "Has the doctor left?"

"A few minutes ago."

With suspicious zest, Lady Ellinwood threw off the covers and sat upright. Reaching for her wire-rimmed spectacles, she perched them on the edge of her nose and waved her granddaughter forward with an impatient flick of her wrist. "Open those drapes, then come here. I want to get a closer look at you and those freckles on your face. What have I said about going out in the sun without a bonnet? We're going to need lemon water, buckets of it," she ordered her beleaguered maid, Janelle, who was never far from her side and generally wore the appearance of a puppy that had been kicked too many times. "Well, what are you waiting for? I haven't all day!"

"Thank you," Rosemary murmured as Janelle hurried from the room. Then her hands crept self-consciously to her cheeks as she reluctantly approached the side of the bed. "I'm sorry. I–I lost my bonnet."

"During your outing with the Duke of Hanover, I presume."

Her mouth opened. "How…how did you know about that?"

"Just because I am confined to this room doesn't mean I am not aware of what my granddaughter is doing or who she is cavorting with," Lady Ellinwood said haughtily.

"We–we weren't *cavorting*. He asked me to drive him into the village to pick up some...some medicine, and I could hardly refuse." Rosemary took a deep breath. Standing up to her grandmother was no small task, but if it made a difference in her health, then she had to do it. "Speaking of being confined to the room, Dr. Shaw said something that I found quite interesting–"

"You went without a proper chaperone."

"What?"

"Into the village. You went into the village with the duke without a proper chaperone." Lady Ellinwood lowered her spectacles to the edge of her nose and stared at Rosemary over them without blinking. "You were alone together in the carriage to and from. Did anything untoward happen?"

"Untoward?" Rosemary shook her head. "I don't–"

"Did he say or do anything inappropriate?" Reaching across the mattress, her grandmother grasped her wrist, her fingers cold and surprisingly strong given her supposed infirmity. "You can tell me, Rosemary. If the duke has done something, if he has compromised your reputation somehow, then we *must* insist that he make amends."

"*Grandmother.*" As she snatched her hand away, everything became clear. And while she was disappointed in her grandmother for putting on such a farce–for that was precisely what it was, what all this was– she was more disappointed in herself for not seeing it earlier.

Rosemary was aware that people considered her to be naïve. The odd little wallflower, sitting in her corner with her books. Occasionally they stared, and whispered, and giggled, but they never bothered her because she wasn't a threat to them. And it did not cause her distress, because she knew herself. She knew that yes, all right, maybe she *was* odd. At least by the standards of the *ton*. But she was also intelligent, and observant, and while she was admittedly ignorant about some things–such as passion–she wasn't nearly as unsophisticated and guileless as everyone thought.

Except in this…in this she *had* been naïve.

Naïve to the lengths Lady Ellinwood would go to secure a husband for her granddaughter. A husband so far beyond Rosemary's reach that the very idea the Duke of Hanover would ever be interested in her enough *to* compromise her reputation was laughable.

Allowing herself to be fooled by her grandmother's scheme, however, was not.

"Is that why we're still here, then?" she asked. "Is that why you've been pretending to be ill? Because you wanted to make a match with the Duke of Hanover?"

"Don't you dare take that tone with me, Child. I was ill. I *am* ill. It is called being old and it is very inconvenient."

Lady Ellinwood was a difficult woman. A hard woman. A resentful woman. A woman who didn't possess an affectionate bone in her body and had the unfortunate habit of moving people around to suit her purposes as she would pieces on a chess board. But Rosemary loved her just the same, for deep down–*very* deep down–she knew that her love was reciprocated. Even if it was an emotion her grandmother was incapable of displaying.

"I was worried for you!" Kneeling beside the bed, she rested her chin on her folded arms and gazed imploringly at the woman who had raised her like a daughter and had never, not once, made her feel as if she were a burden. "Please don't do that again. If you'd told me the truth, I'd have been able to tell you that the duke has no interest in me whatsoever. This was a ploy destined to fail from the start."

"Not even a *hint* of unseemly behavior?" her grandmother sighed.

She thought of the kiss.

The kiss that Sterling was pretending had never happened.

"No. Not even a hint. Can we return to London now?"

"You need to marry *someone*, Rosemary." Lady Ellinwood's lips compressed to form a long, thin line of disapproval. "I am not going to be around forever, and when I am gone, the money will soon follow. You need to be prepared. I would not like all of my hard work to be squandered away should you end up as a governess or a school teacher."

"Wouldn't it be amusing if *men* had to marry *women* in order to secure their future?" Rosemary grinned. "What a different place the world would be if we were allowed to be in charge of our own destinies. To inherit estates and have grand political aspirations and dowries that were given to us instead of us giving them away."

Lady Ellinwood sighed. "You are, and always have been, a strange child. I fear it is to your detriment, as no husband wants a wife with such peculiar ideas."

And no duke would ever want to marry a wallflower, she added silently.

It was true.

Never, in a thousand years, would Sterling ever consider marrying someone like *her*. Someone whose own grandmother considered her to be strange. Such a fact was no great revelation. But what *did* cause her some surprise was the tiny quiver of disappointment she felt at the knowledge that her grandmother's plan (feign prolonged gout so that her granddaughter was stuck under the same roof as a duke), while well-intentioned, had failed.

Miserably.

"But alas," Lady Ellinwood went on, "I'm sure we can find *someone* this Season that is willing to overlook all of your eccentric qualities."

Although her mouth suddenly felt stiff, Rosemary managed a smile. "I'm sure you're right. Should I tell Janelle to begin packing?"

"Yes." Her grandmother's eyes narrowed. "Where *is* that lazy, impertinent girl?"

"You sent her for lemon water."

"That's right. For those ghastly freckles of yours. Honestly, Rosemary. They look like ants marching across your face. No man wants to marry a girl with ants on her face. You *must* remember to wear a hat whenever you go outside."

"I will do my best," she said solemnly.

"One last thing. It has come to my attention through various sources that your...your *cousins*"–Lady Ellinwood spat the word as if it were a curse–"have chosen to remain in England. Word has it one of them even married a private investigator, and the other is engaged to the Earl of Hawkridge, if you can believe such nonsense."

"Joanna has married Mr. Kincaid?" Such was her excitement at the (poorly delivered) news that Rosemary shot to her feet and clapped her hands together. "How wonderful! I was hoping things would work out between them. Evie and Lord Hawkridge as well. Oh, do you think they'll have a winter wedding?"

"If they do, I am certain we will *not* attend."

"But...but they're my cousins." Rosemary did not know the entire story. But she'd heard enough pieces over the years to put most of the puzzle together. Her grandmother had a sister, Mabel, long since passed, who married an American and moved to Boston where they had a daughter, Anne.

After that, things got a bit more convoluted.

When Anne came of age, Mabel brought her to London to debut her amidst High Society. Anne had a brief, secret affair with the recently widowed Marquess of Dorchester...the Earl of Hawkridge's father. When she discovered that she was expecting, Anne returned to Boston and married her childhood sweetheart, Jacob Thorncroft, choosing a quiet life as a wife and mother in the country instead of becoming a countess. Together, they raised the baby–Joanna–without any knowledge of who her true father was, and went on to have two more girls, Evie and Claire.

Anne passed from scarlet fever when the sisters were young, and Jacob during the War Between the States. Nearly destitute, the sisters decided to sell their mother's ring, a ring that had been given to Anne (unbeknownst to her daughters) by the Marquess of Dorchester.

Through a complexing turn of events and some truly remarkable twists of fate, the ring found its way to the Earl of Hawkridge. When Joanna and Evie came across the pond to fetch it back, they hired a private investigator–Mr. Kincaid–to help them.

Not only did Mr. Kincaid unearth the ring's whereabouts, but– with a little help from Rosemary's grandmother–he unraveled the entire mystery surrounding Joanna's real birth father.

Now Joanna and Mr. Kincaid were married, Evie and the Earl of Hawkridge were engaged, and Rosemary was so happy she could burst. She'd always wanted sisters, and now that she had them they were just as wonderful as she had imagined they would be.

It was a perfect happily-ever-after.

Except for one small, teensy tiny problem.

"They are your second cousins once removed," Lady Ellinwood snapped, "and if they are anything like their mother, they are not to be trusted. Anne was an unruly, disobedient girl who invoked scandal wherever she went, and I'm confident her daughters are no different. I had to stomach seeing them here, or else you wouldn't have had the opportunity to get close to the Duke of Hanover. But you are *not* to associate with them once we return to London. Do you understand, Rosemary?"

"But I–"

"I said do you understand?"

"Yes," Rosemary mumbled as her shoulders slumped. "I under-stand."

CHAPTER THREE

A FTER HE WATCHED the third trunk being carried down the stairs, Sterling realized something was happening. Lurching off the sofa in the drawing room where he'd spent the better part of the night guzzling down gin before eventually sliding into unconsciousness, he stumbled to the doorway and leaned heavily against it.

"What's going on?" he asked a passing footman. "What's all this commotion about?"

"Lady Ellinwood and her granddaughter, Miss Stanhope, are departing for London. Is there anything I can get you, Your Grace?" the footman inquired politely. For an instant, his gaze lowered to Sterling's rumpled clothing, then immediately snapped back to his face. "Have a bath drawn, perhaps?"

"Coffee," Sterling muttered, scratching at the thicket of beard on his jaw that he hadn't bothered to shave in…well, he couldn't recall the last time he'd picked up a razor. Not since the end of the house party, at any rate. "Black, no sugar or milk."

"Right away, Your Grace."

As the footman hurried off to fetch his coffee, Sterling glowered at the growing stack of trunks in the middle of the foyer. So Rosemary was leaving, was she? Back to the city for the start of the Season, no doubt. And that was fine. It wasn't as if she were going to stay here forever. Hawkridge Manor wasn't her home. Neither was it his, for that matter. But he could admit, at least to himself, that he'd enjoyed her company. Probably more than he should have.

Rosemary was different from anyone else he'd ever met. She had a pet *squirrel*, for God's sake. And he…he was going to miss her, Sterling realized with a frown. More than that, he didn't want her to go. Which was positively absurd. But not *quite* absurd enough to prevent him stepping out into the foyer when he spied her descending the stairs, her arms awkwardly holding the largest hat box he'd ever seen.

"Give me that before you break your neck," he said gruffly, yanking the box out of her hands as she reached the bottom step. Hoisting the cumbersome thing onto his shoulder, he glared at her beneath it, feeling as surly as an old bear that had been woken from its nap in the middle of winter. "What's in here? The Papal tiara?"

Her bewitching eyes–more blue today than gray in the pale morning sunlight–met his. "No, just hideously ugly bonnets."

Guilt cut through the surliness. Setting the hat box beside the tower of trunks, he turned back to Rosemary with folded arms and a shuttered expression. "A word, Miss Stanhope? I believe the library is currently unoccupied."

They could have easily spoken in the foyer. While servants were milling about like bees in a flower garden, they were trained to turn a deaf ear to conversations above their rank. But Sterling didn't want to share what little time he had left with Rosemary. Not with a maid. Not with a footman. Not with anyone. Besides, if he was going to apologize for his abominable behavior, he'd prefer not to have any witnesses.

"I don't know if the library is the wisest choice," she said, biting her lip.

He lowered his voice to a roguish whisper. "Afraid I am going to kiss you again?"

A delightful shade of rosy pink filled her cheeks. "Then you…then you *do* remember."

Remember?

How could he bloody well forget?

The act had been an impulsive one, as he generally did not make a habit of engaging in stolen moments of passion with blushing wallflowers. Married women who'd grown bored of their elderly husband and were looking for a bit of excitement, yes. Raven-haired actresses with French accents and enormous breasts, most definitely. But shy, plain innocents who turned red at the mere mention of a *kiss*?

Never.

Until Rosemary, he'd been a wallflower virgin.

And for good reason.

Young, well-behaved girls from well-to-do families wanted one of two things out of a man like him. Love or marriage. As hard as it was to believe, some even wanted *both*. But Sterling wanted neither, which was why he ordinarily avoided Rosemary and her ilk like the plague. He would have avoided her, too, if she wasn't so damned easy to talk to. Then there was that mouth of hers. Pink and plump as a strawberry ready to be harvested. He'd never seen a fruit so tempting...and thus, not one to deny himself pleasure, he'd taken a bite. Just a nibble, really. Hardly more than a peck. Except a peck had never rocked him back on his heels with such force that he'd been left nursing a cockstand for a bloody hour afterwards.

So yes, he *remembered* their kiss.

It was all the others that he'd since started to forget.

"A quick chat," he said, gesturing towards the hallway and the library beyond. "Then I'll bid you farewell."

When she continued to hesitate, he rolled his eyes.

"Don't worry, Ruth. I've just enough decency left in me that I won't repeat my prior lapse in judgment. You are safe with me." He used his finger to draw an X over his cold, black heart. "I swear it."

"Very well, but only for a minute." Her gaze darted up the staircase. "My grandmother will be down soon, and she won't be pleased if she has to wait for me."

"A minute," he promised as he followed her into the library and closed the door behind them with a subtle *click*.

Filled with floor to ceiling shelves that held an untold number of books, the room was both vast and intimate, with comfortably oversized chairs upholstered in Italian leather, lush Aubusson rugs in varying shades of deep burgundy and gold, and an entire wall of windows that overlooked the pond where a pair of mated swans paddled through hazy fog that had yet to burn off the water.

Whether by incident or design, Rosemary went to the same settee that she'd been sitting on when he had cupped her chin and lowered his mouth onto hers. When he had temporarily lost his mind and found—just for an instant—whatever remnants of a soul he had left.

Sugar, he recalled. She'd tasted of spun sugar and innocence, with just a hint of spice. Had he not stopped himself when he did, he might have devoured her whole.

"What is it you care to discuss, Your Grace?" she asked, regarding him with the faintest etching of a frown. This time, she didn't sit on the settee but rather stood beside it, gloved hands resting lightly on her hips.

"Ah…" Grabbing a book at random, he shuffled absently through the pages, needing *something* to do with his hands lest they suddenly find themselves peeling that terrible traveling habit off the curvaceous little body hiding underneath of it. "Before you left, I wanted to say that I was sorry. For…ah…"

"Referring to our kiss as a mistake?"

He squeezed the back of his neck. "That probably wasn't the best way to–"

"Continuing to call me by the wrong name?"

"What's a little jesting between–"

"Throwing my bonnet out of the carriage?"

"That was, admittedly, in poor–"

"Keeping me waiting at the tavern?"

"You're right, I should have–"

"Insulting my pet?"

"When did I insult your pet?" he said blankly.

She crossed her arms as temper rippled across her countenance; the first true display of anger he'd ever seen out of her. "You called Sir Reginald, and I quote, 'a rat with a furry tail'."

Of all the ills he'd committed, *that's* what had upset her the most? Sterling started to laugh, saw how serious she was, and coughed into his elbow instead. "Rosemary–"

"Then you *do* know my name."

"Of course I know it," he said, vaguely irritated that she'd ever thought otherwise. "I am a drunk and a degenerate, not a bumbling imbecile. I just like the way your eyes flash when I call you Rebecca, or Ruth, or Renee."

"You haven't called me Renee yet."

"It was next on my list."

She gazed at him intently, as if she could somehow see past the façade he'd carefully erected around himself to the fractured shadow of a man beneath all the cavalier charisma and short, snappy quips. Which was impossible. No one, not Weston or Kincaid or even Sarah, knew how empty he really felt. How bleak and bitter he really was. If they did...if they did, they wouldn't let him out of their sight. Why, then, did he have the uncomfortable feeling that Rosemary saw him for who he truly was?

Except she didn't.

He was confident that she didn't.

Because if she did...if she did, she'd run screaming.

"I accept your apology," she said formally.

"Thank you–"

"On one condition."

Wariness brought his brows together. "What's that?"

"You kiss me again."

Sterling was able to count on a single hand the number of times someone had caught him off guard over the past few years. When you were the worst sinner in the group, not much had the ability to surprise you. But this...this shocked him right down to his rotten core.

"Absolutely bloody not," he said, incredulous.

Her frown deepened. "You did it before. Right here, as it so happens."

"I *know* where I did it." Of its own accord, his gaze went to the settee. It was a fine piece of furniture. The trim was rosewood polished with beeswax, the long cushions sumptuously upholstered in bronze velvet. Rosemary's ivory skin would glow against the rich color as he laid her down upon it, his knees straddling her hips while his teeth nipped the freckle on the side of her neck, just below the delicate shell of her ear. He'd inhale the scent of her, clementine and a fresh spring breeze over the water, as his mouth wandered across the hills and valleys of her voluptuous frame. Lingering here. Nuzzling there. Enjoying the banquet of those soft, lush curves until she was begging him to bring her to sweet release and–

"Your Grace?" Rosemary said uncertainly, drawing his attention to the fact that he was staring with tender adoration at a sofa. Worse than that, he was on the verge of sporting *another* cockstand. Over a bit of fluff and fantasy about an inexperienced wallflower.

How utterly humiliating.

"Another kiss is out of the question," he snapped. "Terrible idea. Worst one I've ever heard."

Hurt flickered in her eyes. "Then I do not accept your apology."

"You can't do that!"

"It's my forgiveness. I can give and take it back as I please."

"Well it's a terrible thing to do. Very bad form."

"So is telling a young woman that her very first kiss was a 'bloody mistake'."

"Stop doing that," he scowled as another shard of guilt poked him.

"Doing what?"

"Quoting me."

"Then stop saying things you wouldn't want quoted."

His jaw clenched. "That was your first kiss?"

She gave a small nod. "It was…not what I was expecting."

Not what she was expecting?

Not what she was expecting?

He muttered a curse under his breath.

Devil take it.

This was why he didn't touch virgins.

There were no expectations with a paramour. Just mindless fucking. As long as they both received their orgasm–make that orgasm*s* for his partner, as never let it be said the Duke of Hanover wasn't a generous man–he didn't care what happened afterwards. Eloise was as close as he'd come to caring for someone who'd shared his bed, and look how *that* had ended up. With blood on the walls and an accusation of murder hanging about his neck like a damned noose.

That all being said, he could hardly leave Rosemary with a bad experience. Which meant he had no choice but to kiss her again. Not because he wanted to. Kiss a wallflower not once, but *twice?* Perish the thought.

No, he *had* to do it. Or else what would happen to his good name once Rosemary was set loose on London and told all her lady friends that he'd called their kiss–a kiss *he* had initiated–a mistake? And a lackluster mistake at that? They'd assume his performance had been substandard. And that couldn't stand.

If the *ton* wanted to believe he'd carved up his mistress like a turkey and fed her to the lions at the zoo, then fine. He had no control over idle gossip. But he refused to let people think he was a poor kisser.

Dear God, his reputation would be destroyed!

Which meant there was only one solution.

"All right," he said graciously. "I'll do it. I'll kiss you again."

She smiled politely at him. "No thank you."

Of all the contrary–

"Why the hell not?" he growled, throwing his arms wide. "Isn't that what you wanted?"

"I understand that I am regrettably ordinary, Your Grace. I'm not a diamond of the first water. My beauty will not provoke wars. Poets will not write sonnets about me. While my peers have set their caps for dukes and earls and the like, I should consider myself lucky if I manage to land a kindhearted doctor or businessman." Her throat visibly tightened as she swallowed. "But that does not mean I shall permit myself to settle for a kiss out of some misplaced notion of pity."

Sterling blinked.

Ordinary?

Pity?

Clearly squirrel dandruff had driven the chit a tad mad. He'd never met anyone as *unordinary* as Rosemary in all his twenty-seven years. As for pity…

"You asked *me* to kiss *you.*"

"Yes," she acknowledged, "and you refused. Now you're only saying you'll do it because you feel sorry for me."

He gave a snort at that. "That's where you're wrong, Reginald."

"Reginald is a boy's name."

"It's the best I could come up with on short notice." His fingers raked through his hair, pulling the inky mess of tangles off his temple. "My point is that I don't feel sorry for anyone. Least of all you. And I am far too selfish to ever do anything out of pity. So if I say that I want to kiss you then damnit, it means I want to kiss you."

Four strides, and he was across the room.

Two more, and she was in his arms.

His hands settled on her waist. His mouth pressed on her lips. The connection was immediate. The fire hot enough to singe. She tasted even better than he remembered, a tantalizing concoction of honey and citrus, sweet and tart, that fanned the flames of his ardor until they threatened to ignite the bloody ceiling.

But even as he thrust his fingers into her hair and slid his tongue into the velvety cavern of her mouth, he cautioned himself to proceed with restraint. Their first encounter with shared passion had been spontaneous, and far too short because of it. Rosemary was not inexpensive gin to be carelessly guzzled, but rather a fine wine to be sipped...and he wanted to enjoy every swallow.

A breathy purr rolled from her throat when he angled his head and deepened the kiss, using his teeth to draw on her bottom lip with just enough force to have her nails digging into his shoulders before he soothed the bite with a lazy stroke of his tongue.

When she did the same to him, albeit with the adorable clumsiness of someone relying on pure instinct instead of expertise, he went absolutely still. Every muscle, every bone...even his breath, frozen in stunned wonderment at the sheer, unadulterated rush of desire that poured straight into his veins.

Sterling had made love to some of the most wanton creatures the devil himself could imagine. The sheer decadence of the acts he'd both performed and had performed on him were...suffice it to say, their iniquity would make a sinner blush. But when Rosemary hesitantly returned his kiss, every other pleasurable act he had ever committed immediately paled in comparison.

On a growl, he threw his vow of self-control to the wind. To hell with caution. To hell with restraint. He wanted now. He wanted this. He wanted Rosemary. Kissing her, being kissed by her, was the closest he'd felt to being alive since he'd watched Sebastian die.

His fingers streaked across her shoulders and around her ribcage to cup her breasts, and his growl turned into a helpless groan when he discovered they were just as soft and full as he'd dreamed they'd be whenever he closed his eyes and hovered in that empty space between sleep and liquor-induced oblivion.

Her nipples were hard, even through the tragic number of layers that comprised her traveling habit, and he encircled them lightly between his thumbs and index fingers, skillfully wrenching a moan from her lips as her head lolled to the side, exposing the slender line of her throat that was simply too tempting to ignore.

He kissed the sensitive juncture where her neck and collarbone met, then trailed upwards until his teeth clasped her earlobe and gave a light, teasing suckle.

Clementines and spring.

She was clementines and spring, and he was…he was enthralled.

Enraptured.

Entranced.

The Duke of Hanover, libertine extraordinaire, was entranced by a mousy little wallflower. The realization of which jolted him out of the euphoric haze he'd temporarily lost himself in and back into cold, unforgiving reality.

He released her with such abruptness that she lost her balance, and it was a good thing the settee was there or else she might have fallen, for he was too busy raking his nails along his scalp and asking himself what in all that was holy he thought he was doing to catch her.

"That was…" *Amazing. Life-changing. The first glimpse of light I've seen in six dark, sunless years.* "That was a mistake. Just another bloody mistake." He dragged a hand down his face. Opened his eyes to find her staring at him, her lips swollen, her cheeks pink, her blue-gray gaze filled with more hurt and bewilderment. Which made him feel like the world's largest arse. But he'd be an even *bigger* arse if he encouraged any type of romantic entanglement between the two of them.

They'd had their kiss.

She could go on to tell her friends how splendidly rakish he was.

And he…he could slink back into the hole he'd crawled out of.

"I wish you well in London, Rhona," he said briskly. "Good luck with the rat. Now I must bid you adieu."

Her plump mouth parted in dismay. "But I lo—"

"Oh God," he grimaced. "Don't say it."

Another reason why he avoided innocents?

The blasted things fell in love at the drop of a hat.

A glossy curl tumbled across her temple as she shook her head. "But—"

"Whatever you *think* you feel, you don't," he interrupted. "Not for me, at any rate. Go and find yourself that nice doctor. Good people, doctors. Always helping those less fortunate. Far better than an arrogant titled leech who offers nothing of substance to Society. Plus if the rat gets sick, you've a doctor in-house."

Her nostrils flared. "Your *Grace*—"

"Off I trot," he said, a tad frantically now. "Farewell, Roxana."

As STERLING BOLTED from the room, Rosemary watched him leave in confusion. All she'd wanted to tell him was that she'd lost her jeweled hairpin while she was being ravished (surely there was no other way to describe what had occurred), and would he mind helping her find it, because if she didn't then her grandmother would notice and ask questions. Questions that she didn't want to answer, given that she'd already skirted around the truth once. But apparently, he'd had important things to do, given that he hadn't allowed her to get more than two words out before he had sprinted out of the library. In all the time they'd spent together these past few weeks, she didn't know if she'd ever seen him move with such speed.

Huffing out a breath, she dropped to her hands and knees, whereupon she quickly found the pin underneath the settee. Using a mirror hanging on the wall beside a portrait of Lord Weston and Lady Brynne from when they were children, she did her best to return her appearance to what she'd looked like *before* Sterling had kissed her...among other things.

He'd touched...he'd touched her *breasts*!

Both of them.

At once.

Even she had hardly done that.

And who knew an *ear* was so directly connected to the warm, pulsing core between her thighs?

It had certainly been an educational experience. She wasn't even upset that he'd called it–once again–a mistake. When you kissed a wolf, you couldn't be surprised when it bit you. What *had* surprised her was how wickedly delightful she'd found his teeth. And how much further she'd wanted to go.

A lady was not supposed to have passionate inclinations.

But then, neither was she supposed to have a pet squirrel.

Having broken one rule...what was wrong with breaking another?

As a shiver of secret delight coursed along her spine, Rosemary wondered if this wasn't what sent people down the road of sin. The thrill of doing something nefarious...something forbidden...something with ruinous consequences...it had a certain addictive quality. Like dessert.

Kissing the Duke of Hanover was the equivalent of sneaking a second piece of red velvet cake.

And she wanted more.

"Your face is more flushed than usual," Lady Ellinwood remarked when Rosemary finally emerged from the library to find her grand-mother, as she'd feared, impatiently waiting in the foyer. "I hope you're not ill. I don't want to listen to you cough all the way to London."

"I'm fine, Grandmother. Thank you for asking."

Lady Ellinwood's mouth thinned. But before she could decide whether her granddaughter was being sarcastic or not–she was, but only a tad–Rosemary wrapped a supportive arm around her grandmother's waist and accompanied her out to their waiting carriage.

A footman helped boost Lady Ellinwood into her seat (earning a rap on his knuckles for his trouble), Rosemary sat beside her, and in a swirl of stone dust and the creak of wood and leather, they set out for London, leaving Hawkridge Manor…and Sterling…behind.

CHAPTER FOUR

S TERLING DRANK FOR the next three days straight. The bottom of a bottle of gin didn't provide him with any lasting solutions to the demons that gnawed at his bones, but it dulled the pain from all those sharp, slicing fangs.

Mostly.

On the fourth day he received a letter from Sarah, which he resolutely ignored. Engaged to be married to Lord Hamlin, a viscount of impeccable reputation who had Sterling's grudging approval, his sister had spent the summer at Hanover Park planning for a Christmas wedding.

How nauseatingly romantic.

As for Sterling, he hadn't set foot on the ducal estate since they buried Sebastian in the family mausoleum. An hour's ride to the east, Hanover Park sat high on a hill with some of the best views in all of England. Bestowed upon the first Duke of Hanover by King Edward III as a reward for protecting his son's flank during the Battle of Crecy where the British army slaughtered over twelve thousand French soldiers, the estate had proudly stood for nearly five generations. A wood and stone testament to the bloodlust and political ambition of Sterling's ancestors.

He'd been born there. Raised there. Had explored the woods, played in the streams, had his first kiss in the massive wine cellar underneath the kitchen there. And his first fuck in the carriage house loft.

There were too many rooms to count and enough turrets to officially make it a castle. The gardens alone were larger than most towns, and the stable, of which Sterling's grandfather, a renowned equestrian, had been particularly proud, was almost an estate unto itself. Ancient oaks lined the long, winding drive. Fountains sprayed water into the heavens. Peacocks strolled the rolling lawns and wandered along the granite paths edged in Italian marble.

And that was just the exterior grounds.

In short, Hanover Park was what dreams were made of.

But for Sterling, it was a nightmare. A bleak reminder of what never should have been his. A yoke around his neck that he didn't want. A sword pointing straight at his chest that he'd just as soon run himself through with than claim what should have rightfully belonged to Sebastian. Which was why he'd turned over the estate and all the duties that accompanied it to Sir Edgar Goulding, a trusted family friend and solicitor who knew better than to plague Sterling with any issue, large or small, regarding Hanover Park unless the entire damned place was on fire...in which case, Sterling would say let it burn.

He had already invited Sarah and Lord Hamlin to live there once they were married, and treat it as if it were their own. If such a thing were possible, he would have made *her* the heir after Sebastian died. Such was his loathing of all that he'd inherited.

He despised every brick, every painting, every bloody peacock, for that matter. Should it all vanish tomorrow, he wouldn't be sorry to see it go. In fact, he'd rejoice. Find a way to get his hands on a bottle of Glenavon Whisky and throw the biggest party the *ton* had ever seen.

Unfortunately, vast estates did not generally disappear into thin air. Which meant he was stuck with Hanover Park until he keeled over, or he managed to find some distantly related male relative to bequeath it to via an act of parliament, or...or he had a son.

For some inexplicable and completely ridiculous reason, an image of Rosemary flashed in his mind. Beside her stood a little boy with her blue-gray eyes and his tousled black hair. Rosemary had that damned squirrel perched on her shoulder, the boy held a bullfrog clutched between his chubby fingers, and Sterling...Sterling was smiling.

Bemused—and a tad annoyed—he reached for his decanter of gin. But when he went to pour it into a glass, only a few drops emerged. His annoyance growing, he staggered out of his bedchamber and down the stairs in search of another source of alcoholic sustenance. By the way his stomach was growling, he needed food as well, especially since he couldn't remember the last time he'd eaten.

With Rosemary here, he'd still been miserable. But at least he'd had someone to talk to. Someone to look forward to seeing. And yes, someone to kiss. With her gone, the manor was depressingly empty. He was almost tempted to travel to London. Not to follow her. He didn't *miss* her. Speaking of things that were ridiculous. But he did miss his favorite gambling hells, and his study with the liquor cabinet he'd had custom made and stocked with the finest spirits money and favors could buy, and all right, maybe—*maybe*—he missed Rosemary the teeniest, tiniest amount.

Her smile. Her little peculiarities. The way she bit her lip if she was anxious about something. The throaty purring sound she made in the back of her throat when he stroked her nipples...

Scowling, he landed harder than necessary on the bottom step, startling a passing maid. Clutching the linens she carried more tightly against her chest, she averted her gaze and hurried past, leaving him to wonder what the staff saw when they looked at him.

He was capable of fooling his peers with a smirk and a drawling snicker. Good old Sterling. A bit rough around the edges, perhaps. But always up for a laugh and a good time. Servants, however, weren't as easy to trick. Not when their very well-being depended on being able to read their employer's wants and needs with pinpoint accuracy.

A crotchety old dowager might say she wanted cream in her tea…but what she really meant was honey, and God protect the poor soul who brought her what she'd asked for.

A clipped tone indicated an earl wanted to be left alone to take off his own boots, thank you very much.

A spill of raucous laughter from an ordinarily subdued debutante called for water to discreetly replace the champagne she'd been guzzling down like a damned pirate fresh off a ship.

And a duke who drank himself half to death every night and quartered himself in his room every day was neither up for a laugh *or* a good time. Rather, he was someone to be avoided. A devil to dance around, not dance with.

His friends didn't understand that.

But the maid did.

So, too, did Rosemary. And yet she'd dared to waltz with him anyway. Which either made her very brave…or very, very foolish.

The Wallflower and the Wastrel, he thought with a bitter twist of his lips. A title that would have done the renowned author Jane Austen proud. Not that he was worthy of being a fictional hero. A villain, more like. In the world of literary characters, he wasn't Mr. Darcy, the brooding protagonist responsible for dampening women's undergarments for the better part of half a century. He was Mr. Wickham, a womanizing scoundrel with no moral compass who had attempted to seduce Mr. Darcy's sister. Except he was even worse than that, because Mr. Wickham hadn't killed his own brother.

"Your Grace." A tall, gangly footman with thinning brown hair atop a pointed scalp approached Sterling in the middle of the foyer. "Someone is here to see you."

Rosemary was his first thought, and he hated that it was. Hated the boyish flutter of anticipation in his chest even more. She was the *last* woman he should have been thinking about. For both of their sakes. Best he push her from his mind, or–better yet–forget she even existed.

To the most of his knowledge, their paths hadn't crossed before the house party. There was no reason to believe they'd see each other now that it was over and she'd gone back to town to begin the Season. Their interlude had been a brief, isolated incident, never to be repeated. And why that should bring him a twinge of sorrow he hadn't the foggiest idea.

"Is it Thomas Kincaid?" he asked, referring to the private investigator he'd hired to clear his name of wrongdoing in regards to Eloise's murder. The two men had first met when Kincaid was a constable for Scotland Yard. Sterling owed him a debt he'd never be able to repay, as it was Kincaid who had recovered Sarah safely after she was kidnapped by highwaymen who attacked his sister's carriage as it traveled from Hanover Park to Bath.

Since then he and Kincaid had become casual acquaintances, if not outright friends, and when Eloise had disappeared, leaving a blood-soaked room behind her and Sterling as the last person to see her alive, he knew that he was in need of Kincaid's particular set of skills once again.

It was the detective who had recommended that he recuse himself from the *ton*. A leave of absence, such as it were, to allow the gossip–not much of which was very complimentary–to settle before the House of Lords reconvened and decided whether or not to charge one of their own.

A trial of peers was exceedingly rare. It made a public spectacle of the nobility, and thus was only reserved for the most egregious of crimes. Dueling, bigamy, treason against the crown…and murder.

Lord James Brudenell, Earl of Cardigan, was the last to stand trial. He was found not guilty of dueling on a technicality, but his good name was forever besmirched and when he died, his estate and title were bequeathed to a second cousin, thus ensuring that the Brudenell name would never be passed on.

Sterling didn't give a damn about his reputation, but all things being equal, he did prefer his head to be *attached* to his neck. Nor did he particularly desire to rot away in Newgate for the rest of his life. Thus, he'd heeded Kincaid's advice and had been twiddling his thumbs in the countryside while he awaited news of how the investigation was progressing.

"No, Your Grace," said the footman, causing Sterling to frown. "It is not Mr. Kincaid."

"Well then, who the devil is it?" he demanded.

"Me," Sarah chirped as she sailed out of the parlor and wrapped her arms around her brother in an embrace that he was too caught off guard to return. "Your favorite sister."

"My only sister," he managed to counter after he'd subdued his initial surprise. "And far from my favorite if you've come here to pester me."

Placing his hands on her shoulders, he set her away from him. While he loved Sarah, he was also wary of her. She may have been six years his junior, but that didn't stop her from taking on the role of a mother hen. Except he was no wayward chick to be brought back into the nest. Nor did he want to drag her into his nest of demons, which was why he'd made it a point to keep his distance. Yet here she was, all the same.

"Pester you?" Sarah's eyes, hazel like their father's and filled with feigned innocence, widened. "I'd never dream of doing such a thing." Then she shook her head sadly as her gaze traveled from his unkempt hair all the way down to his bare feet. "It's clear that I've arrived just in time. You look a fright, Sterling, and you smell even worse. Haven't they water here at Hawkridge? You there"–she pointed at a maid, who stopped dead in her tracks–"have a bath prepared. Extra hot, extra soap. Then I want clothes laid out. Clean ones." She touched Sterling's rough cheek and clucked her tongue. "Where on earth is your valet?"

Swatting her arm aside, he pinched the bridge of his nose where a dull throb had already settled in. "I left him in London."

"That much is apparent. A bath, clean clothes, *and* have a barber called," Sarah told the maid before her gaze shifted back to Sterling. In the depths of those hazel eyes there was exasperation, but also worry. "Won't you walk with me? I've been in a carriage for an hour, and should like to stretch my legs."

"I was just getting ready to take a nap," he grumbled.

"A nap? It's not yet noon. Come along. Some sunlight will do your complexion good. You're as pale as a newborn babe." Linking their arms, she pulled him–still grumbling–outside and onto a flagstone path that led to the rear gardens where fragrant smelling roses were beginning to wilt as the nights grew cooler and the days shorter.

"What are you doing here, Sarah?" he asked.

"Can a sister not visit her brother without an ulterior motive?"

"Some can, I'm sure. But you're not one of them."

"No, I am not," she said, the corners of her lips twitching. Halting in front of a fountain that sprayed a steady stream of water in a graceful arc, she pivoted to face him and took both of his hands in hers. "But I *am* worried about you, Sterling. I've been worried, for quite some time."

As the throb behind his eyes turned into a pounding, Sterling gritted his teeth and looked past her at a green wall of shrubbery. "You needn't concern yourself with me. You've a wedding to plan, and the Season to participate in. Isn't your plate full enough?"

"I've heard the rumors about your mistress."

His gaze cut to hers. "Young ladies shouldn't talk of such things."

"Don't tell me you are going to start playing the part of chaperone *now*. I know what a mistress is, and what they're for. I also know that you didn't kill yours and put her body in a trunk and ship it to America."

He snorted. "Is that what they're saying? Last I heard I disposed of the body by feeding it to sharks. Or maybe it was crocodiles. I can't remember."

It was morbid, to talk of his mistress in such a way. But then, their entire relationship had been morbid from the moment he'd stolen her away from some hapless lord who didn't know his cock from a carrot. All fighting and fucking, with nothing in between. A carnal, animalistic partnership that had suited both their needs perfectly.

He had wanted a way to drown out the demons. She'd wanted a little pain with her pleasure, which he'd happily provided. Along with money, of course. Eloise had always been a greedy little strumpet, and never bothered to hide it.

Now she was gone, taken in the dead of the night after one of their infamous arguments, and while he knew that *he* hadn't killed her, someone most likely had. And in a gruesome manner, if the amount of blood he'd found was any indication.

Yet since her disappearance, he'd been nagged by an unsubstantiated hunch that there was something more to the story. Something that he'd hoped Kincaid's investigation would uncover. Something that would reveal Eloise was actually still alive, and had–for reasons unknown–staged her own death. Which was why he could make light of it. In a dark, twisted way. Because there was a part of him that didn't believe–didn't *feel*–as if she were dead.

A stupid assumption. So stupid that he hadn't even bothered to mention it to Kincaid. But how else to explain the timing of it all, and the fact that nothing had been taken from the house, which ruled out a robbery? No jewelry, no furs. None of those bloody crystal swans with rubies for eyes that she'd insisted he buy her whenever they were out and about town. Nothing of value...except for Eloise. Even then, there'd been no note. No threatening letter. No ransom. She'd simply vanished...leaving him as the prime suspect for a murder he hadn't committed.

Or maybe he had.

Maybe his mind was so far gone, so rotted and filled with filth, that he *had* killed her.

Just like he'd killed Sebastian.

"I don't know why anyone would believe such absurd conjecture," Sarah scoffed, and Sterling might have smiled if his mouth didn't feel so heavy. His baby sister, always coming to his defense. Even when there was nothing left to defend. "Sharks and crocodiles. How ridiculous."

"People like the ridiculous. It distracts them from how small and meaningless their own lives are."

"That's a dark way of seeing the world."

"The world is a dark place."

She squeezed his hands. "Sterling, I know that you blame yourself for what happened to Sebastian. But it–"

"If you're going to tell me it wasn't my fault," he interrupted, "save your breath."

"I just wanted to say–"

"I do not wish to discuss this subject. Choose another."

"Surely it would be better if we–"

"*I said I do not wish to discuss it,*" he snarled, for once using the power of his title to command authority. No one questioned a duke's order. Not even his own sister. Jaw hardening, he went to the fountain and sat on the edge of it. The water hit his back in a light misting spray, but he welcomed the wet as it helped subdue the fire raging inside of him.

After several minutes, Sarah sat beside him, her voluminous skirts spilling across his legs as she rested her head on his shoulder, much like she'd done when she was a young girl and he was a young boy and Sebastian was alive and everything was right and good. "I think you should come to London," she said quietly. "I understand why you've spent the summer here, and your absence did allow some of the gossip to die down. But now I fear the longer you stay out of the public eye, the more that people will begin to assume your guilt."

He sighed. "Haven't they done that already?"

"Some. Not all of them. It's those sitting in the House of Lords that matter most. They are the ones that you need to convince of your innocence. You might begin by repairing your reputation."

"Is something wrong with it?" he asked dryly. "Here I thought I was a paragon of virtue."

She poked him with her elbow. "Anything but. The House of Lords won't want to convict a duke, or even put you on trial. It would bring too much negative attention to the aristocracy. But they will if they think you're more of a risk out of prison than in it."

"What would you have me do? Stop drinking and gambling, start attending mass, find a proper wife, and settle down?"

"Precisely."

"You've got to be jesting." A pained grimace rippled across his countenance when she merely arched a brow. "You're not jesting."

"I wish I were. I wish I'd come here on an amusing whim, and not out of desperation to save my brother. You're not well, Sterling." Lifting her head, she gazed at him in earnest. "You haven't been well for a long time."

Because her words struck a chord of truth deep down inside of his black, rotting soul, he didn't try to refute them. Instead, he clenched his jaw and stood up to pace a restless circle around the fountain before he stopped at where he'd started.

"You're here because you think you can save me, Sarah. And I commend you for it. I love you for it." He drew a breath, dragged a hand through his hair, managed one last, pitiful smile in an attempt to disguise the hurt, the pain, the misery. The raw, aching *emptiness*. "But what if I'm not worth saving?"

CHAPTER FIVE

ROSEMARY HAD FORGOTTEN how *small* London was. For such a large, sprawling city, the streets were impossibly narrow, the houses were uncomfortably cloistered together, and the smells...suffice it to say, she hadn't missed the smells. But she had missed Sir Reginald, and he her, if his frantic chirps at seeing her again were any sign. Or maybe he'd just known she was hiding ginger drops in her pocket. Either way, girl and squirrel were happy to be reunited once again. A good thing, as there wasn't much else to be happy about.

The Season had already started while she'd been in the country...kissing—and being kissed by—the Duke of Hanover. A secret she had already decided to keep to herself, mostly because she didn't want to give her grandmother any more ideas about plotting a grand wedding trap and a little bit because she knew no one would believe her.

Rosemary Stanhope, kissed by a duke?

As if she needed to give people another excuse to laugh.

She *might* have told Joanna and Evie. They wouldn't think she was lying, and they'd probably have some sage advice to offer given that Joanna had landed a husband, and Evie a fiancé, all within four months of coming to London while Rosemary had lived here her entire life without so much as serious courtship.

But alas, she was forbidden from calling on them or inviting them to call on her. A strict rule that her grandmother didn't show any signs of alleviating within the next few days or weeks or even months. Which meant that she was back to having Sir Reginald as her lone source of companionship. And that was all right. It was what she was used to, after all. But having gotten a taste of what it was like to have a sister, someone she could confide in and speak her mind to without fear of being considered odd or strange, she wasn't exactly eager to return to one-sided conversations with a mammal whose preferred activity was climbing trees and stuffing his face with so many acorns that he passed out from the sheer weight of them in his belly.

Although, in that regard she supposed he wasn't too different from Sterling.

Minus the tree climbing part.

What she needed to do—what she *had* to do—was find a way around her grandmother's decree without being caught. And at Lady Garfield's birthday picnic, she had the perfect plan to do it.

An annual event, the birthday party would be held at Crown Top Manor, the formal town residence of Lord and Lady Garfield. Located in the midst of Sheffield Park, a district of old, stately homes overlooking the eastern end of the Serpentine, it was within walking distance of Grosvenor Square where the Earl of Hawkridge lived.

If Rosemary walked quickly, that is.

She had no way of knowing if Evie was even staying with Lord Weston, but it was worth trying to find out. So long as her grandmother's previous behavior held true, Rosemary would have precisely seventy minutes while Lady Ellinwood caught up on all the gossip that had circulated through the *ton* during her absence.

Her grandmother's close-knit circle of friends would start off under the tent in the rear garden as they always did, but the heat and flies circulating around tables filled with lemonade and tea and sweets would soon drive them inside to the front parlor. A parlor that did not offer a clear view of the gardens, giving Rosemary the time and opportunity she needed to dash off to Grosvenor Square.

No one would notice she was missing. To be honest, she doubted anyone would even notice she was there to begin with. No one but her grandmother, but Lady Ellinwood would be too preoccupied with finding out who had flashed too much ankle at the ball the night before to realize that her granddaughter had snuck off.

If her plan went accordingly, Rosemary hoped to have a lovely visit with her American cousin and then return to the birthday party before all of the guests gathered for the presentation of the cake, a seven-tiered monstrosity that seemed to grow taller and more extravagant with every passing year. For Lady Garfield's sixtieth birthday, a flock of *birds* had erupted from the middle of the cake.

It went without saying that Rosemary would be leaving Sir Reginald at home, lest he somehow find himself stuffed into a bowl of frosting.

For a wallflower who ordinarily spent social gatherings playing puppets with the children, it was a daring scheme. But ever since her last encounter with Sterling in the library, she was feeling a bit daring. Up until it came time to actually *act* upon her subterfuge, that is.

"Would you like me to go in with you?" she asked her grandmother nervously as Lady Ellinwood and her acquaintances (whose combined ages teetered north of three hundred) picked up their glasses of lemonade and stood in preparation for their esteemed retreat into the parlor.

The party was a wild crush, with nearly half the *ton* packed into the manicured lawns of Crown Top Manor. A quartet of violinists kept a lively tune, and a few couples danced on a raised wooden platform while the majority of guests meandered about, walking briskly from one shady spot to another in an attempt to escape the unseasonably warm sun. Children splashed and played in the fountains, their delighted shrieks quickly muffled by watchful governesses so as not to irritate the adults. A haughty and tightly closed circle of debutantes observed an equally exclusive collection of titled lords from separate linen tents, and above it all, on a dais in the middle of her stone terrace that overlooked the sprawling festivities, Lady Garfield held court, regal in a gown of deep burgundy while maids, sweaty and pink-faced, vigorously waved enormous silk fans in an effort to keep her cool and comfortable in the sweltering heat.

"There is no need to accompany us, Rosemary. You should be out there," Lady Ellinwood pointed a bony gloved finger at the shrewd-eyed debutantes, "making connections and catching the attention of your future husband. Not joining the dowagers inside for tea."

Rosemary had better odds of being accepted by a pride of lions than she did being welcomed into the midst of *that* savage herd. Better chance of survival, as well. But she merely nodded, as if in agreement, and then waited, nerves tingling, until her grandmother had disappeared inside to put her plan into motion.

For a few minutes, she stood in nervous indecision, wavering between obedience and daring. The only other time she'd defied her grandmother in such a manner was when she had followed Mr. Kincaid to the boarding house where her cousins were staying. But her grandmother hadn't yet forbidden her from associating with Evie and Joanna, and besides, she *did* say she was going on a walk. Which wasn't a lie. Not like this.

"Excuse me," a high-pitched, feminine voice snapped.

Before Rosemary had time to react, she was jostled to the side as Lady Navessa Betram came through, her loyal followers–Rosemary assumed they considered themselves her friends, but Lady Navessa wasn't the sort to have friends, not really–trailing importantly in the wake of her enormous pink and green striped bustle.

That would have been the end of it. A meaningless interaction, swiftly forgotten. But as she was pushed out of the way, Rosemary's arm inadvertently struck a tray of lemonade being carried by a footman. As she watched in wide-eyed dismay, the exceedingly full pitcher sailed up into the air in a rather impressive arc given its size…but if Rosemary had learned anything from devouring Isaac Newton's *Philosophiae Naturalis Principia Mathematica*, it was that all things that went up must come down. Which the lemonade did. All over Lady Navessa.

The sound of her shriek was almost loud enough to shatter glass. It caused everyone to stop and stare, even their hostess. At Lady Navessa who was red-faced and furious, at the poor servant who was trembling head to foot, and at Rosemary who was fervently wishing for a hole to open in the earth that she could hop into.

Unfortunately, no such hole was forthcoming.

But Lady Navessa's rage was.

"You incompetent imbecile," she hissed, rounding on the footman. "How dare you ruin my gown? Do you know how long it took to make it? Or how much it will cost to repair it? You should, as it will be coming out of your pocket! You careless, lazy–"

"It was me." Unable to stand by while the wrong person took the blame, Rosemary swallowed with difficulty before she stepped forward to take the brunt of Lady Navessa's wrath. "I–I accidentally hit his arm."

"I should have known this was *your* fault," Lady Navessa spat, her top lip curling in an unflattering sneer that her followers mirrored as all but a handful of guests gradually drifted away and the violinists struck up a new tune. "Little Rosy Poly. As bumbling as ever, I see. Shouldn't you be in a corner somewhere reading to that rat of yours?"

Rosemary lifted her chin. An assault on her own character, she could manage. But a besmirchment upon Sir Reginald was something that needed to be defended. "He is a red squirrel, not a rat. If you cannot understand the difference between a member of the Sciuridae family, as first classified by the Russian entomologist Gotthelf Fischer von Waldheim, and the clearly distinct Murid family of rats and mice and other ground dwelling rodents, then maybe *you* should be the one to open a book." Gaining confidence from her extensive knowledge of taxonomy, which included the study of various biological organisms grouped together by similar characteristics, she continued on…a bit further than she probably should have. "Moreover, the lemonade was not my fault. Had you not bumped into me, I wouldn't have bumped into the footman, and he wouldn't have spilled it."

Lady Navessa's eyes, the same color as flat silver coins, narrowed to thin slits. "You'd do well to recall your place, Rosy Poly, and not be so stupid as to confuse my tolerance for acceptance. Everyone knows you are only here because of your grandmother and whatever waning influence she continues to yield. On your own, you are nothing. You are no one." Her mouth stretched in a sugary sweet, sympathetic smile. "I hope, for your own sake, you understand that. Even a rat realizes that if it goes where it doesn't belong, it shall not be long for this world. Mind your step, Rosy Poly. I'd hate for you to be crushed under someone's heel."

With that, she snapped her fingers and her loyal handmaidens fell into line. They sailed off into the house and Rosemary, withering beneath the weight of half a dozen smirking stares, had no choice *but* to leave.

She didn't cry as she made her way to Grosvenor Square. But she did wonder, as she often had over the years, what she'd ever done to deserve Lady Navessa's hate. Because it wasn't just Navessa. It was all of them. The popular, the pretty, the ones who put themselves above everyone else. The ones that got to decide who was a diamond to be admired and envied…and who was a rat to be sent scurrying into the shadows.

Rosemary knew that she was different. She'd always known. But why should that make her a target for such maliciousness? Her fascination with science and biology wasn't hurting anyone. Sir Reginald wasn't hurting anyone. And still she was mocked and given cruel nicknames and made to feel like an outsider at every opportunity.

Navessa and her ilk were like the children that yanked the wings off insects. Not for any particular reason, other than they could. And it made them feel superior to cause smaller things pain.

Rosemary, on the other hand, went out of her way to catch spiders in glasses and carry them outside. And gently transfer ladybugs to nearby bushes when they landed on her skirt. And hold grasshoppers in the palm of her hand not to yank off their legs, but to admire the sheer beauty of their shiny green armor.

While it may have earned her ridicule and a seat by herself in the corner, she'd rather be like that than like Navessa. Rather stand up for the weak and the vulnerable than threaten to stomp on them. Rather spend her time with Sir Reginald than be surrounded by a hundred so-called friends who stood by her side not out of true allegiance, but due to fear of becoming the next target of all that vitriol and venom.

She found Lord Hawkridge's house without incident, and after giving her name to a somber-faced butler with long gray sideburns, was issued into an elegantly appointed parlor to wait.

After a terse fifteen minutes, where she debated whether to give up her plan and hurry back to Crown Top Manor before her grandmother noted her absence, the door flew open and Evie, breathless and beaming and carrying an armful of packages wrapped in brown paper and dainty silk ribbon, hurried in.

Rosemary's cousin was short and slender, with shining black tresses set stylishly beneath a felt sailor hat and sparkling blue eyes that were as prone to sharp wit as warmth. She had more fashion sense in her pinky finger than Rosemary did in her entire body, and had graciously used some of that knowledge during the house party to help soften Rosemary's dull, dowdy appearance.

"Had I known you were coming to call I would have made sure to be here to greet you!" she exclaimed, carelessly tossing the various parcels she was holding onto a nearby chair. "Thankfully, I was just on my way back from Blondell Mercantile. Have you been there? It's the largest store I've ever seen! What a marvel. They've everything from perfume to cooking pots. I am trying to find the perfect pair of shoes for–*what on earth are you wearing?*"

"What?" Rosemary said defensively, glancing down. The dress had been waiting when she arrived in London, along with the rest of an entirely new wardrobe her grandmother's modiste had created for her while they were in the country. For today's outing, an apricot gown with lime green piping had been laid out for her to wear. She hadn't thought twice before putting it on. She never did. But if her cousin's expression was any indication, perhaps she should have.

"It's orange. Pumpkin orange. *Blinding* orange." Evie's nose wrinkled. "Heavens, and it's growing mold."

"I think it is supposed to be like that."

"No dress should be like that. Thank goodness you had the good sense to seek me out. And your *hair*. This calls for an intervention. Come with me at once."

Rosemary balked when her cousin grabbed her arm and began to physically drag her from the parlor and up the stairs. "I don't actually have that much time–"

"You've time for this. Sit," Evie commanded once they'd reached her bedchamber, a sun-filled room with a large canopied bed dressed in white linen and pale yellow walls stenciled with pink roses. It was a beautiful room. A room befit for the future Countess of Hawkridge.

Reluctantly, Rosemary sat in front of an elegant vanity littered with various perfumes, creams, and glass vials filled with mysterious powders and potions. A dubious frown settling upon her lips, she met Evie's serious gaze in the oval dressing mirror. "The thing of it is, I've snuck away from a party and if I don't return soon–"

"Why did you have to sneak away?" Evie interrupted as she used a narrow-toothed comb to scrape off the thicker layer of bandoline that had been used to plaster Rosemary's curls to the side of her head. Made of quince seeds, bandoline was an awful, waxy concoction of which Lady Ellinwood was inordinately fond. Rosemary had managed to escape wearing it while her grandmother was on bedrest, but now that she was back on her feet and the Season was underway, she'd ordered it brought into the house by the bucketful.

As someone who did not pay much mind to outward appearances, particularly her own, Rosemary had never given much attention to the clothes that her grandmother ordered her to wear or the way she instructed her hair to be styled. At least not until Evie had pulled her aside at the house party and pointed out that her old-fashioned, oversized dresses were doing her no favors.

"You needn't dress provocatively to be noticed," Evie had said kindly. *"But your clothes should reflect your personality, and from what I know of you thus far, you're much more bright and beguiling than your gown would suggest."*

To date, it was the nicest compliment Rosemary had ever re-ceived. Which made her loath to tell her cousin the real reason why she'd had to steal away from Lady Garfield's birthday picnic like a thief into the night. Evie and Joanna had been so welcoming of her, so accepting, that she didn't want to hurt their feelings by revealing her grandmother's opinion of them. Especially since her grandmother's opinion was wrong. But neither could she keep lying. Any more half-truths and they'd begin to tangle up, like a knotted piece of thread.

"My grandmother doesn't like you," she blurted, and immediately winced. She could have said that better. She *should* have said that better. But Evie didn't look offended by her bluntness. If anything, she appeared amused.

"I received that impression when Lady Ellinwood refused to speak to me at Hawkridge Manor. At first, I feared she was deaf, but as it seemed she was capable of hearing everyone but me, it appears her hearing loss is selective."

"I'm sorry," Rosemary said miserably, hunching her shoulders. "As

I've mentioned, she can be rather…difficult."

"*I'm* sorry that you've had to live with her all these years." Giving up on the comb, Evie switched to an ivory brush with short, stiff bristles. "It must not have been easy. Growing up without your parents. I lost my mother when I was young, but I still had my father. Without him…without him, I don't know what I would have done. What *we* would have done, my sisters and I." The corners of her mouth twitched in a quick grin. "Killed each other, most likely."

"I don't remember them. My parents." There was a touch of wistfulness in Rosemary's tone, but no pain. How could you hurt from the loss of something if you possessed no memory of ever having had it? "It is a miracle I survived the fire, as young as I was. Barely three, and already an orphan. I am fortunate that my grandmother took me in."

"What else should she have done? Tossed you onto the street? Doing the bare minimum is hardly cause for celebration. Family takes care of family." Evie set the brush on the vanity, then placed her hand on Rosemary's shoulder and squeezed. "*You're* family now. Whether you want to be or not. And the Thorncrofts take care of their own. If you'd ever like to get out beneath Lady Ellinwood's thumb, you've a home here for as long as you need. I'm sure Weston wouldn't mind."

Leave her grandmother? The thought had honestly never occurred. But now that it had, she found herself feeling tempted. Tempted…and terribly guilty.

"My grandmother had already raised one child when I came to live with her. She never expected to be burdened with another." Biting her lip, she laced her fingers together on her lap. "While it's true that she isn't prone to fits of affection, she's taken good care of me. I've not wanted for anything."

Which was, she reflected, rather sad. What did it say about her life, what did it say about *her*, that twenty years of existence could be summed up in five words or less? Were she to die tomorrow, her gravestone would be every bit as unremarkable as her journey thus far.

Herein Lies Rosemary Stanhope
An ordinary woman who wanted for nothing
May she rest in peace

"You are not a burden." Evie lifted the brush and resumed dragging the bristles through Rosemary's stiff, unwieldy curls. "But I suppose someone who allows a squirrel to take up residence under their roof cannot be *all* bad. How is Sir Reginald?" Her hand stopped as her voice took on a guarded edge. "You haven't brought him here with you, have you?"

"No, he is at home, taking a nap. Lady Garfield is not very partial to squirrels. That is where I was," she explained when Evie lifted a questioning brow in the mirror. "Every year, she throws an elaborate garden party for her birthday."

"I think we received an invitation, as the name sounds familiar, but Weston had a matter to attend to with his solicitor and I've been far too busy preparing for the wedding to attend any social functions during the day." Finally finished with brushing the bandoline from Rosemary's hair, Evie grabbed a handful of pins and, holding them between her teeth, began to fashion a loose coiffure. "Had I known you'd be there, however, I'd have made certain to attend. I could have brought Joanna as well. Although it sounds like your grandmother wouldn't have been pleased to see us."

"She'll eventually come around." *I hope*, Rosemary added silently. "I wish I hadn't gone, to be truthful. The other ladies there...they weren't very...erm..."

"Pleasant?" Evie said dryly. "So I've gathered from my brief experience with the *ton* thus far. And I thought the women in Somerville were malicious and spiteful. The ones here would devour them for breakfast with a side of tea. It appears an American with some scandal attached to her name was not their first choice to marry the Earl of

Hawkridge."

Aghast, Rosemary twisted in her chair. "Has someone said something untoward to you?"

"Nothing that I cannot handle. Now stop moving." Fingertips lightly grasping Rosemary's skull, Evie gave her head a firm turn back towards the mirror. "I'm almost finished and if I don't set these pins correctly it's all going to come tumbling down. They are just jealous, you know."

It was like observing a magician work, Rosemary marveled as she watched her cousin deftly turn her hair from a flat pancake into a three-tiered cake. Freed from the waxy bandoline, her curls shone in the sunlight, appearing chestnut and mahogany in color instead of their usual mousy brown. Loose tendrils framed the side of her face, emphasizing the natural arch of her cheekbones while the rest had been gathered at the crown of her head to give her countenance, which tended towards roundness, more length. And all of it accomplished with nothing more than a brush and a few hairpins.

"Who is jealous?" she said absently, scratching an itchy spot on the inside of her elbow.

"The ladies at the garden party, and the ones who went out of their way last evening to remind everyone through pointless questions that I was born and bred in America. As if we didn't soundly trounce you in the War of Independence." Evie hesitated, then added belatedly, "No offense, of course."

"None taken. But no one is jealous of *me*. Least of all Lady Navessa," she muttered under her breath.

"I've found that spitefulness is nothing more than a symptom of jealousy. If someone wants what you possess, they try to take it from you by whatever means are at their disposal. Men fight with their fists, women with their words." Sliding the final pin into place, Evie put her hands on her hips and stepped away to cast an admiring eye upon her handiwork before her gaze lifted to Rosemary's in the flat, silvery glass. "If this Lady Navessa was acting unkindly towards you, then she is almost positively jealous. And why wouldn't she be?"

Rosemary gave a startled laugh. "Why *would* she be? Navessa is a diamond of the first water and has already received too many marriage proposals to count. Not to mention, she's a favorite of Queen Victoria. I'm just…me."

Selecting a small brown vial from the myriad of bottles and tins that covered her vanity, Evie used a dropper to release a thin layer of oil upon her fingertip and then, leaning in close to the mirror, dabbed it on her lips. "You're witty and charming and unique. Animals adore you, which I've always found to be a good sign of someone's character." She smiled at her reflection and, apparently satisfied with what she saw, returned the dropper to the vial after offering some to Rosemary, who gave a hesitant shake of her head. "How is my darling Posy, by the way?"

"Growing by leaps and bounds. She's moved out to the barn and has taken up well with a small herd of yearling ewes. I made sure they all got along before we left."

"I did want to bring her here, but I knew she'd fare better in the countryside. Lambs don't belong in London." Evie gave a small sigh. "But I do hope she remembers me."

"I'm sure she will. Animals have wonderful memories. Some even better than people." By sheer happenstance, Rosemary glanced at a clock in the corner of the room. When she saw where the minute hand was positioned she gasped aloud and surged to her feet. "Oh, no. I've been here much too long. My grandmother is going to be wondering where I am."

"I'll walk you out. But," Evie complained as they made their way down the stairs and into the foyer, "I don't like how you have to sneak around. I am not some secret lover that you're visiting. I am your relative, and soon to be the Countess of Hawkridge. What's the point of having a fancy title if it doesn't get me what I want? And what I want is more time with my one and only cousin."

"I can try to come back again. At the end of next week, perhaps. My grandmother is visiting a friend out of town, and she should be gone for most of the day."

The corners of Evie's lips, shiny and plump from whatever she'd applied to them, jutted downwards in disapproval. "That's far too long. I've ordered fabric samples that are arriving tomorrow and I am going to need to see them against your complexion. How else am I supposed to choose between pearl and alabaster? With your skin tone, I'm leaning more towards alabaster, but you never know."

"Aren't pearl and alabaster the same color?" Rosemary ventured.

Evie stared. "They most *certainly* are not. Moreover, I've no idea how I am supposed to find a silhouette and neckline that will compliment you, and Joanna, *and* Brynne." Her eyes narrowed accusingly. "It doesn't help that you've all different colored hair."

Rosemary touched a brunette curl dangling in front of her ear. "I'm...sorry?"

"Apology accepted." Evie waved her arm in the air. "Although I suppose, strictly speaking, it's not your fault. Besides, if anyone is up to such a gargantuan task, it's me. You might even say I've been preparing myself for this since I was a little girl designing outfits for my dolls. If I have to, I *might* be able to cut a piece of your hair and choose the shade of ivory and type of fabric based on that. But I absolutely *must* have the dresses fitted in person. That is not up for negotiation."

Rosemary's fingers tightened protectively around her curl. "Excuse my ignorance, but...what are the dresses for?"

"For the wedding," Evie replied, as if it were the most obvious thing in the world. "You're going to be one of my bridesmaids, aren't you? Which means you need a bridesmaid's dress. Along with my sister and soon to be sister-in-law."

She said it so matter-of-factly that it took a moment for the enormity to settle. For Rosemary to comprehend what Evie meant, and to understand what was being asked of her. What *had* been asked of her, without a question ever being spoken. Because it hadn't needed to be. And that type of inclusivity, the kind that she'd never experienced before, was enough to bring a rush of unexpected tears to Rosemary's eyes.

"What's this?" Evie asked when Rosemary embraced her in a hug.

"To thank you," Rosemary sniffled.

"For what?"

"For wanting me to be in your wedding."

For just wanting me.

At this point, Rosemary was accustomed to being alone. Most times she even preferred it that way. Especially when it came between staying in the corner of the room with a book and being forced to dance in the middle of it. But choosing to be alone did not mean that she wasn't often lonely, and she had long yearned for someone to fill that loneliness with her.

When she was young, she'd desperately wanted a sister to play with. To giggle with. To conspire with. As she'd grown older, and come to the difficult realization that she was forever destined to be an only child, she'd wished for a friend. Just one. A best friend who knew her better than she knew herself, and accepted all of the oddities and little eccentricities that set her apart from everyone else. But that friend never came either. Until all at once, and without much warning, she had two of them. Two best friends. Two sisters (who were technically second cousins, but she wasn't exactly in a position to be picky). Two women who accepted her *as* she was, for *who* she was.

Minus a few hair and wardrobe alterations.

"I've never been asked to be in a wedding before," she went on, and when a fresh torrent of tears threatened–heavens, where were they all coming from?–she drew a ragged breath and used the green lace hem of her sleeve to dry her face. "I'll find a way to come to the dress fitting. I promise."

"Dress fitting*s*," Evie corrected. "There's also to be a formal luncheon, and a dinner party, and an engagement ball. Then the wedding itself, naturally, which is to take place at Hawkridge, with a hunting expedition the day before for the gentlemen, and an afternoon of leisurely activities for the ladies."

"That all sounds…wonderful," Rosemary said dazedly.

Evie gave a rueful grin "It's a lot. I know. Truth be told, Weston would be happy running off to the nearest church. He wants me, and could not care less about all of the pomp and circumstance. But I've dreamed of this day my entire life, and I want more than a quick elopement to Gretna Green." She gasped and clapped her hands together. "Speaking of Gretna Green, have you heard the news?"

"No. I'm not usually privy to much gossip," Rosemary admitted.

Evie clucked her tongue. "This isn't gossip. It's fact. As it turns out, Brynne–Weston's twin sister, you know–is married. And has been, for nearly two years! To a *very* handsome Scot. Lord Lachlan Campbell."

The name sounded vaguely familiar, although Rosemary couldn't place a face to it. "I take it they eloped to Gretna Green?"

"They *did*," Evie said in a hushed voice even though it was just the two of them in the foyer. "No one knew. Not even Weston. Best to not say anything about it to him, as it remains a bit of a sore subject. He *punched* Lachlan when he found out. In the *face*. But isn't it romantic?"

"Lord Weston punching Lord Campbell is romantic?" Rosemary said, confused.

"No, no. The *elopement*. After which, it appears there was some kind of estrangement, but that's all water under the bridge these days. I've never seen a happier couple except for Joanna and Kincaid, who are absurdly perfect together." Evie held up a finger. "Don't tell her I said that."

"I won't," Rosemary said solemnly.

"Anyway, Brynne and Lachlan's secret marriage is the talk of the *ton*. I am surprised you haven't heard about it, although I suppose you've not been in London very long. Things are quite fast-paced here, aren't they?" She bounced lightly on her heels. "I must admit that I adore every ounce of drama. It's most entertaining."

What Rosemary found entertaining was how different Evie and Joanna were. They may have been sisters, but they were as opposite as night was from day. Evie cared about appearances...in a good way. She valued her beauty, and the beauty in others. Whereas Joanna would have likely worn trousers if Society allowed her to get away with it. The eldest Thorncroft sister was as impulsive and headstrong as Evie was calculated and charming. Yet they both had one thing in common: loyalty to those that they loved.

A circle that now included her, hard as it was to believe. All that time spent yearning for a family when she'd already had one an ocean away. She just hadn't met them yet.

"I am exceedingly pleased for you, and Brynne, and Joanna. From what little I've seen thus far, you've all found husbands that are perfect for you." Even as she said the words aloud, Rosemary encountered an unfamiliar tightness in the back of her throat. Followed by an unpleasant burning reminiscent of gin. The feeling was *so* foreign that she wasn't even sure what it was at first...until it came to her in a startling wave of recognition.

Jealous.

She was *jealous* of her cousins.

How terrible!

Here they had been nothing but kind and accepting, and she was jealous of the joy they'd found with Weston, and Lachlan, and Kincaid. Jealous that they'd already had their happily-ever-afters written while hers was hardly past the first chapter. Hardly past the first paragraph, really. And while she'd wanted to ask Evie for advice on what to do about Sterling, suddenly she was loath to share what had happened, for a rushed kiss in a library paled in comparison to finding one's soulmate.

Whatever she and Sterling had, it obviously wasn't anywhere close to the bond that Evie shared with the Earl of Hawkridge. And if, in the back of her mind, she'd thought...even for a moment...that *maybe*...well, it just went to show how truly little she knew about true love.

"Look at the time," she said, a tad desperately. Especially since there wasn't even a clock in the foyer. "I wish I could stay longer, but–"

"Go, go." Oblivious to the uncontrollable envy that continued to rise up in Rosemary like an awful green sickness, Evie placed her hand in the small of her back and ushered her towards the door. "I don't want you to get in any trouble on my account. We'll see each other soon enough. Will you be attending the Marigold Ball?"

Held every autumn, the famed Marigold Ball was a traditional event dating back to the wedding of the very first Duke and Duchess of Clemson. As the story went, the duke had won his bride's favor after defeating all challengers in a jousting tournament held at the bequest of King Edward III. As a token of her love, she'd given him a marigold to wear on his armor. Miraculously, the orange flower had survived countless duels without losing so much as a petal. When the fighting was done and the Duke of Clemson declared the victor, he and his lady were married that very afternoon whereupon she wore the marigold in her hair.

From that day of celebration a tradition was born, albeit one that had shifted and changed over the years. Somewhere along the way the tournament was replaced with a ball; one that was still held on the same field that had seen the duke and duchess wed all those centuries ago.

At the beginning of the night, every unmarried woman in attendance was given a marigold, which she could then bestow upon whichever suitor struck her fancy. If he accepted the flower, it was a sign the two would soon be husband and wife. If he declined, then she would suffer a month of bad luck. Two, if at the end of the evening she hadn't found anyone to take her marigold.

To date, Rosemary had given out precisely three flowers.

All of which Sir Reginald had happily eaten.

Handing out a marigold to a squirrel instead of a man wasn't *exactly* in line with the rules, but neither did it break them. Besides, to the best of her knowledge, she'd not yet suffered any bad luck as a consequence. And Sir Reginald did enjoy the treat, so what was the harm?

"Yes," she said, nodding. "My grandmother and I will be there."

Evie beamed. "Excellent! I'll bring the fabric samples."

CHAPTER SIX

D ESPITE RETURNING TO the birthday celebration later than
intended, Rosemary's absence was not detected. Her grandmother did not even comment on her change in hair, other than to say
that it had turned frizzy with the heat and more bandoline was in
order.

It was strange, how observant Lady Ellinwood could be at times
and how oblivious she was at others. Once she had made an enormous
fuss–and nearly fired a servant–because her son's portrait, which hung
above the mantel in the drawing room, had somehow shifted half an
inch to the right. But when her granddaughter hid an injured hedge-
hog in an empty chamber pot for the better part of a month, she
hadn't noticed at all.

To this day, Rosemary suspected that her grandmother *had* known
about Mr. Trinkets...but had decided, for reasons unknown, to look
the other way whenever she heard scurrying and loud chirping.

It went without saying that Lady Ellinwood was a complicated
woman, her iron demeanor forged by the loss of her husband, son, and
daughter-in-law. If she was too strict on occasion, too overbearing,
Rosemary understood it was only because she was being protective.
And if she'd never made any attempt to coddle her granddaughter, or
hug her goodnight, or read her stories or kiss her bruised knees, what
was that but another type of protection? A preparation, rather, for the

cold, unforgiving world that Rosemary would be forced to face as she grew older. A world that embraced those who swam with the current, but didn't quite know what to do with the odd ducks who paddled against it.

That night, after tucking Sir Reginald into his box stuffed with bits of cotton and leaves and his favorite toy, a miniature bear that Rosemary had lovingly stitched herself, she combed out her hair and reflected on her conversation with Evie. A conversation that had unearthed a few complications of her own. The largest of which being the envy she'd felt...and the tender nerve that had been exposed when she realized that despite having found her sisters, there was a piece of her that was still on the outside looking in.

She was honored to be Evie's bridesmaid. Elated to be able to participate in what was sure to be a beautiful day filled with many blessings. But she also couldn't help but think...*why not me? Why am I unlovable? Why am I forever the one left out and left for last?*

Courtship, love, marriage–or the notable lack thereof–had never bothered her before. A wise choice, as it turned out, for now it was *all* that her mind wanted to dwell on. But self-pity was not a quality that Rosemary permitted herself to have, and with a brisk yank of the brush through her curls that would have undoubtedly made Evie cringe, she cast such thoughts aside and climbed into bed.

After a long, emotionally draining day, sleep was anything but elusive. As her eyelids grew heavy and her breathing evened, she tumbled straight into slumber. Dreaming, as she had every night since coming to London, of a duke with haunted gray eyes and the devil's own smile...

LONDON WAS EXACTLY as Sterling remembered it. A loud, cluttered juxtaposition of new money and old, purity and sin, decorum and decadence. Over by Fleet Ditch, the poor worked themselves to death in factories that spewed black coal dust into the air while in Grosvenor

Square the wealthy sipped champagne out of crystal flutes and congratulated themselves on their success despite having done nothing to earn it. In a ballroom filled with debutantes and their eager mothers, a flashed ankle might mean social ruin, while in the infamous pleasure gardens orgies took place under a full moon.

Before Sebastian died, Sterling had navigated the narrow path between sainthood and sinner with expert skill. He'd cultivated a reputation as a perfect gentleman in public while allowing his wilder appetites to be sated in private. The expectations were never as high for a second born son, but he'd met them nevertheless, as much to avoid disappointing his big brother as to maintain his good name. Then the duel happened and, in his grief, he didn't just fall off the bloody wagon.

He plunged.

Headfirst.

Into waters dark and deep.

There was a part of him–a terrifyingly large part–that wouldn't mind drowning in that water. That would be perfectly fine with closing his eyes and holding his breath and sinking all the way to the bottom never to rise above the surface again.

Hell, he was already halfway there. Slowly but surely, he'd been slipping a few inches further every day since Sebastian left him. Smiling above the waves even as his legs failed to tread water underneath. Another few weeks, a month, maybe half a year, and he'd be too far gone to ever claw his way back up to the light.

The only time he'd felt like he *wasn't* on the verge of succumbing to the inky depths of oblivion was when he had been at Hawkridge Manor.

With Rosemary.

Fucking, gambling, drinking…he'd turned to every vice he could think of in the hopes of either yanking himself out of the water or putting himself out of his misery once and for all. Anything but this constant, unabating state of *nothingness*.

Nothing but the weight of his guilt crushing down on him and the gnawing sounds that the demons made as they picked at his bones.

And then…then there was Rosemary.

His proverbial light in the darkness. His squirrel-loving wallflower who drank gin and drove carriages and boldly asked for kisses in the library. Who had been on the brink of telling him that she loved him before he'd had the good sense to stop her.

The only noble thing he had done these six years past.

Since she left, he'd told himself–*commanded* himself–to stop thinking about her.

To stop walking into rooms in search of the faintest remaining hint of citrus.

To forget the sweet, heavenly taste of her lips.

To forget he had ever *met* her.

Which was exactly why he'd come to London. Not because he knew that she was here as well. That was so absurd that it didn't even deserve comment. No, their being in the same place at the same time was a complete coincidence. *He* had come on the advice of his sister. Whom he hadn't listened to in over half a decade, but in this instance she was right. If he had any prayer of staying out of Newgate, he had to rehabilitate his image. Beginning with a successful Season.

Balls, dinner parties, attending theater shows where women were fully clothed…everything he detested but needed to do if he wanted to show what a shining pillar of Society he was. A shining pillar that was responsible for the death of his brother, but couldn't possibly have murdered his mistress. Whatever bloody sense that made. But Sarah seemed to think it would work, and who was he to disagree with his beloved little sister?

So he was here.

In London.

The world's largest city where the odds of bumping into *one* person out of a million were…one in a million.

Which was why, if sometime during his ridiculous redemption tour, his path just *happened* to cross with Rosemary's, it could hardly be considered *his* fault now could it?

He was just doing what his sister had asked of him.

Loyal, obedient brother that he was.

To avoid the inevitable fanfare and speculation that would accompany his return to High Society, Sterling arrived in the wee hours of the morning and stumbled, drunk on gin and exhaustion, into his bed where he slept for the better part of three days.

He would have slept four, had he not been roused by an incessant pounding at the door.

"I'm coming, I'm coming," he muttered, and nearly walked naked out his bedchamber before he remembered to grab a robe. He was immediately joined by his valet in the hallway, whose flustered appearance was atypical of the sixty-year-old servant's generally stoic, unflappable disposition.

"I sincerely apologize, Your Grace. They refused to leave or even give a card. I tried repeatedly to have them sent away, but–"

"It's all right, Higgins," Sterling interrupted, waving off the valet's profuse apology with a careless jerk of his arm. "I'm up now, and I can see what all the damned ruckus is for myself." So saying, he paused at the open banister overlooking the two-story foyer and studied who was waiting for him down below. A man and a woman, both dressed in the plain, sensible clothes of the working class.

"Do you know them?" Higgins said anxiously. "I can have the constable called–"

"No need for that. The constable is already here." Leaving his valet at the top of the steps, Sterling descended the staircase in a loose, lanky stride as he tightened the knot around his waist that was holding his robe closed. He'd no sooner reach the bottom than he found himself besieged by Thomas Kincaid and his pretty red-haired wife, Joanna, who he'd not yet met but immediately recognized as she shared enough similar traits with her sister, Evie, who he had met *and* attempted to seduce. An endeavor that had obviously failed, as she was now engaged to be married to Lord Weston.

"You can go," he said, squinting blearily at Kincaid through blood-shot eyes. "It's too early for business. But your wife can stay, as it's never too early for pleasure." A lazy grin slid across his mouth as he openly admired the detective's American bride. She was taller than Evie, with a more willowy build, but the sisters had the same blue eyes and striking, bred-into-the-bone beauty. "You don't have another sibling, do you?"

"As it so happens I do. Her name is Claire, and I wouldn't let her within an ocean's reach of you." Although Joanna's words were stern, the twitch of her lips revealed a strong sense of humor lurking behind her austere façade. A good thing, as Kincaid was far too practical by half and could greatly benefit from a touch of frivolity in his life. "You're every bit as disreputable as my husband warned me you'd be, Your Grace." Forgoing the more traditional and ladylike curtsy, she stuck out her hand. "It's wonderful to finally meet you."

"I'd say the same," Sterling said with an amused glance at Kincaid after he'd shaken her hand, "if your husband wasn't currently looking as if he wanted to take out his pistol and shoot me with it."

"Strangle, not shoot," Kincaid remarked with the mild calm of a man who was anything but. "It'd take too long to get the blood out of the marble."

"Now that pleasantries have been exchanged, shall we adjourn to the parlor?" Joanna suggested brightly. "There's much we need to discuss." She used her elbow to give her husband a not-very-discreet nudge in the ribs. "With our *paying* client."

Kincaid's eyes, a clear, intelligent amber behind round spectacles, remained pinned on Sterling. "Our paying client should have remained in the country as I advised him to."

"Too many birds. They kept waking me up at ungodly hours." He lifted a brow. "Is that a feather sticking out, Kincaid, or are you just pleased to see me?"

Joanna snickered. "Make that *two* ocean's distance."

Once they were settled in the parlor, a large room with mahogany paneling that had always been a bit too somber for Sterling's taste, he and Joanna sat across from each other on matching divans in emerald velvet while Kincaid remained standing, his arms behind his back and a frown fixed on his face.

"Go on," Sterling sighed. "Best get the lecture of the way. I should have stayed at Hawkridge Manor as you told me, blah blah blah. But I'm not a bloody prisoner, am I?"

"You're in the presence of a lady," said Kincaid. "Please mind your language."

"No ladies here," Joanna put in cheerfully. Cupping a hand to her mouth, she leaned forward out of her seat. "Besides, I've said much worse."

Kincaid grumbled something unintelligible under his breath, and then in a louder voice said, "I knew I shouldn't have brought you with me."

"Maybe *I* shouldn't have brought *you*," Joanna said with a haughty toss of her head. "Ever consider that?"

"I like her," Sterling decided. He nodded at Joanna. "I like you."

"The feeling, Your Grace, is mutual."

"Please, call me Sterling."

"Don't call him that." Kincaid jabbed a finger at Sterling. "And you, stop flirting with my damned wife."

Sterling held up his hands, the very picture of degenerate innocence. "I'd never dream of it." He lowered his voice. Added just a touch of consternation to it. "Please mind your language. We're in the presence of a lady."

Joanna snickered.

Kincaid growled.

Sterling sat back and grinned. Reaching for the coffee that a maid had brought in on a silver serving platter along with a smattering of breads still warm from the oven and various sides of jam, he raised a cup of the black brew to his mouth.

And nearly spat it out all over the antique Aubusson rug.

"Dear God," he shuddered. "That's terrible."

"What's wrong with it?" Joanna asked, red brows collecting over the bridge of her nose in concern. "I found mine quite lovely compared to the sludge that…ah…someone I know makes."

"There's no whiskey in it," Sterling said, scowling at his cup as he returned it to the platter. "There's supposed to be whiskey."

"It's half past nine in the morning," she said blankly.

"Your point being?"

"Maybe it would be best to hold off on the liquor until you hear what we've recently discovered," Kincaid cut in. Sitting beside his wife, he slanted her a sideways glance out of the corners of his spectacles and frowned. "My coffee isn't *that* bad, is it?"

"The worst I've ever tasted." She patted his knee. "But that's neither here nor there, as I didn't marry you for your culinary skills."

As he watched the newlyweds, Sterling felt an unexpected pang in his heart. At least, where his heart *would* have been if he still had one.

Love was never something he aspired to. Not since he had lost Sebastian, at any rate. Any traces of genuine feeling he had left in him these days was reserved strictly for Sarah. He didn't plan to take a wife. Mayhap not even another mistress, given what had happened to Eloise. Of course, he wasn't going to give up a good rutting now and again. He was dead inside, not insane. But there was a marked difference between blindly fucking for the sake of pleasure and the sweet, subtle affection that Kincaid and Joanna so clearly shared.

Unbidden, his mind conjured a picture of Rosemary. As sharp and vivid as if she were sitting right next to him with *her* hand on *his* knee.

In her adorably oversized clothes and ugly bonnet, her blue-gray eyes filled with warmth and adoration and the tiniest inkling of exasperation.

They were both smiling. Laughing over a private joke that only the two of them understood. And he knew, as surely as he knew his own name, that he loved her. He *loved* her, and she loved him, and they were happy.

Annoyed by the sudden and unwanted direction his thoughts had taken, Sterling picked up his whiskeyless coffee and drained it to the dregs in an attempt to clear his head of useless, fanciful imaginings.

Because even *if* he wanted to fall in love (which he didn't), and even *if* he wanted to get married (which he wouldn't), it would *never* be to the likes of Miss Rosemary Stanhope.

She deserved the moon and every bloody star in the sky. While he...he was a comet hurtling towards earth, burning everything in its path on the way down.

"Well?" he snapped, more forcefully than he'd intended, but who the devil cared? It was all meaningless, anyways. Even if his name was cleared, he wouldn't be any further ahead than he'd been before. Sebastian would still be dead. His life would still be a crack all pile of shite. And his future...his future would be as empty tomorrow as it was today. "What have you come here at the crack of dawn to tell me? What is it you've discovered? Something large, I hope, given the inordinate sum I've paid you thus far."

A smaller man prone to intimidation might have cringed, or stuttered, or even gotten up and left. But Kincaid was neither small, nor easily intimidated, and even though his lack of a title put him far below Sterling in the all-important British social hierarchy, he met the duke's harsh gaze without so much as a flinch.

"*You* came to *me* for help. Or have you forgotten?"

Shame collected in a ball of red heat at the nape of Sterling's neck. Unable to meet Kincaid's cool stare, he glanced to the side as his hands curled into fists and he wondered, not for the first time, how he'd gotten here. To this place of bleakness and rage and hopelessness. When he wasn't sloshed, he was angry. When he wasn't angry, he was...he was nothing. Nothing but a shell of a man pretending to be something he wasn't for the sake of people who didn't give a fuck about him. And those few who did–Sarah, Kincaid, even Rosemary–he pushed away. For surely it was better for them to hate him than to see what he'd really become.

"I've not forgotten," he said stiffly. "Nor did I come back to London on some heedless whim. My sister encouraged my return, as she maintains the naïve belief that my reputation can be salvaged."

"Interestingly, your sister is why we've come here today."

Everything inside of Sterling went hot and then freezing cold. He gripped the curved armrest of the divan with such strength that his nails punctured the velvet, and would have leapt to his feet if there was anywhere for him to go. "What's wrong? Has she been taken again? Why didn't you–"

"Lady Sarah is fine," Joanna interrupted. "Perfectly fine. I spoke with her just yesterday. We had an enjoyable conversation over the most *delightful* pastries filled with cream and–"

"I don't think the duke cares about the pastries, my love," said Kincaid, his gaze on Sterling, who had sagged limply into his seat as the blood began to once again pump through his veins. "Joanna set up a meeting with your sister because we think there may be a connection to her kidnapping and Eloise's disappearance."

A connection? The two incidents had occurred years apart. He still remembered the fear that had sliced through him when he received word that Sarah's carriage had been besieged by highwaymen. Reading that ransom note had cut him to the bone. The fear. The horror. The bloody unfairness of it all. How much was one family expected to endure? First their parents, then Sebastian, and now Sarah. Pure, innocent, adorable Sarah. The *one* person in the world he'd been charged with to keep safe. And he'd held a crudely written letter threatening her life in his hands.

The bastards had demanded a hundred pounds for her safe return.

Sterling would have given them ten thousand.

Ten thousand and his own life, if it came to that.

It hadn't. The three days they'd held her were a blur, even now. He had paid them at once and then paced a hole through the rug in this very parlor as he waited for them to uphold their side of the bargain. Except they hadn't, and when the clock ticked half past midnight, he'd gone straight to Scotland Yard where he had met a constable with wire-rimmed spectacles and a serious air about him that had reassured Sterling despite the panic clawing at his insides.

He had handed Kincaid the note, told him all that he knew, and then waited some more.

For the rest of the night and all the next day he hadn't eaten, hadn't slept, and hadn't even drank. When Sarah was safely delivered, he held her in his arms and wept. Only the third time in his life that he'd cried. The first two due to overwhelming grief, this time out of sheer, unspeakable relief.

"What kind of connection?" he asked, baffled as to how his sister and his mistress–two women, it went without saying, that had never met–might be intertwined.

"*You*, Sterling." Kincaid's mouth flatted into a thin, grim line. "The connection is you."

CHAPTER SEVEN

O N THE NIGHT of the Marigold Ball, the weather was cool and
clear. If one tilted their head, they could almost see the stars
through the manmade fog that spewed from the massive textile
factories lining the Thames. But from her seat on a stone bench at the
far end of the field, the only thing Rosemary saw was the flash of Sir
Reginald's bushy tail as he vanished into the leafy branches of an oak.

"*Sir Reginald!*" she hissed with no small amount of alarm. "Sir
Reginald, get down here this *instant!*"

Just a few minutes ago he had been fast asleep, curled in a ball
inside the pocket she had secretly sewn into the waist of her burgundy
ball gown. But the unexpected boom of a firework had caught them
both unawares, and while Rosemary had jumped and then composed
herself, Sir Reginald had panicked and bolted. Out of her pocket, along
her arm, and straight up into a tree.

It wasn't the first thing to have gone wrong this evening, but it was
definitely the worst. As Rosemary had been preparing to leave, she had
received a hastily written note from Evie filled with apologies. She and
Weston, it appeared, would not be attending the Marigold Ball as
planned. Neither would Lady Brynne or Lord Campbell, or Joanna and
Kincaid, which meant that Rosemary would be left to face the *ton*
alone.

Which was why, naturally, she'd brought Sir Reginald.

As her grandmother gossiped with a bevy of crotchety old patronesses bemoaning the direction High Society was taking (*"have you heard, women actually want to participate in* Parliament, *of all things?!"*) and Lady Navessa made her rounds in search of the most eligible bachelor with which to bestow her marigold upon, Rosemary had taken her pet and retreated as far from the dance floor and white tents and paper lanterns as she possibly could.

She'd thought the little enclave she'd found, complete with a bench and trickling fountain to drown out the shrill laughter and vicious gossip flowing from the main courtyard, was the perfect place to while away the hours. Until a firework was accidentally discharged, and Sir Reginald abandoned her warm, cozy pocket for a precarious perch high overhead and far out of reach.

What was she to do now? She couldn't leave him here! Not by himself, out in the dark, where there was no telling what predators lurked in the shadows waiting to sink their teeth into a tasty squirrel-sized snack. Oh, what a disaster tonight was shaping up to be! If only she'd kept him at home. If only *she'd* stayed at home. But her grandmother had been quite insistent that she attend, as if the outcome of this Marigold Ball would be any different from the previous three. As if Rosemary weren't going to do anything other than sit in the proverbial corner and read a book.

Which, given her current circumstances, she *wished* she was doing. Instead she was anxiously swinging her arms from side to side as she walked back and forth underneath the oak trying everything she could imagine to coax Sir Reginald down.

She offered him a lifetime supply of peanuts. Sleeping under the covers instead of in his box. A day spent in Hyde Park climbing whatever tree he wished. Just not *this* tree. On *this* night. At *this* estate, the prestigious London residence of the current Duke and Duchess of Clemson. A couple renowned for being remarkable hosts...and excellent hunters.

During Rosemary's first Marigold Ball it had started to rain halfway through, and all of the guests had been rushed out of the field and into the main ballroom by way of the side foyer. There'd been mass confusion and, in the melee, Rosemary had gotten turned around and somehow found herself in a wide, dark hallway...with dozens of black, glassy eyes staring at her.

When her eyes adjusted to the low lighting, she was appalled to find herself gazing at a plethora of stuffed animals. Where portraits ordinarily hung there were deer heads instead of all shapes and sizes. Ones with antlers and ones without. Ones with their mouth open and ones with their mouth closed. There was even a full-sized stag beside which stood a bear towering on its hind legs, massive brown jowls frozen in a fearsome snarl.

If the Duke of Clemson was capable of killing a *bear*, what would he do to a tiny, defenseless squirrel?

Rosemary didn't plan to find out.

"Sir Reginald!" Hands on her hips, she implored her pet to listen to reason. "Please come down. I know you're frightened, but it's really not safe up there. I know you believe it to be safe because you are a squirrel and it is a tree, but you're not an ordinary squirrel, are you? You're a tame squirrel, which is completely different."

A quick chitter, a scrape of nails on bark, and then...nothing.

Stubborn creature.

"Fine." On a huff of determined breath, Rosemary lifted her skirts and climbed up onto the bench. Eyeing the lowest branch, which appeared wide enough to sustain her, she tentatively stretched her fingers out and, much to her surprise, managed to grab it. "If you won't come down, then I'll come up."

No sooner had her feet left the smooth, flat surface of the bench and she found herself suspended three feet above the ground with nothing but her quickly fading strength to prevent her from tumbling into the bushes than Rosemary realized her mistake. Namely, that she hadn't an athletic bone in her body and while climbing a tree was a simple matter of defying gravity for a squirrel, it was a much more difficult task for a woman.

Particularly if that woman was wearing a bustle the approximate size of a small pony.

"Well, well, well," a familiar voice drawled from behind her. "What have we here?"

Not him, was her first thought.

Anyone but him!

Her grandmother, Lady Navessa, the Duke of Clemson…anyone, *anyone* but the one man who was guaranteed to gain the most amusement from her unfortunate predicament.

"Aren't you supposed to be at Hawkridge?" she said through gritted teeth.

"Aren't you supposed to be dancing?" Fallen leaves crunched beneath Sterling's boots as he approached and although he didn't touch her, didn't lay so much as a single finger upon her body, she tensed as if he had for his mere *presence*–his scent, the cadence of his breathing, the burning pressure of his stare–immediately brought her back to the library and the passionate kiss they'd shared.

A kiss that he'd called a mistake before he had all but run out of the room. Her last glimpse of him before she'd left the manor. And while she'd be lying to herself if she said that she hadn't dreamed of seeing him again, she certainly hadn't dreamed of it happening like *this*. With her dangling helplessly off a branch while her legs kicked feebly in the breeze and Sterling quite literally laughed behind her back.

Don't fall. Don't fall. Don't fall.

A ridiculous command, really.

A piece of her had been falling for him ever since their first kiss.

"I don't like to dance," she replied tartly. Ignoring the growing ache in her arms, she struggled to maintain her grip as the only thing worse than being caught hanging in midair was tumbling onto her rump. At least if she didn't let go she could retain a shred of her dignity. Although admittedly it, and she, was on rather precarious footing.

"No, I can see swinging about like a monkey is far more preferable than a waltz." Sterling paused, and in the long shadow he cast in front of him she saw his head cant to the side. "What *are* you doing up there, by the by?"

"Isn't it obvious?"

"Not the least little bit."

"Sir Reginald." Her arms were *really* starting to hurt now. Was the pain worth saving herself the humiliation of falling at the Duke of Hanover's feet?

Yes.

Yes it was.

"Who?" he said blankly.

"My pet squirrel!" she cried.

"Ah, the rat."

Were such a thing possible, steam would have whistled from Rosemary's ears. Her legs kicked as she tried to twist her body to see Sterling's face, but he remained elusively removed from her line of sight. There but not there; his existence proven only by the surge of annoyance that filled her breast...and the dampness between her thighs. "We've been over this more than once. Sir Reginald is *not* a rat."

"Hmmm. I suppose you may be right, as last I checked rats don't climb trees."

"I *am* right. Furthermore–*ahh!*" Before Rosemary could jump into another lecture illuminating the various differences between the Rodentia families, her left hand–numb from the point of her elbow to the tips of her fingers–abruptly slid off the rough bark. She made a desperate attempt to save herself with her right, but as that wrist had all the strength of a dull potato, it was a failed effort to say the least. With an embarrassing screech, she fell back...straight into Sterling's waiting arms.

They closed around her like steel. Strong, immovable bands that pressed her spine flush against his chest and left her feet suspended several inches above the ground. She felt the steady thud of his heartbeat. She felt the comforting weight of his chin on the top of her head. She felt the gradual ebb and flow of his chest as it rose with each breath that he took. But most of all...most of all she felt *safe*. In a way that she hadn't in a very long time.

It was an odd sensation, as Rosemary had never really thought of herself as *unsafe*. Aside from a few snaps with a wooden cane now and again, her grandmother had never beaten her. She was in no danger of suffering homelessness, or starvation, or being forced to do something that would test her morals in order to survive.

But like a bird that had been displaced during a storm and was made to grow up in a tree that wasn't its own, she never felt...she never felt like she fully *belonged* where the wind had planted her. Until she let go of a branch and landed on a duke.

Sterling...Sterling was her tree.

And wasn't that a miraculously terrifying thing to discover?

"Are you all right?" he asked gruffly.

"Y-Yes," Rosemary said, even though she wasn't. Not at all. How could she be? How could she be all right when she'd just come to the conclusion that she was in love? In *love*. With quite possibly the worst man she could have ever fallen in love *with*. Yet here she was, wrapped in his arms like some sort of fairytale princess. Except in this story, the heroine was a book-addicted wallflower and the hero...well, he was as much a hero as she was a princess.

Which was to say, not at all.

He lowered her slowly onto the grass and the leaves. Her toes touched first, then the balls of her feet, and finally her heels. When she was standing of her own volition he didn't release her, as she might expect he would, but instead grasped her shoulders and turned her towards him, leaving her with nowhere to look but up. A gasp wrenched itself from her lips.

"You...you shaved." Without thinking about what she was doing, her hand rose between them and she touched the edge of his jaw. It was hard, but also somehow soft; the thick scruff of stubble he'd sported at Hawkridge Manor nowhere to be seen. The difference was startling, even though she was sure she must have witnessed him clean shaven before. At a ball they'd both attended, or a play they'd both watched. But she hadn't paid him any mind then, and she was positive he hadn't noticed her.

Certainly not like he was noticing her tonight.

He laid his hand upon hers, and his muscles flexed and rippled as his mouth bent in a wry smile that made her heart skip a beat. "My valet refused to let me out in public without taking a razor to my face first. What do you think?"

"I think he did a very good job," Rosemary replied seriously. She searched his countenance, focusing on his square, handsome chin and the straight line of his jaw. "I don't see a stray whisker anywhere."

"What about now?" he asked, leaning into her hand as his eyes dropped to her mouth and the air between them suddenly crackled with delicious tension.

Rosemary wet her lips, and his gaze darkened. "As–as I said, he did a very...very good–*ah.*"

This time when she fell, she didn't scream so much as whimper. Perhaps because she wasn't falling *out* of something but *into* something.

And that something was Sterling.

He cradled her against him with all the infinite care of a shepherd tending to a lost lamb. Except Rosemary wasn't a sheep, and the Duke of Hanover had more in common with the wolf that stalked the flock than the man who cared for them.

His tongue slipped lazily between her lips and heat shot through her with the archaic force of a lightning bolt scorching the earth. Almost immediately, this kiss went further, farther, faster than the two preceding it. They were a wildfire racing across an open field that hadn't seen rain in a fortnight, and Rosemary…Rosemary wanted to burn.

Thrown off balance all over again, she clung to his torso as she'd clung to the tree, holding on to the narrow lapels of his emerald green jacket while his hands, devilish entities unto themselves, followed her body's natural curves from her shoulders all the way to her waist where they settled, thumbs hooked on the sloping ridge of her hipbones as his fingers splayed across her backside, delving through untold layers of satin and muslin and wool until he reached her bottom.

Sterling squeezed her plump flesh and heat shot through her anew when she found herself pressed intimately against his loins, that sweet, slick area between her thighs rubbing on a rigid, pulsing staff.

On a muttered oath, he abandoned her hips to cup her breasts, strumming across nipples already hard and all but begging for his touch.

Bright flashes of light danced behind her closed eyelids when he dropped his head while simultaneously yanking on her flimsy bodice, exposing her skin to moonlight and feverish madness before his wicked, wanton mouth closed around a swollen rosebud.

Her knees buckled, and his breath fanned across her breast in a velvety chuckle as he prevented her from sliding to the ground in a boneless heap of delirious desire.

"Clementines," he rasped. "You taste like clementines."

He kissed her other nipple, tongue swirling around the puckered point in a waltz all of his own making as she did her best to remain on her feet. Swathed in sin and draped in shadow, she and Sterling abandoned themselves to a passion that refused to be denied. That *couldn't* be denied, no matter how irregular or inconvenient it was to catch fire for a scoundrel who was hard-pressed to remember her name half the time.

But that wasn't important.

When flames licked across her skin, nothing was.

Tit tit tit tit tit.

Except for that.

"Sir Reginald!" she gasped, wrenching free of Sterling's embrace as her pet's anxious call threw a bucket of cold water onto the fire. Like a mother that had heard the cry of her child late at night while the rest of the house slept, every fiber in her being instantly went on alert. Yanking her dress into place and lifting her skirts, she hopped back onto the bench and tried in vain to spy the squirrel amidst the dark, leafy branches. "Sir Reginald, not to worry. I'm here!"

"What the devil is going on?" Scowling, Sterling shoved both hands through his hair, scraping the inky curls off his temple as he stepped beside the bench and followed her frantic stare upwards into the maze of limbs and leaves. "Who are you yelling at?"

"Sir Reginald." She bit her bottom lip–a lip swollen from Sterling's kisses. "I cannot reach him, but he's frightened. Too frightened to come down on his own. What am I going to do? I must get him. It's far too dangerous for him to stay here overnight."

A muscle ticked high in Sterling's jaw. "Have you tried reminding him that he's a damned *squirrel*?"

"He already knows that," she huffed.

"Are you certain?" the duke said skeptically. "Seeing as he's oh, I don't know. *Stuck in a bloody tree?*"

"You don't have to take that tone."

"What tone?"

"*That* tone."

"You mean the tone of a man who was just cock robbed by a rat?"

Rosemary nodded. "An exceedingly crude way of putting it, but yes. And Sir Reginald isn't–"

"A rat. Yes, yes, I'm aware." Sterling's sigh was long and agonizing. "He is a member of the prestigious *Sciuridae* family which includes the American prairie dog and marmot."

Some women wanted diamonds and rubies.

Others, lavish furs.

But for Rosemary, Sterling's unwitting admission that he'd actually listened–and retained–what she had told him about Sir Reginald was the most wonderful gift she could have ever hoped to receive.

"What's happening *now?*" he asked in alarm when she impulsively leapt off the bench and looped her arms around his neck.

"I am giving you a hug." A gold button pressed into her cheek as she laid the side of her face flat upon his coat. "Because you're not nearly as horrible as you think you are."

She felt him stiffen. Then after a long moment, during which neither spoke, he began to relax. Like a hard ball of clay being worked by the skilled hands of a sculptor, it didn't happen all at once, but rather in degrees. First he let out the breath he'd been holding. The tightness in his shoulders unraveled next, followed by a subtle release in his ribcage. At last, he reached behind her to pull her snug against his chest, not in a manner that was provocative or sensual, but tender and endearing, which somehow made it even more intimate than the kiss they'd just shared.

"Your Grace?" she whispered, lifting her chin to gaze at him under a thick sweep of mahogany lashes.

"Aye," he murmured, brushing a curl behind her ear. "What is it?" For once, his voice wasn't derisive and mocking. Instead there was a note of vulnerability in it that she'd never heard before. A chord of fragileness that delved far below the surface of his charming exterior to whatever traces of goodness and humanity that still lingered beneath.

"Could you…that is to say…might you be able to retrieve Sir Reginald for me?"

CHAPTER EIGHT

A ND THAT WAS how Sterling found himself climbing a tree at the
Marigold Ball.

In the dark.

Wearing his formal attire.

While a wallflower waited anxiously below yelling instructions
that were less than helpful.

"Have you spotted him yet?" she said. "Try clucking your tongue!"

"I'm not going to cluck my tongue at a *squirrel*."

"I've a few cranberries in my pocket. Sir Reginald loves cranberries."

Grabbing on to the lowest hanging branch, Sterling managed to
wrap his legs around the base and, from there, pivot–after much
grunting and cursing–into a crouching position. Squinting, he shoved a
collection of leaves out of his face as he tried to locate the whereabouts
of Rosemary's runaway pet. "Sir Reginald is going to end up on the
end of a stick roasting over an open fire if he doesn't get his arse down
here this bloody second," he muttered sourly.

"What was that?" she called out.

"I said throw me a damned cranberry."

The first bounced off the branch above him, but he managed to
catch the second. As he plopped it into the middle of his palm and
extended his arm while clucking his tongue, Sterling wondered how

he'd gotten here.

There was only one answer.

Rosemary.

A glance into those beguiling eyes of hers and how could he *not* give her whatever it was that she desired? Had she asked him to walk to Istanbul and steal a crown from the Ottoman sultan he'd have done it. Hell, at least there would have been Turkish wine there.

But no.

Not his Rosemary.

His Rosemary didn't want crowns or jewels or pretty trinkets.

She wanted a rat with a furry tail.

Because of course she did.

"Do you see him yet?" Hands clutched beneath her chin, she peered up at him, her eyes twin pools of shimmering blue fog set in a face pale with worry. "Are you clucking?"

Sterling gave a curt nod, realized she most likely couldn't see him through the oak's twisted maze of limbs, and bit out, "*Yes. Yes, I'm clucking. It isn't working. Maybe if we return tomorrow–*"

"Sir Reginald can't spend the night *outside*," she said, aghast.

Once again, Sterling considered the merits of reminding Rosemary that while domesticated, her pet was a wild animal. But it was clear that neither of them were capable of thinking sensibly at the moment, or else why would he be in a tree clucking at a squirrel like some lunatic escaped straight from Bedlam?

It was the kiss. It had addled their minds. Or maybe his mind was already addled to begin with. That would help explain why he hadn't been able to keep his hands to himself. Why no sooner had he seen Rosemary again than he was possessed with the urge to taste her. To touch her. To pick up right where they'd left off at Hawkridge Manor as if not a day had passed.

Bollocks.

What was *wrong* with him?

Had he no redeeming qualities left?

Every rogue worth his salt knew that you never, ever kissed an innocent at a ball. Besides being the plot of every country house novel gone awry, it was simply a bad idea. No good could come of it. No good *had* come of it, given that he was currently ten feet up in the air holding on to a tree for dear life while trying to coax a belligerent squirrel onto his shoulder.

If he told this story later at the pub, not a soul was going to believe him. And he wouldn't blame them a bit. He hardly believed it himself. If Sir Reginald didn't show his whiskery little face in the next five seconds–

Tit tit tit tit tit.

"Did you hear that?" Rosemary yelped excitedly. "That was–"

"Quiet," he ordered as he cupped his ear and tried to decipher where the sound had come from. Directly above him, he thought. But it was hard to tell for certain. "Sir Reginald? Is that you, mate? Be a nice fellow and come on down, now. You've worried your mistress, and it's getting late."

Tit tit tit. Tit?

"It's a brave lad you are. Handsome as well, I'm sure. Why don't you come here and let me see what a fine coat you have?" Vaguely, Sterling registered that he was deploying the same soft, crooning voice he'd used to lure many a vixen into his bed. Here he thought he'd been fine tuning his art of seduction all those years to secure himself the most beautiful and talented mistresses money could buy, when in actuality he'd been preparing to seduce Sir Reginald.

Never, he decided then and there. Never would this story see the light of day, in a pub or otherwise. Forget murder. His reputation wouldn't ever recover if it became public knowledge that the Duke of Hanover had attempted to flirt with a squirrel.

"Have you got him?" asked Rosemary. "What are you *doing?*"

Sterling ground his teeth together. "Would you care to come up here and give it a go? Because you're more than welcome. I'm doing *you* this favor, in case you've forgotten, and it's not my fault your squirrel is the stupidest, most slow-witted creature that I have ever had the misfortune to–"

And that was when Sir Reginald bit him.

A sharp nip, right on the inside of his left thigh.

In the retelling of this incident (because it would be retold, over and over again), Sterling continued to deny that he screamed. But he did. Like a little girl. Loud and shrill, the high-pitched sound of his feminine screech carried all the way to the manor where the Duchess of Clemson was being serviced by the Earl of Coatesville in her private study.

"Did you hear that?" she frowned.

The earl lifted his head from between her thighs. "Hear what?"

"I'm not sure. Perhaps a maid dropped a tray on her foot?" She patted the top of his head. "Carry on."

The only thing Sterling carried with him as he fell out of the tree and landed on the ground in an unceremonious heap was regret. *This* was why he didn't help people. This was why he preferred to be alone. Because the moment you held out your proverbial hand, a squirrel tried to bite it off.

"Sir Reginald!" Rosemary cried out joyfully when her pet came flying down the trunk of the tree, streaked across the grass in a red blur, and leapt straight onto her shoulder. "You're all right. Thank heavens."

Staggering to his feet, Sterling scowled as he brushed leaves off his clothes and yanked a twig out of his hair. "*I'm* fine, thank you for asking."

He almost wasn't. A few inches higher, and Sir Reginald might have–

No.

Best not to even think about it.

"You were very courageous." Rosemary's dress rustled as she

approached. Rising onto the tips of her toes, she closed her eyes and placed a kiss upon his cheek. "My own knight in shining armor."

To Sterling's horror, he *blushed*. Like a schoolboy who'd just groped his first pair of tits behind the stables.

How mortifying.

"Just keep that damned animal away from me," he said, glaring at Sir Reginald who stared back at him nonplussed, black eyes bright and suspiciously cheerful. If he didn't know better, he'd suspect the squirrel was *smirking* at him. "If it gets itself stuck in a tree again, you'll have to find someone else to rescue it."

"Of course," she said solemnly.

This was where Sterling should have walked away. He'd saved the day. There was nothing keeping him here. The party–and the Duke of Clemson's private stock of bourbon imported straight from some godforsaken place called Kentucky–was under the tents a hundred yards away. *That's* what he had come for. To drink, and socialize, and take the first step towards clearing his name. Not to do…whatever it was he'd done with Rosemary.

Kissing, and fondling, and nearly having his bollocks bitten off by a smirking squirrel.

He should have been walking–nay, running–as fast as his legs could carry him. Instead, he remained rooted to the spot, reluctant to leave his wallflower behind. Never mind that she wasn't *his*. And he didn't want her to be. He just…he just enjoyed this particular bench. That was all. And if Rosemary *happened* to be standing by it, and he *happened* to kiss her again, well, that was nothing more than sheer coincidence. An act of fate, such as it were. Completely out of his control, really.

"How long are you staying in town?" she asked before she sat on one end of the bench.

Excellent craftsmanship, Sterling noted as he sat on the other end. Who *wouldn't* want to take advantage of such a fine piece of outdoor furniture? It didn't hurt that its maker had obviously intended the bench to suit a person who was by themself...which meant that there was hardly more than a hair's width between him and Rosemary. Less, when he decided that he just *had* to stretch his arm out along the back which brought them together like two puzzle pieces fitting snugly into place.

It was strange, this need he had to be close to Rosemary. Not that he ever didn't *want* to be close to women. But that was generally in a purely physical capacity. Lustful appetites, and all that. With Rosemary, though...with Rosemary, it was different. Yes, he wanted to kiss her again. And admittedly do a great deal more than kiss. They'd been moving in the right direction before Sir Reginald's untimely interruption. But now...now he was content simply sitting beside her. Which was as foreign a notion to him as deciphering ancient Sanskrit.

The truth was that as much as she irritated and bewildered him, she also soothed him. Being in her presence was a cooling balm to his hot, restless soul. A balm that he'd sincerely missed this past fortnight. Especially given what he'd learned from Kincaid.

"Tell me about yourself," he said abruptly. "I don't know anything about you."

"Tell you about myself?" she asked, visibly bemused. Even Sir Reginald looked taken aback.

Sterling couldn't blame her. Or the squirrel. Since when did the Duke of Hanover care about anyone but the Duke of Hanover? And he didn't. Care about Rosemary, that is. But she was a distraction he badly needed. Both from past demons and future uncertainties. So if he could sit on this bench for a while and forget everything but the present, why wouldn't he? He was an arrogant, self-entitled arse. Not a masochist. He didn't crave pain. It just happened to follow him wherever he went.

"Yes," he said in a clipped, no-nonsense tone. "I can hardly go about kissing every wallflower I meet without knowing something about her first. What if you ruin my reputation?"

Rosemary blinked. "What if *I* ruin *your* reputation?"

"Indeed. I'm not sure if you're aware, but being accused of murdering one's mistress does put one in a position of social vulnerability. I need to be on my best behavior from this day out. Which means I cannot consort with…" He gave a vague wave of his hand. "Unsavory types."

Tit tit tit!

Sterling glared at the squirrel still sitting atop Rosemary's shoulder. "Quiet, you. Before I make you into a hat."

"Please don't threaten him," Rosemary said with a frown.

"*He* started it," Sterling said grumpily.

"He is a squirrel, and infinitely smaller than you. Surely you can be the bigger person in this situation." Digging into the small satin reticule tied around her wrist, Rosemary procured another cranberry and held it out. "Go on. If you want to know more about me, the first thing you should learn is that I admire those who treat animals with kindness and respect."

Sterling stared dubiously at the red fruit. "He's going to bite me again."

"He's not." She gave Sir Reginald a stern glance out of the corners of her eyes. "You're not."

Tit tit. Tit tit tit! Tit.

"What did he say?" Sterling demanded.

The corners of Rosemary's lips twitched. "He said he is willing to try if you are. Sometimes that is all it takes, you know. Someone willing to set aside their differences and look past all the obstacles in their path and just try."

Why did he have the impression that she wasn't only talking about a squirrel?

"Here," he said grudgingly, holding out his hand with the cranberry in the middle of it.

After a brief hesitation, Sir Reginald slowly tiptoed across Rosemary's arm and teetered, black eyes darting, on his hind legs. Reaching out with his tiny paws, he snatched up his prize and darted into the folds of her gown where he promptly disappeared.

"Where did he go?"

"I have a squirrel pocket," she explained.

"Why am I not the least bit surprised?" Absently, Sterling's fingers began to play with a curl that had come loose from Rosemary's coiffure and was dangling in a tempting spiral of silky brown down the middle of her neck.

Again, he questioned how he'd ever perceived her as plain. Given, she hadn't the striking, stop-dead-in-your-tracks beauty of her American cousins. Few women did. Nor did she have the alluring, enticing appeal of Eloise. A woman who had exuded sexual arrogance with every long, sweeping pass of her tongue along her bottom lip.

Rosemary wasn't a shiny red apple, ripe for the plucking.

She was…she was the first taste of warm bread. The kind that Cook used to put out by the window to cool when he was a boy, knowing full well that he'd run by and grab a chunk straight from the middle, burning the tips of his fingers as he sank his teeth into all that delicious, freshly baked dough.

She was the first tug of a fish on his line when he and Sebastian were gangly lads sitting on a flat slab of rock with their bare feet dangling in the water and the sun hot against the nape of their necks.

She was his first sip of whiskey. That initial burn that had made his eyes water and his throat hurt, before it mellowed and he tasted the individual notes of honey, smoke, and brine.

Rosemary was warmth, and goodness, and comfort. She wasn't beautiful like a rose or a diamond. Those were things. Objects. Pretty in their own right, but what was a rose without its petals or a diamond when it lost its shine? Rosemary's beauty stemmed from the soil. From the water. From the first ray of sunlight after a storm. Standing in her glow was a reminder of what he'd been, and all that he had hoped to one day become.

When he was with her, his shadows didn't seem quite so long or the night so dark. And it was selfish of him to borrow her light. To let himself believe, for even more than a moment, that he was worthy of her. That someone as angelic as she could ever be with a devil like him. But what *was* a devil, if not selfish? He was already damned. Why not enjoy the ride on his way down to hell? So long as he didn't bring Rosemary with him.

"Why aren't you under the tents dancing?" he asked. "Surely there's at least a few suitable gentlemen who would be willing to overlook a squirrel pocket."

She sighed. "If you happen to meet one, please let my grandmother know. She's started to think that I'll never find a match."

"And what do you think?" he said, genuinely curious to hear her response. Was there a lord somewhere out there in the mellow glow of the torchlight that Rosemary was sweet on? If so, he'd like to know the fellow's name. Not for any purpose, really. Just so that he could pull whoever it was aside and inform him, in no uncertain terms, that if he ever dared to harm a hair on Rosemary's head then he was a dead man.

"Having already met every person in attendance tonight at some function or another, I can say with confidence that my match is decidedly *not* under the tents. But my grandmother was still insistent that I show my face and make some attempt at socialization. In the hope, I suppose, that an earl might suddenly be struck with amnesia and forget that I am a quaint little mouse destined for spinsterhood."

Sterling frowned. "Who called you a quaint little mouse destined for spinsterhood?"

I'll grab them by the cuff and–

"*You* did," she said pointedly.

"Ah." Releasing her curl, he scratched sheepishly under his chin. "That does sound like something I'd say."

She made a humming noise of agreement under her breath, then asked, "Why aren't you under the tents dancing?"

"Because I'm a quaint little mouse destined for spinsterhood?" he offered, and was rewarded for his cheek when she smiled.

"I am certain there is a long line of ladies waiting for you to sign your name on their cards."

But I don't want them, he thought silently. *I want...you.*

His jaw tightened. What pure, utter romantic rubbish. Clearly when Sir Reginald bit him on the thigh the squirrel had transmitted some kind of horrible disease. The symptoms of which included fawning over a wallflower as if he really were some love-struck schoolboy.

"You are correct," he said as he surged to his feet. It was apparent now that he was deathly ill, and it was equally apparent that the only antidote was to put as much distance between himself and Rosemary as possible before he did something truly absurd, like kiss her again.

Inadvertently, his gaze fell to her mouth as her smile faded.

"I...I am?" she said.

Wrenching his stare free of those tantalizing plump, perfect lips, he glared instead at a spot halfway up the tree he'd tumbled out of. "Indeed. There are probably dozens, nay, hundreds of women waiting impatiently for me to make my grand arrival. I wouldn't want to disappoint them."

Her head tilted to the side. "Does it cause you digestive upset?"

"Does what cause me digestive upset?"

"Having such a high opinion of yourself," she said innocently.

"Ha ha." His eyes narrowed. "Very amusing, Ramona."

From somewhere inside her pocket, Sir Reginald gave a loud chirp as Rosemary stood up. She absently patted the side of her skirt, and the squirrel quieted. "You did not come here to practice your Viennese Waltz any more than I did. So why *are* you at the Marigold Ball? My grandmother forced me, but I cannot imagine anyone who would have the power to make the great Duke of Hanover do anything he didn't want to do."

"Did you just miss the part where I climbed that bloody tree to rescue your rodent?"

Moonlight glimmered on her skin as she lifted her shoulder. "I didn't force you to help me. You did it because you wanted to. Because deep down, you're not nearly as self-absorbed or pretentious or wicked as you pretend to be."

"I am wicked," he said, offended that she'd dare suggest otherwise. "I'm *very* wicked."

"Are you?" she asked skeptically. "To some, maybe. I've no way to see how you act with others. But with me you have been, while admittedly vexing at times, quite kind."

Kind?

She thought he was *kind?*

He didn't know whether to feel amused or insulted.

"I am afraid you're mistaken, Roxanne. There's not a kind bone in my body." His eyebrows wiggled suggestively as he took a step towards her and lowered his voice to a velvety growl. "But by all means, if you don't believe me, you're welcome to check for yourself. I'd start with my trousers first."

Her gaze softened. "You don't need to do that with me."

"Do what?"

"Use blatant sexual advances to disguise your vulnerabilities."

Sterling gaped.

Kind *and* vulnerable?

This was really starting to get out of hand.

"Should I show you just how wicked I can be?" He meant it as a threat. A way by which to set Rosemary onto her heels and remind her that he wasn't some trained puppy looking for sticks to fetch, but a feral beast with fangs and claws. If she thought he was another pet to be put in her pocket, she was sadly mistaken. He was a bastard in every sense of the word but one. A blackguard. A devil in duke's clothing. A–

"By all means." Seemingly unperturbed by his bared teeth and raised hackles, she gestured at the oak tree. "Should I send Sir Reginald back up there so that you can save him again? I'm sure that would be a true display of your terrible wickedness."

The impertinence was almost too much to be borne.

"You're wrong," he snarled. Hands on his hips, he began to pace. "You think you see something redeemable in me because that's what you want to see. But there's nothing here, Rachel. Nothing but darkness and rot. Whatever kindness I had in me disappeared a long time ago, and the only vulnerable person out here is you."

"Maybe," she said quietly. "Or maybe *you're* wrong."

Chest heaving, he stopped short, corded muscles bulging in his neck and shoulders as the guilt he carried, the guilt he always carried, nearly caused him to drop to his knees. "You have no *bloody* idea what you're going on about. You know nothing about me, or the things I've done. If you did…"

"If I did?" she whispered.

Slowly, he raised his head. From behind the shadows and the weight of his own sins he stared at her. His beacon of light. His ribbon of hope that he didn't deserve. His second chance at happiness that he could never take. "If you did, you'd already be gone."

She took a bold step forward, the silly chit. Then another, and another, until she was standing directly in front of him. Reaching out, she grabbed the lapel of his jacket. As if she were anchoring herself to the mast before her ship set sail into the midst of a storm. She lifted her chin. Met his gaze. And said four little words that set both their worlds on fire.

"I'm not going anywhere."

CHAPTER NINE

*S*O *THIS*, ROSEMARY thought silently as she waited with her breath held for Sterling's response, *was how the mouse felt as he'd scurried up to the lion to pluck the thorn from his paw.* A combination of exhilaration, and fear, and emboldened recklessness.

Truth be told, she'd never done anything so daring in her life as to purposefully provoke a man as dangerous as the Duke of Hanover. A single snap of his ferocious jaws and she'd be in the bottom of his gullet wondering where she'd gone wrong. Where she had turned left when she should have turned right. Except what if…what if no matter what path she took, they all brought her here? To a starry night with Sir Reginald in her pocket and Sterling at the end of her arm.

He stared at her, his expression a mixture of disbelief and thinly veiled anger. But there was something else there. Something dancing around the hard granite edges. A yearning. A wanting. Like a starved child with his face pressed up against the glass of a baker's shop window dreaming of all the treasures contained within.

"You should be running in the opposite direction," he rasped even as he skimmed his fingers along her cheekbone and then sank them into her hair. "Any other wallflower would be."

"That's true," she acknowledged. "But in case you haven't noticed, I am a tad unconventional."

His mouth, a mere inch from hers, stretched in a mirthless grin. "A tad? You're the definition of the word."

"I shall take that as a fine c-compliment," she gasped, her voice catching when he angled his head and took her earlobe between his teeth. A sharp nip, followed by a soothing lick of his tongue and she went wobbly at the knees.

"Renata," he murmured against her neck.

"Y-Yes?" she moaned.

He kissed his way to her shoulder. "Before we proceed any further, you need to know that there is something wrong with–*bollocks*."

"Oh, dear." Her knees straightened. "There's something wrong with your bollocks?"

"What? *No*." He pulled back to scowl at her. "That's not what I...there's nothing wrong with my bollocks. My bollocks are in perfect working order, thank you very much."

She nodded seriously. "That's good to hear."

"What the devil would give you the impression that–never mind." He raked a hand through his hair, then pointed at the tents. "*That's* why I cursed."

Rosemary turned automatically to follow the direction of his finger. What she saw–or rather *who* she saw–marching straight at them with all the single-minded determination of a foot guard regiment in the British infantry caused all of the blood to drain from her face. "Bollocks."

"Exactly," Sterling said grimly. "You should get behind me."

"What will that do? They've already seen us!"

The "they" she was referring to was none other than Lady Navessa and her trio of handmaidens. Somehow, someway, Navessa had spied Rosemary and Sterling standing under the tree. While a more benevolent person might choose to discreetly look the other way when confronted with evidence of an indiscretion, especially at a ball where secret moments of passion ran rampant, it was apparent that the reigning queen of the *ton* was not about to let this opportunity pass her by.

She would be ruined, Rosemary registered dimly. Being caught sans chaperone in the dark with a renowned rogue was going to destroy her reputation. By the time Navessa got done pummeling her good name into the mud, she'd never be able to show her face in Polite Society ever again. Her grandmother would be humiliated. Any slim chance she might have had at making a successful match would be gone. Forget the Earl of Hawkridge revealing he had an American half-sister. *This* would become the Scandal of the Season.

Navessa would make sure of it.

"There's only one thing left to do," Sterling said matter-of-factly as Navessa continued her descent across the sloping lawn, her yellow gown billowing in the breeze.

"Disappear into thin air?" Rosemary suggested.

"Marry you."

"*Marry–*" No. She couldn't even complete the sentence. It was too farfetched. Too preposterous. Too...too *insane* to even contemplate. Marry the Duke of Hanover? Marry *Sterling?* It would never work. They would never work. He was too...*him* and she was too...*she*. Yes, his kisses made her literally weak in the knees and, yes, she enjoyed being in his company and, yes, she really did believe there was good to be found in him. But *marriage*. Marriage was a different chapter entirely. A different book, really. And she wasn't even sure whether she was ready to pull it down off the shelf, let alone read it.

"Give me your marigold," he said, shoving his hand under her nose.

"I-I-I can't," she stammered.

His eyes flashed with annoyance. "Why not?"

She bit her lip. "Because Sir Reginald already ate it."

"Do you know," he said through clenched teeth, "I am beginning to genuinely dislike that squirrel."

From within her pocket, Sir Reginald gave an indignant squeak.

"He didn't mean it," she soothed, stroking his tail.

"I bloody well did."

Navessa was nearly upon them now. Close enough for Rosemary to see the gleam of malicious triumph in her gaze.

She squeezed her own eyes shut as she thought of what her grandmother would say. How ashamed she'd be. How all of her hard work and sacrifice would be for naught. "There has to be another solution," she hissed desperately. "What if–what if we just tell the truth?"

"That your pet squirrel was stuck in a tree and I retrieved it for you and we've been kissing ever since?" Sterling said dryly.

"Maybe not *that* truth. But...but we could say the part about Sir Reginald. He was stuck in a tree, and you came to help me, and that's it. That's all that happened."

"It would never work."

"Why not?"

"First, because you're a terrible liar."

Her shoulders hunched. She *was* a terrible liar.

"Second, because if I am not mistaken that is Lady Navessa Betram baring down on us and she's been after me since the day I became a duke. I won't begin to speculate on how all women's minds work, but I've a good idea on how hers does. She will view you as a threat, and will do everything in her considerable power to dishonor and discredit you. You'll be ruined, she'll take it as a chance to make her move, and I'll be congratulated for seducing a wallflower."

Rosemary's mouth opened. Closed. Opened again.

As much as she hated it, he was right.

Every word.

"It's not fair," she said.

"No, it's not." His expression gentled as he touched the small of her back. "But that's life, isn't it? We'll say I just asked you to be my wife, and we were taking a moment by ourselves to celebrate before we announced it to the *ton.*" He shrugged. "All things considered, it's not the *worst* idea in the world."

"All things considered," she said faintly.

"Indeed. My sister has been on me about doing what I can to re-pair the family name. *That's* why I came here. To socialize, and hobnob, and do all the useless, meaningless things expected of a duke. Given the new virtuous path I've undertaken, I suppose it is only a matter of time before I'm expected to marry. If I have to do the deed with someone, why not you? At least I'll stop being hounded by my sister, and you'll get to be a duchess." He paused expectantly, as if he were waiting for her to drop to his feet and weep with gratitude at being offered such a wonderful position. "What say you?"

She'd have liked to say that of all the proposals ever given in the history of the world, that was quite possibly the worst. It wasn't even a proposal so much as a business proposition devoid of love or faith or passion. Like reaching into a bin of apples and pulling one out that was slightly squishy on the side but eating it anyways because what did it matter, really? It was just an apple. Not all that important in the grand scheme of things.

That was how Sterling saw marriage. As a slightly squishy apple. Whereas she saw it as an entire banquet of fruit waiting to be sampled and enjoyed. Plums and peaches and pineapples. Pomegranates, too, if she wanted to continue with her alliteration. Pears. Papaya. Plantains.

Heavens, but there was a lot of fruit that began with P, wasn't there?

Stay on track, she told herself. *You haven't much time to make the most important decision of your entire life.*

Navessa was all but breathing down their necks. Another ten yards, and there'd be no more hiding. The moment of judgment would be upon them. Upon her, that is, since Sterling was a man and the same societal pressures that applied to her didn't affect him in the slightest. If the rumors were to be believed, he stood credibly accused of *murdering his mistress*. Which she knew he hadn't done. Yet despite his presumed misdeeds, Society was waiting to welcome him back into their fold with open arms while in the same breath they would cast her aside without a second's thought for the simple crime of a kiss.

How convenient for men to make rules by which they did not have to abide.

"What if I don't want to be a duchess?" she asked Sterling softly.

"Don't be ridiculous," he scoffed. "Every woman wants to be a duchess."

He was right about one thing. He *didn't* know how the female mind worked. At least not hers, at any rate.

"But–but I don't know the first thing about it," she said, her panic rising. "The duties it would entail. The balls I'd have to throw. I can't host a ball. I don't even *like* balls."

"Surely your dislike doesn't extend to *all* balls," he teased, and the vulgarity of such a statement was enough to puncture the pressure rising within her and coax a startled laugh from her lips. "It won't be all bad," he continued. "Given how much of a ruddy duke I am, the expectations for you as a duchess won't be very high. Plus, I won't care what you do. Host balls here in London or take Sir Reginald and live in the country. It doesn't matter."

"But...what about us?" she said blankly.

"Us?" His brow furrowed. "What do you–"

"Your Grace! I was told you might be attending tonight," Navessa trilled as she swept in on a wave of self-righteousness and lemon-colored skirts. The dress she'd chosen to wear for the evening showcased her generous bosom and hugged her tiny waist before expanding into a bell shape that was so wide and so broad courtesy of the petticoat boning beneath the layers of fabric that Rosemary wondered if she was able to fit through doorways.

A question best saved for another time, she decided, when Navessa's icy gaze flicked across her with unmistakable contempt.

"And Miss Rosemary Stanhope. We meet again, I see. Do you have any glasses of lemonade you'd like to throw at me?"

"I didn't throw lemonade at her," Rosemary told Sterling when he lifted a brow. She frowned at Navessa. "I didn't throw lemonade at you. If you'll recall, after you jostled past, my elbow accidentally hit a platter with a pitcher of lemonade on it and yes, it did spill, but–"

"Oh Rosy Poly," Navessa interrupted in a voice that was a tad too loud and a touch too sweet. "I was only *jesting*. What's a bit of fun between friends?"

That gave Rosemary cause to hesitate. "I...I wasn't aware that you considered me your friend."

"But of course I do! Didn't we make our debut together? Haven't we gone to every Marigold Ball together?"

"I don't know if I would say we've gone *together*–"

"We're practically sisters," Navessa cooed while her handmaidens suppressed snorts of laughter behind pink satin gloves. "Which is why, when I saw you alone with the Duke of Hanover, I knew that I had to come over straightaway. No offense intended towards His Grace"–she batted her lashes at Sterling–"but my dear, you must understand that a young, unmarried woman such as you should not be in the company of, dare I say it, a scoundrel." Her lips puckered to form a perfect "o". "What might people *say*?"

"The duke and I didn't do anything." Even as she spoke the words aloud, Rosemary felt a betraying flush begin to creep up the nape of her neck and spill across her chest in large, blotchy pieces of red. "I mean, we did talk. About–about things. But there's no harm in talking, is there? And yes, he did help me find my squirrel, but–"

"Is that what we're calling it these days?" Navessa smirked as her companions burst into giggles and Rosemary's entire face turned the approximate shade of a ripe tomato.

"That's enough," Sterling interceded flatly. "You've had your fun, Lady Navessa, while proving just what a cruel, vindictive shrew you are. You mock Rosemary because you perceive her as less than you, but what you don't realize is that she's so much more than you could ever hope to be."

Navessa gasped.

The handmaidens abruptly stopped laughing.

"Your Grace, I–I came over here out of concern," Navessa sputtered indignantly. "I can assure you there was no mockery intended."

Sterling merely rolled his eyes. "If anyone believes that, I've a three-legged racehorse to sell them."

As the redness slowly began to recede from her cheeks, Rosemary tentatively touched Sterling's wrist. "It's all right," she murmured. "I am accustomed to it."

"It's bloody well *not* all right," he snapped. "They don't get to bully and belittle you and get away with it. Not while I'm standing here."

"Bully and belittle?" Navessa's blonde head canted to the side as the sugar slipped from her voice and was replaced with cool, calculating spice. "I'd never do such a thing to poor Rosy Poly. Not to say that others won't once they learn of what she's been up to all the way out here in the dark with none other than the Duke of Hanover." She clucked her tongue. "It's always the quiet ones, isn't it? Such a shame."

"A shame," her companions echoed in eerie synchronicity.

Ignoring Navessa, Sterling looked straight at Rosemary. His gray eyes were impossible to decipher, their swirling depths filled with a myriad of emotions, but she read the question in them nevertheless. A question that would no longer wait for its answer.

Did she allow Navessa to ruin her? To ostracize her from a Society that had already pushed her to the outskirts? Or did she accept Sterling's proposal? A marriage where, by his own admission, it wouldn't matter what she did or where she lived so long as he could say that he had a wife.

Banishment or a loveless marriage.

Neither choice was very appealing.

But she had to pick one.

"I..." She stopped. Wet her lips. Tried again as inside her chest her fragile, hopeful heart beat madly. "I will. I mean, I do. I mean–"

"Excellent," Sterling said curtly, and was that a flash of relief in his gaze? Before she could tell for certain, he fixed his attention on Navessa. A predatory smile, one that Rosemary did not recognize, claimed his mouth. It made him harder than she knew him to be. Colder. And far more intimidating. "How fortunate that you can be the first to offer your congratulations."

"My congratulations for what?" Navessa said, the corners of her lips pinching.

"Our betrothal." He put his arm around Rosemary's waist, resting his hand with familiar assertion on the curve of her hip. "Before you interrupted us, I asked Miss Stanhope to marry me. She has agreed."

"M-*Marry* you?" Navessa looked as shocked as Rosemary had felt when Sterling first announced his ridiculous plan to save her from ruin. A ridiculous plan that had just become reality, even though she could still hardly believe it. Wouldn't believe it, she imagined, for at least a few days, or even a few weeks. By then maybe–just maybe– she'd be able to wrap her head around the idea that she was engaged to the Duke of Hanover.

"Indeed. Won't she make a marvelous duchess?" Turning his head, Sterling kissed the top of her head in a gesture of affection that she thought was a tad overdone until she caught Navessa's reaction out of the corners of her eyes.

How interesting. She'd heard of turning green with envy before. Until this very second, she had always been under the assumption that it was a metaphor. But there was a definite emerald tinge to Navessa's countenance. Or maybe it was a trick of the moonlight. Either way, it was obvious that she wasn't taking the news well. Neither were the handmaidens, if their wide open mouths were any indication.

"You–you cannot be *serious*," Navessa managed after a long, stricken pause.

"Why not?" Sterling asked.

"Because...because it's Rosy Poly. She can't marry a *duke*." Navessa looked to her loyal subjects for confirmation and, in unison, all three nodded. "There. Do you see?"

"The only thing I see is a woman consumed by jealousy. I hate to be the one to tell you this, but it's not a good look on you." He lowered his voice to a conspiratorial whisper. "Your skin. It's gone all pasty."

Navessa gasped and clapped both hands to her cheeks. "No it hasn't."

"Yes," he said gravely. "I am afraid it has."

"But Rosy Poly–"

"For all future encounters, you will refer to my betrothed as Miss Stanhope." Hard steel replaced the humor in Sterling's voice. In the dim lighting, Rosemary could have sworn his eyes burned black. The hand at her side tightened, the muscles in his arm flexing. "After we are married, she is to be Her Grace, The Duchess of Hanover." He paused, then smiled coldly. "Let me hear you say it."

"I...I..." Once again, Navessa looked at her friends, but this time they averted their gazes.

"Well?" Sterling asked. "You see, it's easy to pick on someone you perceive as weaker than yourself. To call them names and belittle them. To make yourself feel better when you make them feel small. But the truth is, people of your ilk are always the small ones. That's why you're so bloody desperate to hide it."

Navessa's mouth trembled. "Her Grace," she whispered. "The Duchess of Hanover."

"That wasn't nice," Rosemary chided gently after Navessa had turned on her heel and fled back up the hill towards the tents with her handmaidens hurrying to keep pace.

Unwinding his arm from her waist, Sterling backed up until he was leaning against the tree with the heel of his boot casually resting on the trunk. Leafy shadows obscured the upper half of his countenance. His eyes were gray again. His mouth curved in a familiar roguish grin. "What about me remotely suggests that I am a nice person?"

Oh, I don't know, she thought silently. *Perhaps the fact that you climbed a tree to rescue a squirrel that you profess not to like and then proposed to a woman you claim not to care about.*

Could he truly not see the light inside of him that she did? He was like a rock with slivers of gold peeking out through the cracks and crevices. Rough and hard on the outside, but so bright and shining within. The only thing to do, she supposed, was to keep chipping away. One piece of stone at a time. An arduous endeavor, no doubt. But what else was she to do? They were to be married. And if there was a single thing she'd ever wished for in a husband, it was to be loved and to love in return.

"What are we to do now?" she asked, almost shyly. How was it that before their hasty engagement she'd felt perfectly at ease with him alone in the dark, but now that they were permitted to be together (although the *ton* would have still liked a chaperone present) she had goose pimples on her arms?

"We go spread the news far and wide, of course." He tilted his head at her; flashed that infamous Duke of Hanover smile that showed all his teeth but fell just short of his eyes. "You're about to become a very popular woman, Reagan."

"Popular enough for my husband-to-be to remember my name?"

"I am not sure if I'd go *that* far." He extended his arm, but after a brief hesitation she gave a tiny shake of her head and linked her hands behind her back instead.

"I should find my grandmother and escort her home. Before word gets out, I'd like to tell her privately, if that's all right with you. She...she should hear it from me." Rosemary wasn't sure how Lady Ellinwood was going to take the news. Hopefully her excitement at such an excellent match would overshadow any questions on the circumstances *leading* to such an excellent match.

"Are you sure?" Sterling asked.

No.

No, she wasn't sure about anything.

"Yes." Although her mouth felt inexplicably tight, like it had after Evie talked her into trying a witch hazel-based astringent designed to lessen the appearance of her pores (whatever that meant), she managed a smile. "Perhaps you can call upon me tomorrow and we can begin to discuss our future?"

"I generally don't rise before eleven unless it is a dire emergency."

"Then I shall expect you sometime in the afternoon."

They stared awkwardly at each other.

"I'll just go this way–" Rosemary started.

"I should probably head up to the–" Sterling began.

They both stopped.

Exchanged the quick, fleeting smiles of strangers passing each other on the street.

"Until tomorrow," she said.

"Until tomorrow," he repeated.

Without another word, they both set off on their separate ways…a fitting punctuation to the strangest, most unexpected, most unbelievable night of Rosemary's life.

CHAPTER TEN

THE NEXT MORNING, Evie and Joanna were enjoying coffee and buttered toast on the stone terrace overlooking the gardens when Evie gave a loud shriek and leapt from her chair, sending the paper she'd been reading over the edge of the balcony.

"What?" Joanna exclaimed, startled. "What is it?"

"Rosemary," said Evie, her eyes as wide as the saucers their porcelain teacups were sitting on. "It's our cousin, Rosemary. She…she's engaged."

"But that's wonderful news! Although I was not aware she was being courted by anyone. Still," Joanna took a bite of bread and then dabbed at her mouth with a linen napkin, "these things can happen quite quickly. You and I should know that better than anyone. Who is she to marry? Not that I'd know him. You're much more up to date on the who's who of High Society than I am. Well? Out with it!"

"The…" Evie paused for dramatic effect. "Duke of Hanover."

"Oh. *Oh.*" As comprehension dawned, Joanna slowly lowered her napkin. "Are you certain?"

She gave an indelicate snort. "Am I certain? It said so in black and white! Right in the *London Caller* gossip column, which is *never* wrong. Apparently, Hanover proposed to her last night at the Marigold Ball."

"Wait." Joanna pinched the bridge of her nose. "Weren't you there?"

"No. Weston and I were supposed to go. But we had an afternoon, ah, appointment." Her cheeks pinkening, Evie glanced down at her feet. "Followed by an evening appointment. And then a late night–"

"I get the idea." Grimacing, Joanna held up her hand, palm facing outwards. "There should be a law against having to hear about the sexual practices of one's sister and half-brother. It's...icky."

"Icky?" Evie said dubiously.

"Yes. Icky."

"Why weren't you and Kincaid at the ball? Weston made sure you received invitations."

"We had to follow up on a lead for a case that we're working. Besides, you know I've never enjoyed large functions and Kincaid would rather have his tooth pulled than wear a formal dinner jacket."

"So neither of us attended."

Joanna shook her head. "It would appear not. Are you sure this gossip column contains accurate information? Maybe whoever wrote it is only speculating."

Evie gasped and put her hands on her hips. "Lady M would *never* speculate."

"Who is Lady M?"

"The woman who writes the gossip column."

"You don't even know her *name* and we're supposed to trust everything she tells us to be correct?"

"She wouldn't dare make a mistake as big as this. Just because you're a private detective now doesn't mean you need to independently verify every single source."

Joanna arched an auburn brow. "That's *exactly* what it means."

"Well, I am telling you that if Lady M has said that Rosemary and the Duke of Hanover are betrothed, then they are betrothed. If you want to go track down witnesses and take their statements, fine. Go ahead. But you'll just be wasting your time." On a huff of breath, Evie resumed her seat and poked at her toast, but refrained from taking another bite. With her wedding looming ever closer, she was watching how much she ate. Especially since she'd been absolutely ravenous as of late. Nerves, she assumed. "We need to decide what to do."

"About what?" With no such compunctions in regards to her eating habits, Joanna happily applied a thick layer of butter onto another piece of toast (her third, but who was counting?) and bit into it.

"Rosemary and her engagement!" Evie said in exasperation. "Haven't you been listening?"

"Why do we have to do anything? Rosemary seems like a practical person. While Hanover wouldn't have been *my* first choice for her, I'm sure she has her reasons for accepting his proposal."

Evie stared at her sister.

Were they even talking about the same person?

"She has a *squirrel.*"

"A very practical pet. Small, tidy, doesn't require a lot of care like a dog or a horse or a pig."

"Who do you know that has a pet pig?" Evie demanded.

Joanna lifted her shoulder in a careless shrug. "I am just saying, of all the animals that Rosemary *could* have chosen, a squirrel is hardly the worst. From everything she has said, Sir Reginald is quite well behaved."

"That may be true, but Hanover isn't. I had the opportunity to have a long conversation with him during the house party at Hawkridge Manor, and while he is admittedly handsome and charming and affable, he drinks like a fish and chases anything in a skirt." Evie sipped her coffee. "Did I ever tell you that he asked me to be his mistress?"

Joanna dropped her toast. "No you most certainly did *not.* Honestly, I don't know what's more shocking. The fact that you wouldn't tell me, or that you refused his offer." Her eyes narrowed. "You did refuse, didn't you?"

"Of course I did. I had my heart set on Weston by then and love makes you do stupid things, like refusing the attentions of a duke." Evie gave a long, wistful sigh. "The Duchess of Hanover *does* have a nice ring to it. But I'm firmly settled on being the Countess of Hawkridge."

Picking up an orange nectarine from a bowl of fruit in the middle of the table, Joanna began to peel it with quick, efficient swipes of her thumbnail. "I'm so sorry you have to be *just* a countess. How horrific for you."

Having grown used to her sister's jests after a lifetime of sibling sparring, Evie smiled thinly. "I am sure I'll manage. But what about Rosemary?"

"We should definitely find a way to speak to her." Joanna popped a slice of nectarine into her mouth and then drummed her fingers on the table as her brow creased in thought. "Especially given Hanover's current...*entanglement*."

"You mean the murder of his mistress. He told me about that."

She nodded. "Kincaid has been working on clearing his name for some time. Almost since the day he and I met, actually. The case has been a mystery since it began, and nothing is as it seems. We've recently discovered some unnerving facts that might even place Hanover's life in danger. But since he asked Rosemary to be his wife, I'm sure she knows all about it."

The two sisters exchanged a skeptical look. Having both met Sterling, neither were confident in the duke's willingness to be forthcoming. While he presented himself as an open book on the outside, those tormented gray eyes contained more than a few secrets.

"I'll get my hat," Evie announced.

"I'll get my reticule," said Joanna.

A servant was opening the front door for them when Weston came strolling out of his study and into the foyer. Noting his fiancée's pelisse and bonnet, he notched a brow as an amused smile toyed with the corner of his mouth.

"Off to do more wedding planning?" he asked, walking up behind Evie and gently nudging her coiffure to the side so that he could place a light kiss upon the nape of her neck while Joanna mimed gagging into her glove.

"No," said Evie, glaring at her sister, "we're actually going to see Rosemary."

"Your cousin?" Weston remarked with mild surprise. "I was under the impression that Lady Ellinwood wasn't overly fond of her granddaughter's recalcitrant American relatives."

"Recalcitrant," Joanna repeated. "I like the sound of that."

Evie turned into Weston's broad chest and adjusted the lay of his four-in-hand tie. "Lady Ellinwood may not like us, but given that Rosemary is soon to outrank her, the decision on whether or not we are allowed to pay call is no longer hers to make."

"I don't understand."

"The Duke of Hanover proposed to Rosemary last night at the Marigold Ball," Joanna explained. "If Lady M is to be believed, Rosemary accepted and they are now engaged."

"The devil he did!" Weston said with such uncharacteristic virulence that both Evie and Joanna stopped and stared. A composed and oft times aloof man (unless he happened to be in the company of his recalcitrant American fiancée), the Earl of Hawkridge was rarely given to fits of emotional outburst.

"I thought Hanover was your friend," Evie ventured.

"He is." A vein pulsed on the side of Weston's temple. "But that doesn't mean I want my family eternally connected to his. Sterling is a scoundrel. He's always been a scoundrel. He'll always *be* a scoundrel. Which makes for an entertaining companion at the gaming hell. But not a good husband for your cousin."

"That's why we were on our way to pay her a visit and try to find out how this came to be," said Joanna, gesturing at the door. "Evie? Are you ready?"

"I'll join you outside in a moment." Evie waited until her sister had left and the door had closed to wind her arms around Weston's neck, rise up on her toes, and claim his mouth with hers in a long, slow, drugging kiss that left them both breathless and panting by the end of it.

"What was that for?" he said gruffly, tucking an ebony curl behind her ear.

"For opening your heart to me *and* my family. I love you, Weston Weston, and I cannot wait to marry you." She kissed him again, just a light brush of her lips across his cheek, but when she turned to follow Joanna out of the foyer, he grabbed her wrist and pulled her back.

"We could be married by the end of the week, if you wanted." He nuzzled her neck, then slid his hand inside her pelisse to fondle her breasts. "Just say the word and I'll have a carriage readied to take us to Gretna Green."

Twisting in his arms, she poked her finger into the middle of his chest. "I am a greedy, selfish woman, Weston. I want you, and I want my big wedding, and my beautiful dress, and my white doves. I want all of it. And then I want a lifetime of happiness."

"Then that's what you shall have." A flicker of suspicion rippled across his countenance. "What doves?"

"The ones I've ordered to be released as we walk out of the village church."

"I don't recall agreeing to any doves. They're nothing more than glorified pigeons."

"They're a symbol of love and hope," she corrected. "And they'll be lovely."

"If one takes a shite on my head–"

"It wouldn't dare," she said even as a grin tugged at the corners of her mouth. "Besides, Posy will be there, and she'll want some other animals for company."

Weston's sigh was long and suffering as he cast his gaze to the vaulted ceiling. "The things men do for love."

"I'll let you know what we find out about Rosemary and Hano-ver." A final kiss, and Evie hurried out the door after Joanna.

FOR THE SECOND time in less than a week, Sterling woke to the sound of pounding fists at his door. Grumbling and growling, he rolled out of bed, stuck a hand in the face of his apologetic valet, and marched down the stairs to tell whoever was brazen enough to come calling at the ungodly hour of half past ten in the morning that he'd see them straight to hell.

"Out of the way," he muttered at the three footmen who were physically attempting to hold the door closed while whoever was on the other side of it used Herculean strength to shove it open. "I'll take care of this."

Looking relieved, the servants moved to the side, the door slammed open, and none other than Weston and Kincaid stumbled inside, their forward momentum nearly causing them to fall onto the marble tile in a tangle of limbs while Sterling watched in cool amuse-ment from a safe distance.

"Uncivilized louts," he remarked. "Haven't you ever heard of a calling card? Obviously your American brides are having a poor influence."

Weston regained his balance first and turned on Sterling with the cold, implacable expression of a boxer right before he stepped into the ring. While shorter by a few inches, the dark-haired earl had the muscular build of a bull and fists of iron that a man would be foolish to place himself on the other side of. "We've been friends a long time, but if you say another word about Evie ever again it will be your last."

"Duly noted." Sterling's gaze flicked to Kincaid. "What about you? Care to make any threats?"

The private detective removed his spectacles, polished them on the sleeve of his tweed jacket, and carefully placed them back on his face. "My wife *is* a bad influence, so I've nothing to say to that regard. We've come to discuss your sudden engagement."

His engagement.

To Rosemary.

Bollocks.

The enormity of it hadn't sunk in yet. Or maybe it had, but the weight of it had gotten lost somewhere in the bottom of the second bottle of the Duke of Clemson's excellent Kentucky bourbon.

While Rosemary had left the Marigold Ball early, Sterling remained behind to spread the good news of their pending nuptials. News that had been received with equal parts amazement, disbelief, and despair. He was even fairly certain he'd caught a bevy of debutantes and their mothers weeping behind a potted palm tree.

In hindsight, he should have retired then and there. But his mood had been high, his spirits jovial, and when Clemson and Lord Andover, an old mate from Eton, invited him to join them for a rousing night on the town, who was he to refuse?

They'd started at the Carlton Club in St. James's, a private meeting house for the conservatively minded members of Parliament (shockingly, Sterling had never been awarded a membership in his own right), and ended up at Crockford's right down the row, a gambling hell started by a common fishmonger who'd risen to prominence and obscene wealth by routinely emptying the pockets of drunk aristocrats.

Crockford had certainly lightened Sterling's coffers by a considerable amount. He wasn't even sure how much money he'd lost at the tables, or what time his valet had finally come to collet him. All he did know was that he had awoken in his own bed...and he was engaged to Rosemary. The latter of which was apparently not sitting well with either Weston or Kincaid if their stern, unforgiving expressions were any sign.

"Is this going to be an entire conversation, or can we get it over with in ten words or less?" he asked, scrubbing a hand across his face. "Because I was up late, and–"

"A conversation," Kincaid interrupted.

"A *long* conversation," Weston said with emphasis.

Sterling sighed. "I was afraid you were going to say that. Well, come on into the drawing room and I'll ring for some food and drink. No need to be savages about it. What's your preference? Wine, whiskey, gin…"

"Coffee. Black," Weston said as he preceded Sterling into the drawing room and helped himself to a chair. "Which is exactly what you'll be having, as we need you sober for what we're about to say."

"Or at least more sober than you are now," Kincaid added before he sat down beside Weston, leaving a settee open across from them which Sterling reluctantly took even though it made him feel as if he were a young lad at school again being brought to the headmaster's office for trying to start a fire in the common area.

"Barely more than a puff of a smoke," he mumbled under his breath. "No need for so much fuss."

"What was that?" Weston asked sharply.

"Nothing." He slumped in his seat and let his head fall back until he was staring at the ornate chandelier hanging from the ceiling. "Get on with it then. The lecture, or whatever it is you're doing here. I've more sleeping to do."

A long, terse silence, and then…

"You've fucked up, Sterling."

A humorless smile twisted Sterling's mouth as he lowered his chin to meet Weston's cool gray eyes. "Tell me something I don't know. The past six years of my life have been a combination of fuck ups. Which particular one are we discussing this morning?"

Kincaid crossed his arms. "Your proposal to Miss Stanhope."

Of all the things he'd done, all the sins he'd committed, and they were here to pester him about his one *good* deed? And it was good. He needed to believe that. Needed to believe he'd helped Rosemary more than he'd hurt her. Needed to believe that, for once, just once, he'd chosen the honorable path. The right path. Because of Rosemary. *For* Rosemary.

"What about my proposal?" he said warily.

"You never should have made it. What the devil were you thinking?" Weston asked.

Sterling scowled. "What does it matter to the two of you who I marry?"

"It wouldn't," said Kincaid.

"Except you've picked the only woman in all of England directly related to the women *we* have chosen to marry."

"And?" Sterling pressed.

"And as you are, you're not fit for marriage." There was no rancor in Weston's tone, which almost made it worse. "Miss Stanhope is a naïve innocent. You're…not. In more ways than one. It isn't a suitable match."

"Do you think I don't know that?" Sterling demanded as he shot to his feet. Outside the windows, a light rain had begun to fall from a gloomy, dismal sky that was rapidly matching his mood. To think he'd actually gone to bed feeling *happy* for once. He should have known it wouldn't last longer than a few hours. "I am well aware that Rosemary is far better than I. But what else could I have done after Lady Navessa Betram stumbled upon us? You may not be aware, but she's quite possibly the worst gossip this side of the Thames. Had I not asked Rosemary to marry me, she would have been ruined. Would you rather public exile than marriage to a duke?"

"By God," Weston exclaimed in disbelief. "Is that what happened? You took the poor girl's virginity at a *ball*?"

Sterling knew that he was far from perfect. As far as a person could probably get. But it still hurt to realize just how low of an opinion his so-called friends held of him. "No. I didn't take her virginity at a ball," he snapped. "Nor anywhere else, for that matter. Not that it's a damned bit of your concern. But I did kiss her after I tried to rescue her squirrel from a tree and—"

"You did what?" Kincaid asked politely.

"A round of fireworks went off prematurely and scared Sir Reginald. He ran up into a tree and Rosemary was attempting to retrieve him when I found her. Instead of watching her break her neck trying to balance on a bench or fall from a limb, I offered my services. Afterwards we, ah, allowed ourselves to become momentarily distracted." He stuffed his hands into the deep pockets of the dressing robe he'd thrown on before leaving his bedchamber. "Before we decided to go our separate ways, Lady Navessa spied us from the tents. A marriage proposal was the only thing I could think of in the heat of the moment to save Rosemary's reputation."

Another round of silence.

Once again, Weston was the first to break it.

"Miss Stanhope has a pet rat that she's named Sir Reginald?" he said, his brows knitting in bemusement.

Was *that* all they'd gotten from his long-winded explanation?

Bloody hell.

Why even bother?

"He is a red squirrel, not a rat," he said, not wanting it to get back round to Rosemary that someone had denigrated her pet and he'd not stood in Sir Reginald's defense. His bride-to-be did not anger easily—or at all, for that matter—but he knew from firsthand experience that she did bristle whenever anyone dared take aim at her beloved squirrel.

"Is there a difference?" Kincaid wondered.

"Is there a difference?" Sterling scoffed. "For your information, they're not even from the same family. Ah, here's the coffee."

As he went to the sideboard to fix himself a plate of eggs, roasted red potatoes, and a generous slab of bacon along with a steaming hot cup of coffee stirred through with cream, Weston and Kincaid gazed at each other in astonishment.

"Are you seeing what I'm seeing?" Kincaid asked in a low voice.

Weston nodded slowly. "If you're seeing that Sterling might actually love someone other than himself, then yes, I am. Who would have ever foreseen that he would ever be brought to heel, let alone by some woman with a squirrel?"

"Not me. But then I didn't see myself falling for a stubborn red-haired American, either."

Weston snorted. "*No one* could have seen the Thorncrofts coming.*"

"What are you ladies gossiping about?" Balancing his food in one hand and holding his mug of coffee in the other, Sterling started back across the drawing room, neatly sidestepping a pedestal with a marble bust of some angel or another sitting on it. He wasn't a religious man by nature–his faith had abandoned him long ago–but that hadn't stopped Sarah from buying him the bust as a Christmas present three years ago. He suspected she'd done it as a joke, even though she insisted to this day that it was a serious gift.

"We were discussing your fiancée, Miss Stanhope," Kincaid supplied.

"And the fact that you're in love with her," said Weston.

It was a testament to Sterling's quick reflexes that when the mug slipped from his hand he managed to catch it before it hit the floor.

"*Hell and damnation,*" he cursed when coffee sloshed over the edge and burned his fingers. Setting both the mug and plate aside on a table, he rounded on his unwanted guests with a clenched jaw and an uncomfortable tightness in his throat. "Take that back. I don't love Rosemary, and I don't want a servant to get the wrong idea and spread a rumor across town. What the devil do you think talk like that would do to my reputation?"

"There are no servants in the room," Kincaid said mildly. "Even if there were, isn't it expected that a man should love the woman he is to marry?"

"Some men, yes. But not *this* man. I already told you why I am marrying Rosemary. To save her from the sharp teeth of the gossip hounds. There's nothing more to it than that."

There couldn't be, he thought silently as something akin to panic skittered under his skin with tiny, prickling claws.

Love?

He didn't *love* Rosemary.

Hadn't he been careful to tell her as much? Hadn't he made it clear–because he didn't want to be accused of misleading her–that they weren't entering an indissoluble union so much as they were putting pen to paper on a mutually beneficial business arrangement?

She'd get to maintain her good name and become a duchess. He'd get to extricate himself from the marriage mart and trick his peers in Parliament into believing that he was fully reformed. After all, how could a man who married a wallflower be capable of violently murdering his mistress? The two things did not equate. So long as feelings didn't get in the way, it was an excellent solution to all of their problems. Honestly, he should have thought of it sooner.

"Is Miss Stanhope aware that you claim not to be in love with her?" asked Kincaid.

"I don't *claim* anything. I *know* I am not." Retrieving his coffee, he took a mindless swig. "And yes, she's very much aware, as I've done nothing to indicate otherwise. Rosemary and I have an…understanding."

Didn't they?

He was fairly certain they did.

"Then you've done this–asked her to marry you to prevent Lady Navessa's vicious tongue from spewing lies–out of the kindness of your heart," said Weston, studying him closely.

"I don't know if I'd say *kindness*–"

"Good on you, Sterling," Kincaid cut in. "I'm proud of you."

"I haven't done anything," he said, vaguely alarmed by the unwarranted praise. "People become engaged every day. You've both done it." He pointed at Kincaid. *"You're* married."

"But it's different for us." Weston rose from his chair and went to the sideboard. His back to Sterling, he poured himself a cup of coffee. "I am an earl. Kincaid isn't even titled. You'll have much larger expectations placed upon you, as will Miss Stanhope. I am glad to hear you've considered all that, and have decided to mend your ways."

"Sorry?" said Sterling, tapping his ear. "I don't think I heard you correctly. Mend my what?"

"Your ways," Weston said with the calm, dangerous pleasantness of a father who was about to give his wayward son a serious ultimatum in regards to his future inheritance. "Your excessive drinking, to begin with. Your gambling. Your fornicating with anything in a bustle. Now that you are engaged to be wed, those...activities will have to stop. Especially since you are to marry my wife's cousin."

"And mine," said Kincaid.

Weston delivered a rigid smile. "Welcome to the family."

Talk about a bloody awful welcome.

"No drinking? No gambling? No fornication? What's left to do?" Sterling said blankly.

"I am confident you'll find something." Joining Weston at the sideboard, Kincaid browsed the various plates and trays before filling a crystal bowl with freshly cut fruit. He stabbed a strawberry with a miniature silver fork and raised it to his mouth. "There's also the matter of what we discussed in regards to your pending case. Do you mind if we speak openly in front of Weston?"

Sterling gave a belligerent wave of his arm before he collapsed onto the middle of a sofa and let his head fall against the thinly padded back with a resounding *thump*. "Why stop now?"

In brief, practical terms, Kincaid shared with Weston what he and Joanna had already explained in great detail to Sterling. "When the blood was first discovered in Eloise's bedchamber, the natural assumption was that she'd been murdered and the body disposed of elsewhere. While never formally brought up on charges–"

"Not yet," Sterling muttered as he closed his eyes and wished desperately for a nip of gin.

"–Sterling was presumed to be the killer. A crime of passion following an argument that several servants overheard. Which was why he hired me to clear his name and find the *real* killer. Something that I have not been able to do, because it is my belief that Eloise isn't dead."

"Are you sure?" Weston frowned.

"Given that I have determined the blood found in the room belonged to a butchered pig, I am nearly positive."

"Then where is she?"

Sterling slanted an eye open. "That's what *I* asked."

"Her whereabouts are thus far unknown," Kincaid admitted. "Though we've tracked down a few leads, Eloise remains elusive. Strange, given that she is a woman without means or a fortune to use in order to remain hidden. Which leads me to my current theory: Eloise was but a pawn is a much larger, much more deceptive game." He paused, then finished grimly, "A game whose end goal is to completely destroy the Duke of Hanover."

Complete and utter silence reigned.

For all of two seconds.

"Stop laughing, Sterling," Kincaid said through gritted teeth. "This is not a time for amusement."

"Oh, but it is." Openly guffawing, Sterling slapped his knee and wiped tears from the corners of his eyes. "*A game whose end goal is to completely destroy the Duke of Hanover,*" he quoted in a deep, mocking parody of the detective's voice. "You've obviously been reading too many of those American dime novels. How could someone want to destroy me when everyone adores me? It'd be like walking into a house party and dumping out the best bottle of champagne."

"As loath as I am to stroke his ego, Sterling has a point." Weston popped a grape into his mouth. "No one that I know holds a grudge against him and, to the best of my knowledge, his ledgers are clean at all the gambling hells."

"I pay my debts," said Sterling, sobering.

Weston nodded. "He pays his debts."

"Be that as it may, Eloise's death *was* staged to make it appear as if she were the victim of a violent murder." Tipping his spectacles to the edge of his nose, Kincaid scowled first at Weston and then at Sterling. "Given the timing and the location of the act, it cannot be sheer coincidence. Someone wants to cause you considerable harm, Sterling."

"Then why not just kill me?" he asked. "That would be harmful."

"I don't have the answer to that yet," Kincaid admitted. He pushed his spectacles back into place. "But I do believe that this is connected to your sister's kidnapping. Call it a hunch, or instinct, or blind intuition. Whatever you like. It doesn't change the fact that your life is most likely in danger, and not because of a trial that may or may not happen."

"How can you even be sure it really was just pig's blood?" Sterling was no expert investigator, but to him all blood–whether it be human or animal–looked exactly the same.

"Because I took a sample. And under detection of my compound microscope, the viscosity was completely different."

"What the devil is–you know what, no," he said with a grimace. "I'm sure I can live my entire life without completing that sentence." Lifting the back of his hand to his mouth, he yawned into it. "I need a nap. Which means you two need to leave. Your concern for my welfare is touching. Truly. But if someone wanted to hurt me, they're about six years too late."

"Just promise you'll be careful," Kincaid said seriously. "Don't go out alone at night, and pay attention to those around you. If there's a person who starts acting suspiciously, or you receive word from Eloise–"

"Eloise, greedy harpy that she is, probably found another benefactor and thought it would be amusing to paint me as a villain. I'm sure she is bathing naked in diamonds at the castle of some grossly rich count as we sit here bollocks in hand." Even as Sterling spoke the words aloud, he didn't really believe them. Eloise had been hotheaded, impulsive, and even malicious at times. But she wouldn't have taken on a new protector without rubbing his face in it. That would have removed all the fun.

Still, he didn't–he *couldn't*–honestly believe that a cloaked stranger was out there plotting some grand scheme to ruin him. No matter what evidence or instinct Kincaid had to the contrary. But he did, very much, want a nap. And so he said what his friends wanted to hear.

"All right. I'll be careful. Vigilant, even." He smiled thinly. "Every night, I shall have my valet check under the bed, and I'll hold hands with the doorman when I leave the pub. Why are you looking at each other like that?" he said when Weston and Kincaid exchanged another meaningful glance. "Stop it. Nothing good ever comes after. Not for me, at any rate."

After ingesting another grape, Weston approached him with all the stealth of a lion closing in on its prey while Kincaid kept his vantage point from the high ground. Otherwise known as the sideboard. "There are a few rules we need to set out in regards to Miss Stanhope…"

CHAPTER ELEVEN

L ADY ELLINWOOD RECEIVED the news of her granddaughter's
engagement with far less enthusiasm than Rosemary had been
expecting.

It wasn't that she'd wanted her grandmother to jump and shout
for joy. She did not desire a broken hip on her conscience. But she *did*
feel that a little bit more than "that's nice, please pass the blanket, the
carriage is chilly" was warranted. After all, it wasn't as if she had
announced she was marrying a baker or a doctor or–even worse, at
least in her grandmother's eyes–an entrepreneur.

Sterling was a duke.

And even though Rosemary genuinely wouldn't have cared if he
was a baker or a doctor or a candlestick maker, the small child still
living deep inside her had wanted to see a flash of approval in Lady
Ellinwood's sharp blue eyes. Maybe (as farfetched as it seemed) even a
congratulatory embrace.

She should have known better.

When they arrived back at the house, her grandmother promptly
excused herself and went straight to bed, leaving Rosemary feeling
oddly deflated. What was the point of having something exciting
happen to her if she had no one to share the excitement with?

That night was one of the rare times she wished with all of her
might that her mother were still alive. That she had a comforting lap

she could rest her head upon as she shared all of her hopes and doubts and dreams. That she had someone to stroke her head, and gently kiss her temple, and whisper to her just before she drifted off to sleep that it was all going to work out.

Instead, all she had was Sir Reginald. Who was surely better than no one, but a squirrel wasn't a mother or a father or even an aloof grandmother, for that matter. Which was why she was so elated the next day when Joanna and Evie came to call.

As luck would have it, Lady Ellinwood had stepped out earlier in the morning for tea with her embroidery circle, allowing Rosemary to receive her cousins in the parlor without any undue strife (so long as they left right before luncheon).

"Would you care for anything to drink?" she asked brightly. "There's both cold tea and lemonade. Or hot tea and coffee, if you'd prefer. At the beginning of next month, our cook will begin boiling and mashing apples for cider. It's an old family recipe that I'll have to share with you. The trick is to add the nutmeg–"

"Before you strain the apples so that it soaks straight through the skins into the fruit," Joanna finished with a smile. "We've always made our cider the same way."

It was such a small connection. Inconsequential, really. But Rosemary's heart swelled nevertheless because it was yet another thread connecting her to a family she hadn't even known existed four months ago. And family meant everything, especially to someone who hadn't gotten to experience the full breadth of what it was to belong to something larger than yourself.

"I didn't give much consideration to who handed it down over the years," she said, "but the recipe must have come from our Great-grandmother, Lady Beatrice Ellinwood."

"Do you have a picture of her, by chance?" Evie asked as she sank gracefully onto a divan upholstered in pink and mauve striped silk. The rest of the parlor–the entire house, really–was similarly designed in soft pastels that ranged from a sandy blush Aubusson carpet in the formal dining room to salmon curtains in the parlor.

Only Rosemary's bedchamber was a different color palette. She'd chosen the bright yellow walls (achieved by mixing turmeric with linseed oil to bind in the pigment) and Prussian blue ceiling as a means to distinguish her room from what was unmistakably her grandmother's domain. Until recently, it had stood as her singular small act of defiance. Aside from the litany of furry creatures she'd nursed back to health in secret, of course.

"I do not, unfortunately." Her eyes widened. "But my grandmother might! I'll be right back."

Off Rosemary dashed, up the stairs and down the hall until she reached Lady Ellinwood's private suite of rooms at the far eastern corner of the house. Even though she knew her grandmother was out, habit compelled her to knock.

A young, freckle-faced servant with carrot orange hair stuffed under a white cap immediately opened the door. Behind her was a pile of linens and two other maids, their faces red and sweating as they struggled to flip Lady Ellinwood's heavy mattress stuffed with horse hair and wool. It was a difficult task that needed to be done once per month lest the mattress begin to sag on one side or the other.

"Do you need help?" Rosemary asked automatically. "I can hold that end–"

Greta, the red-haired servant, shook her head. "It's no trouble, Miss. We're nearly finished. Are you looking for Lady Ellinwood? Because she left about an hour ago."

"To have tea with the embroidery ladies. Yes, I know. But I'm not searching for her. I'm looking for a picture." It struck Rosemary as she stepped past Greta and went to a mahogany escritoire on the far side of the room that she'd only entered her grandmother's private chambers on a handful of occasions, and then only when specifically summoned to do so. Nightmares, thunderstorms, and the like were a reason to call for her governesses–*not* to come running in here and disturb Lady Ellinwood's precious sleep.

In the scary dark, she'd never had someone who loved her uncon- ditionally to go running to. Never had the bed of her parents to climb into when thunder boomed and lightning flashed. Never had a mother guide her trembling hands while she drank a warm cup of milk, or a father to carry her back to her room and tuck her in before he gave the monster lurking under her bed a stern talking to.

That wasn't to say her governesses had not taken splendid care of her. Because Mrs. Armstrong had been wonderful, and Rosemary was in contact with her still. But a paid position did not invoke the same feelings of comfort and security that a loving family member did. As a result, she'd grown up believing she didn't need that sort of comfort.

Why waste time and energy missing what you'd never had?

But she *did* need it.

More importantly, she wanted it.

And perhaps that was the real reason she'd found herself inexplica- bly drawn to a most unsuitable scoundrel. Not because he needed her. But because *she* needed *him*. Perhaps Sterling wasn't the only wounded creature seeking a safe, warm nest. Seeking a sense of family. A sense of home. A sense of belonging.

"Miss…Miss Stanhope? Do you need help finding what you're looking for?" Greta asked uncertainly and, with a start, Rosemary realized she was standing frozen in the middle of her grandmother's bedchamber. The one place in all the house she really ought not to be.

"No, thank you. I'm fine. I'll be out of your way in a minute." She hurried to the escritoire, a desk with various drawers and secret compartments in addition to a hinged, slanted front that could be lowered for writing. She knew this was where Lady Ellinwood penned all of her private correspondence, and if she had any photographs or mementos then surely they'd be in here somewhere as they weren't to be found anywhere else around the house. With the exception of the portrait of her son in the drawing room, Rosemary's grandmother kept no other pictures of family past or present.

That included her granddaughter.

But when Rosemary pried open a long, narrow drawer nearly sealed shut with beeswax, indicating it had been polished many times over without being used in between, she was stunned to find that Lady Ellinwood *did* have paintings and photographs of her family. For some inexplicable reason, she'd just chosen to keep them hidden away.

Tears pricked the corners of Rosemary's eyes and her breath lodged in the base of her throat as she unveiled detailed miniatures of her father as a baby, and a boy, and a man. There was a grainy photograph, yellowed and curled at the edges, of her parents on their wedding day. Lord Gregory Stanhope and Miss Lilly Davidson. Both so young. So serious. So *alive*. To the best of her knowledge, it was the first–and only–picture of them standing together.

Underneath it she found another photograph. The last before they all turned to sketches and oil paintings. This one depicted a middle-aged man sitting on a stool, his eyes dark and somber even as the hint of a mischievous grin lifted the side of his moustache.

This had to be her grandfather, Lord George Stanhope. A man she'd never met as he was already gone well before she was ever born…but she had an inkling that if they'd had the opportunity to know each other, they would have gotten on splendidly.

There were stains at the bottom of the picture. Stains that had caused the ink to blur and run and fade. As if somehow the photograph had sustained water damage. Or–

"*Tears*. They're tears," Rosemary whispered as she very carefully returned her grandfather to the drawer before continuing on her impromptu journey through the past.

The next miniature, cut in the shape of an oval as if it had once sat inside of a brooch, showed two girls side by side, one with fair hair and one with dark. Despite their different coloring, it was obvious they were sisters. Dorothea and Mabel, if Rosemary had to guess. Painted long before Mabel fell in love with an American and sailed across the Atlantic to start a new life with a new family.

Had Dorothea felt abandoned when her only sibling left her? They were so close in age, they must have had their debuts back to back, or maybe even together. Every holiday, every milestone, every ball and party attended together, until Mabel moved to an entirely different continent.

In some way or another, Lady Ellinwood had been left by everyone she'd ever loved. Her parents, of whom Rosemary could find no picture. Her sister. Her husband. Her child and daughter-in-law.

Naturally, Rosemary knew all of this already.

But she hadn't really felt the breadth of the loss her grandmother had suffered until now.

How awful it must have been.

How awful it must *still* be, if she remained compelled to keep these pictures, these memories, tucked away in a drawer to gather dust month after month, year after year, decade after decade.

Swallowing past the lump in her throat, Rosemary dashed at the tears that had collected on her cheeks and rushed past Greta out into the hall where she took a few minutes to compose herself before returning to her cousins in the drawing room.

Immediately, they both sensed something was amiss, but they were wrong about what it was.

"I knew it," Evie said triumphantly, rising from her chair in a spill of lavender silk. Stylishly attired in a long-sleeved jacket with green piping along the arrow-tipped collar and a matching skirt, she was every inch a countess-to-be. "I knew you didn't want to marry him. How did he coerce you into it?"

Rosemary's engagement was so new that for a split second she hadn't the vaguest idea what her cousin was referring to. "Who coerced me into what?"

"See?" said Joanna, and now she was the one who sounded triumphant. Plainly clothed in a blue dress sans piping or lace or fancy embellishments, she had her auburn hair knotted in a twist on top of her head with only a simple gold pin for decoration. "I *told* you Lady M was mistaken. It's all nothing more than a big misunderstanding. Maybe the Duke of Hanover became engaged to a different Rosemary? Or to someone who looks like her. There's any manner of much more reasonable explanations than–"

"Oh, yes," Rosemary interrupted belatedly once she came to understand what the topic of conversation was regarding. "Sterling did propose to me last night."

"–that," Joanna finished weakly. "It's true, then? Are you sure?"

Evie sniffed. "Don't be put out just because you wanted Lady M to be wrong. If anyone's sure if Rosemary is engaged or not, it's *Rosemary*. Congratulations, darling! I wish we had wine or champagne to toast with, but tea will have to do for now." She lifted her cup of black currant tea that a maid had poured while Rosemary was in her grandmother's chambers. Her lips pursed as she took a sip, then flattened when she lowered the cup and regarded Rosemary over the curved porcelain brim. "Congratulations *are* in order, aren't they?"

"Yes, I think so." Rosemary's brows knitted in confusion. "Why would you believe I was coerced?"

Her cousins shared a quick glance.

"Should I...?" Evie asked.

Joanna nodded. "By your own admission, you know him better than I."

"All right, but it's going to sound more bluntly spoken coming from me."

"*Everything* sounds bluntly spoken coming from you."

"What is this about?" Rosemary inquired politely. She'd walked further into the drawing room while her cousins were...discussing, bantering, fighting? It was hard to tell sometimes...and she positioned herself in front of a window wet from rain. What had begun as a light drizzle in the early hours of the morning had intensified to a steady soaking, a subtle shift that hinted at cooler, damper months to come as Mother Nature shed her summer cloak and reached for a warmer autumn shawl.

"Your engagement. To the Duke of Hanover." Evie nibbled on her bottom lip, an uneasy habit Rosemary might not have noticed if she didn't often engage in it herself. "I must admit, it caught Joanna and me...off guard. The last we were together, you didn't mention you were being courted by anyone, least of all a duke."

"Least of all *that* duke," said Joanna with a meaningful arch of her brow.

Evie glared at her sister. "I thought we agreed I was going to do this part?"

"By all means, go right ahead."

"Thank you. As I was saying–what was I saying?"

"That I never mentioned I was being courted by anyone," Rosemary supplied helpfully. "And that's because I wasn't."

"Then how did you and the Duke of Hanover come to be engaged?" Joanna wondered aloud.

"Because he asked, and I said yes." Summarized into seven words, her relationship with Sterling seemed remarkably straightforward. In truth, she could not begin to untangle the knot of emotions that tied them together. The more she tried, the more complex the knot became.

"We didn't realize you even *knew* him," said Evie. "And it's not that we doubt your intentions, but having had a few interactions with Hanover at the house party, I'd be remiss if I did not share my...*our*"– she glanced at Joanna, who inclined her chin–"...misgivings."

"Your misgivings," Rosemary repeated.

"That's right."

Lifting herself up onto the deep windowsill, she let her feet swing aimlessly as the back of her skull pressed against the cool window pane. "Because I am a wallflower and he is a duke?"

"No! That's not it at all. Well...yes," Evie admitted after a brief pause. "That's partially it. But mostly our concern stems from the fact that Hanover is a bit of a...rogue. And by a bit, I mean that his reputation is terrible."

"My husband has quite literally been tasked with clearing him of murder." Although Joanna's blue gaze was filled with compassion, her firm tone caused Rosemary to stiffen and immediately jump to the defense of her fiancé.

"Sterling is innocent. If Mr. Kincaid cannot prove that, then he isn't very good at his job." Her eyes went huge as her mouth dropped open. "I–I cannot believe I said that. I'm sorry. I did not mean to imply–"

"Not to worry," Joanna assured her. "Really. Had someone said that about Kincaid, I'd have reacted much the same way." Her thick russet lashes pressed closely together as she studied her cousin with a scrutiny that made Rosemary want to squirm. "You love him, don't you? Hanover."

Evie started to laugh. "Don't be ridiculous–my God," she gasped when Rosemary's entire face flushed a dull shade of pink. "You *do* love him."

"I don't know if I do or not." Fingers twisting anxiously together, she sat up straighter on the sill. "It's all culminated rather rapidly, and I've never been in love before, so I cannot compare. One minute he was kissing me at Hawkridge Manor–"

"He kissed you at Hawkridge Manor?" Evie practically yelped. "When? Where? *When?*"

Rosemary's color heightened. "In the library during the house party."

"Before or after the receiving dinner?"

"Ah..." Perplexed by the specificity of the question, Rosemary thought back, counting off the days in her head. "After. Several days after."

"That's fine, then." Evie glanced at Joanna, who gave a small shrug.

"I wouldn't see why not," she said.

Rosemary's perplexity grew. "What are you talking about?"

"Should I tell her?" Evie asked.

"Probably best if you do," Joanna replied.

"Tell me *what?*"

Evie gave a deep sigh. "On the night of the receiving dinner, I could not sleep. Earl problems, you understand. So I went for a walk and encountered Hanover on the terrace. A very drunk Hanover, mind you, and during the course of our conversation he…he inquired into whether or not I'd be interested in becoming his mistress."

"Oh." Rosemary's stomach sank. "*Oh.*"

"Nothing came of it," Evie said hurriedly. "He was well into his cups. Honestly, I'd be surprised if he even remembers he spoke to me. But it was a very roguish thing to do, and that's why Joanna and I were naturally worried when I read about the engagement this morning in the paper. We just wanted to ensure that you weren't coerced into something you weren't keen on."

Rosemary's teeth clacked together as she slipped off the sill and the soft soles of her walking shoes came into contact with the hard floorboards. "What paper announced our engagement?"

"All of them, I imagine, although I read about it in the *London Caller.*"

Her face paled. She'd known word would get out soon enough. Gossip traveled fast when it was spread by many mouths. But she had been under the naïve impression that she'd have a few days, mayhap even a week, before Sterling's proposal became public knowledge.

"Let's get back to the kissing." Evie clapped her hands together. "You already said he kissed you during the house party. What occurred after we all left?"

Rosemary's head was spinning. "We kissed a second time in...in the library. And again last night, at the Marigold Ball, before he...before he asked me to marry him."

"I cannot believe this. Rosemary! You–you *minx*," Evie cried with no small amount of delight. "This is better than anything I've yet to read in Lady M's column. Now that we know you and Hanover have been carrying on a delightful little dalliance this entire time, your engagement makes perfect sense. And to think we were worried!"

"I don't know if I'd call it a dalliance–" Rosemary started to protest.

"It also explains why Hanover came to town despite Kincaid warning him to remain in the country," Joanna interrupted. "He gave us some nonsensical excuse about his sister asking him to partake in the Season to repair the damage done to his name, but all the while he *really* came here for you. How...uncharacteristically genuine of him."

"Wait," Rosemary interjected as a flicker of alarm cut through the overwhelming knowledge that her engagement was likely the topic of conversation in every parlor and drawing room across London. "Why did Kincaid want Sterling to stay at Hawkridge Manor?"

The corners of Joanna's mouth jutted sharply. "You mean he hasn't said anything?"

"Said anything about what?" she asked blankly.

Joanna looked at Evie. "Should I tell her?"

"Probably best if you do."

Joanna took a deep breath, then smiled kindly at Rosemary. "You might want to sit back down..."

CHAPTER TWELVE

ROSEMARY PINCHED HER eyes shut as she exhaled through her
nose. Behind her, the rain lashed at the windows in a steady roar
of water as the storm continued to gain strength, but the sound of the
rising tempest was nothing compared to the pounding in her head.

"So what you're saying," she murmured, slowly opening her eyes
to find her cousins watching her with identical expressions of concern,
"is that Sterling has been—what's the word you used?"

"Framed," said Joanna.

"Framed," she repeated. "Like a picture, but not."

"No, in this instance, it means he was set up. Someone went to
great lengths to make it appear as if he'd killed his mistress when, in
fact, he not only had nothing to do with her murder, she most likely
isn't even dead."

"And you think…you think this person is trying to harm him specifically?"

"Yes, that is the conclusion Kincaid and I have drawn."

"But…why?" Rosemary asked in bewilderment. She knew that
Sterling was far from flawless, but she'd never heard anyone speak a
bad word about him. Aside from calling him a wastrel, rogue, and
ne'er-do-well, that is. Even then, such insults were levied with a
general sort of complimentary affection. To the best of her knowledge,
prior to his mistress' bloody disappearance, he'd been an exceedingly

popular figure amidst the *ton*. For what reason, then, would anyone try to frame him for murder? "Have they demanded money or other means of compensation?"

"Not yet, which is why we're led to believe this is a personal grudge. Especially after we began to consider what happened to his sister. There was no ransom then, either. Which is very strange, looking back at it now. Why else take a duke's sister if not for money? Unless they were after something far more nefarious. Thankfully, Kincaid foiled whatever plot they were brewing before it had the chance to come to fruition, and Hanover hired an ex-soldier's guard that has discreetly kept watch over Lady Sarah ever since."

"I never knew his sister was kidnapped by highwaymen." A frown captured Rosemary's mouth. "Sterling never said a word."

He'd never said a word about *any* of this. And that troubled her almost as much as knowing that someone wanted to cause him serious harm.

How could they possibly hope to have a real marriage if they didn't share the intimate details of their lives with each other? She wasn't asking for him to reveal every secret that he held. Not after being engaged for less than a day, anyway. But was it too much to ask that he bother to mention some crazed madman had arranged for his mistress to disappear and the walls of her bedroom to be slathered in pig's blood all in an attempt to have him blamed for a murder he hadn't committed?

Unless...unless he hadn't told her because he didn't *want* a real marriage.

In which case, she wasn't sure if she wanted their engagement to continue.

It would mean complete and utter ruin, to end it now. The social fallout would be even worse than if he'd never proposed to begin with and Navessa spread word of their indiscretion far and wide. But wasn't public humiliation better than private heartbreak?

"I need to see him," she said abruptly. "I need to see Sterling."

"Right this minute?" Joanna cast a glance out the window. "But it's pouring buckets."

"I'm sure he'll come to call on you sooner rather than later," Evie assured her. "You have a wedding to plan. Speaking of that…"

"You didn't," Joanna groaned as her sister reached behind the sofa and lifted a large leather satchel that Rosemary hadn't even seen her bring in.

"I most certainly did." Humming happily under her breath, Evie reached into the bag and began to pull out a wide assortment of fabric swatches which she laid out on the cushions in a long, neat line. "Now," she said, turning to face Rosemary. "I realize I mentioned ivory before, but what's your opinion on mauve…"

MUCH TO ROSEMARY'S consternation, her fiancé—how peculiar it felt, to think of Sterling that way—did not call on her the next day, or the day after that. Even when it eventually stopped raining and the dismal weather could not be used as an excuse to explain away his absence, he did not come to see her. Nor did he send a letter, or a note, or a messenger pigeon.

That didn't stop other people from coming to visit her, though.

Ladies who hadn't cared enough about her to even say hello when they passed her in the park were suddenly clamoring to have tea every afternoon. The poor butler, an elderly man by the name of Dunbridge, who hadn't done much more over the past ten years than hand Lady Ellinwood her gloves and hat whenever she went out, found himself inundated with countless calling cards and visitors and invitations.

By the fourth day, he'd taken to hiding in a broom closet whenever the doorbell chimed.

Rosemary was giving serious consideration to joining him.

She had no interest in pretending to smile for women who only wanted to be in her good graces now that she was to become a duchess. Women who had giggled at her behind their fans. Who had stood idly by while Navessa had openly berated her at Lady Garfield's birthday picnic. Who wouldn't have hesitated to slice her to the quick had Sterling *not* offered to marry her.

Now that she had Joanna and Evie (both of whom had taken a short holiday to Campbell Castle in the Highlands to visit Brynne and her husband), she'd a better grasp of what real friendship was…and what it wasn't. This simpering, idolized attention wasn't real or genuine. It wasn't even very flattering, when she considered that they weren't the least bit interested in who *she* was but rather who she was marrying.

The invisible man, as it so happened.

At least that was what it seemed like these past few days.

When they were at Hawkridge Manor, she couldn't turn a corner without bumping into Sterling. Now that they were engaged to be married, he was nowhere to be found.

Odd, how that worked.

Finally, after an entire week had gone by, she decided that if Sterling would not come to her then she would go to him. It was the nineteenth century, after all. Why couldn't she call upon the man who had, for all intents and purposes, already jilted her before they'd had a chance to walk down the aisle? And so, after ensuring that Sir Reginald was tucked safely in the inside pocket of her pelisse and wouldn't be swept away by the sharp, cutting breeze whipping through the streets like the flat edge of a blade, that was precisely what she did.

Rather, that was what she *tried* to do.

After a long, chilly walk to Grosvenor Square with leaves dancing in the air, she discovered that Sterling was not in. A quick peek past the footman who had opened the door for her revealed that he most likely hadn't been in for a while, unless he favored sitting on furniture draped in broadcloth.

"I do not understand," she said. "This *is* the residence of the Duke of Hanover, is it not?"

"Aye, Miss," the footman replied. "But His Grace rarely comes here."

"Where does he stay, then, when he is in London?"

"I'm sorry, Miss, but His Grace doesn't like us sharing his whereabouts. If ye wanted to leave a card, I can see that he gets it."

Had Rosemary not already waited seven days, she might have been content to wait some more. But she had, and she wasn't, and her voice rose an octave as she said, "I am his fiancée and I would like, *very* much, to learn where I can find my husband-to-be!" She stomped her foot for emphasis, and immediately felt guilty. "I apologize. I shouldn't have yelled like that. It's just that I must speak with him. You see, he proposed rather impulsively, and we haven't seen each other since."

The footman tugged on his collar in confusion. "Then ye aren't engaged?"

"No, no, we are." She hesitated. "To the best of my knowledge. But we should talk about it, don't you think? I'm not sure how all this works, to be honest. I've never *been* engaged before. But it seems to me that you cannot just ask someone to marry you and then disappear. Unless that is what couples typically do. Except that's not what my cousin and her fiancé, the Earl of Hawkridge, have done. They're living together. Oh, not *together* together," she corrected hastily. "Completely separate bedchambers. But they're in the same house. His sister is there, too. Not right this minute. They've actually all gone off to the Highlands. I was invited, but on account of my recent engagement, my grandmother wanted me to remain in London to receive visitors. I was hoping one of those visitors was going to be the duke, but as you can see–"

"10 Cherry Lane in Mayfair," the footman cut in somewhat desperately.

Rosemary's brow creased. "Sorry? What was that?"

"10 Cherry Lane in Mayfair," he said again. "His Grace keeps a townhouse there."

"Oh." She smiled brightly. "That wasn't too difficult, was it? Thank you very much. If for some reason he comes here before I get there, can you tell him that I stopped in?"

"I will, Miss." By the way the footman had started to close the door, it was obvious he wanted her to leave. "Have a good day."

"Thank you again," she said, stepping out from under the marble portico. "You've been exceedingly helpful."

"Ye're welcome, Miss. I–" The footman stopped. Stared. "Is that a *rat* in yer pocket? Me brother Tim had one of those when he was a boy."

"Who, this?" She patted between Sir Reginald's ears as her pet poked his head out to see what was happening. "No, this is a red squirrel. But I *have* heard that rats make good companions," she said generously.

"Aye, me brother had him for almost six years before he died. In all that time, he never bit him. Not once. Our mum hated that rat. Tried to drown him in a bucket of water a few times. But he was always too fast for her."

"Sir Reginald bit the Duke of Hanover on his leg," Rosemary confided in a whisper. "It wasn't very nice, was it, Sir Reginald?"

It was impossible, of course, but she would have sworn that her pet rolled his eyes.

"So His Grace knows that ye have a squirrel ye keep in yer pocket?" the footman asked.

"Oh, yes. It was one of the first things we discussed, actually."

"And he *still* asked ye to marry him?"

Rosemary nodded.

"Wow." The footman gave a low whistle. "His Grace must really be in love with ye."

Her smile faltered. "10 Cherry Lane, did you say?"

"Aye, Miss. Should I call ye a carriage?"

"No, that's fine. I do not mind walking." What she *did* mind was Sterling having such little regard for his fiancée that he'd not shared he kept an entirely different household from his ducal manor in Grosvenor Square, leaving her no means by which to contact him except to track him down on foot.

Perhaps he had a viable excuse as to why he hadn't told her about the direction the investigation had taken or the danger he was in. Maybe he was trying to protect her. But how could he excuse away his absence these past seven days, or the fact that they were to be married and she didn't even know where he lived?

Rosemary was aware that in a vast array of subjects, she was greatly naïve. In her solitude and her loneliness, she'd cut out a small corner in the world and she had filled it with books, and daydreams, and furry creatures to raise. In that corner, there'd been no room for courtship, or passion, or popularity. So maybe those things were unfamiliar to her, and there was nothing she could do about that. But she *did* know about common decency and respect. And she knew that Sterling needed to explain why he'd given her neither.

Maybe she wasn't the fiancée he'd expected to have. Certainly the entire *ton* was flabbergasted by their union. But she was the fiancée he'd chosen…and the fiancée he'd resolutely ignored for a week, leaving her to solider the social burden of their sudden engagement by herself.

Biting the inside of her cheek and ducking her head against the howling winds, she set off back towards Mayfair.

STERLING COULDN'T STOP shaking.

The tremors had started in his hands. Small, involuntary vibrations that radiated all the way down from his head, through his arms, and into his fingers courtesy of the demon elf that had taken up residence in his skull and was swinging merrily away at bone and brain with an axe.

His heart alternated between utter stillness and bouts of frenzied activity where it slammed against the wall of his chest with such terrifying force he wouldn't have been surprised to look down and see it go bouncing off across the room.

When someone knocked on the door, at first he thought it *was* his heart. *Boom. Boom. Boom.* The light tapping of a fist against wood was like the blast of a cannon to his poor, tortured, elf-riddled head. Mouth already curled in a snarl, he sat up on the sofa he'd substituted for his bed–stairs were out of the question–and looked for a servant to send whoever the hell had come to pay him a visit far, far away. To another country, preferably. On a different continent. Until he remembered that he'd given the entire household staff paid leave for an as-of-yet undetermined length of time. He didn't want anyone to witness him in this condition. Not a footman, not a scullery maid, and especially not Higgins, the judgmental arse.

Once a day, Cook delivered a basket of meats, bread, and fruit which he picked over, but ultimately ate very little. His stomach wouldn't allow it. More than an apple slice or a cube of cheese and he was running to the privy to hurl his guts into the fathomless depths of a stone basin.

It wasn't very pleasant.

Actually, shy of losing Sebastian, this was the most *un*pleasant experience he'd ever had in his entire life. And he placed the blame squarely on the self-righteous shoulders of Kincaid and Weston.

"A detoxification," they'd called it before they jaunted off to Scotland on holiday, leaving Sterling to deal with the consequences of their barbaric ultimatum.

And it was barbaric.

Probably illegal as well.

If it wasn't, then it should have been.

He'd make it a point to bring it up at the next Parliamentary session.

"Gin or Rosemary," Weston had said in no uncertain terms. "You cannot have both. Our cousin will not be married to a wastrel drunkard."

He had tried to bargain, as desperate men do. What if he cut back? A bottle of whiskey a day. He'd take gin right out of the equation. All right, all right. Half a bottle. A nip or seven on special occasions. Drinking only after twelve o'clock. Ten on Sundays. But all his wheedling had done was prompted them to say the ten words that he'd never, ever wanted to hear.

"No alcohol of any kind, Sterling. Henceforth, you are sober."

Sober.

Him.

It was unthinkable. It was irrational. It was completely unnecessary. Yes, maybe over the past year or so he'd started to drink a *little* too much. But it wasn't a problem. Other men drank, didn't they? He'd never walked into an empty pub. Sometimes Weston and Kincaid had even accompanied him, the hypocritical bastards.

He would show them that he was perfectly capable of staying off the bottle for a few days, and then they'd see that their concern was utterly misplaced. If they wanted to help someone, they could take a trip to Seven Dials and pull some poor drunkard out of a ditch. He was the bloody Duke of Hanover, and if he wanted to have a damned scotch with his dinner then he'd have a damned scotch! He didn't need it. He didn't rely on it, like some sort of crutch. Which he'd prove by simply giving it up for a week. Whiskey, gin, wine, port. Everything.

So he'd watched, arms folded, while Weston and Kincaid carried every bottle, glass, and decanter out of the house. Then he had settled in for a quiet evening in his study going over dusty ledgers like a proper, responsible landowner.

By sunrise, he was drenched in sweat and was incapable of standing upright. His first indication that maybe the earl and the private detective were right, as much as he was loath to admit it. Maybe he *did* have a problem. A problem that was much larger and much more insidious than he'd let himself believe.

What was one bottle, until it turned into two?

What was one drink, until it turned into ten?

Somehow, someway, he'd lost control. Over his impulsions. Over his cravings. Over himself.

Gin or Rosemary.

On the third night of his sobriety, delirious with fever and hearing the voices of people who were no longer living, he reached for the silver flask he kept hidden underneath his desk. He unscrewed the top. He lifted it to his dry, cracked lips. He smelled the gin; wood and winter. He opened his mouth…and released a guttural bellow of rage and self-disgust as he threw the flask across his study where it smashed through the glass front of a curio cabinet.

Gin or Rosemary.

He rose on the fifth day feeling slightly better, although too weak to do much more than lay curled in a ball on the floor. It was the coolest part of the house, and with his face pressed flush against a wide pine board he let himself dream of blue-gray eyes and a wallflower's sweet, shy smile.

Gin or Rosemary.

When the sun rose on the last day of his first hellish week without alcohol, he'd made it all the way onto the sofa. A small triumph marred by the arrival of an unwanted guest. Struggling to rise, he reached for the water he'd taken to keeping within arm's distance at all times and guzzled straight from the pitcher. A few drops dribbled down his chin which he carelessly wiped away with the back of his hand. Still the knocking persisted, and with a grimace and a growl, he staggered to the front door and wrenched it open.

Gin or Rosemary.

"Rosemary," he breathed, and suddenly the choice wasn't a choice at all, but a forgone conclusion. And every second of hellish, indescribable agony was worth this one single moment of clarity. Because he'd never seen her when he was sober.

Less drunk was still drunk, like wearing spectacles in a light drizzle. But now the clouds had parted and his lenses were crystal clear, allowing him to see Rosemary as he never had before.

He saw her face, the roundness of her cheeks and the adorable tilt at the end of her nose and the freckle underneath her ear. He saw her hair, wisps of it blown free from her chignon to dance and curl around her jaw in ribbons of rich mahogany and tawny brown. He saw her eyes, the same soft morning fog framed with thick black lashes that he'd focused on in his dreams. And he didn't know it then. Wouldn't know it, for quite some time. But that was when he fell.

In the foyer of his Mayfair townhouse, on legs barely strong enough to hold him, in front of a woman with a squirrel peeking out of her pocket, the Duke of Hanover fell in love.

Completely.

Utterly.

Irrevocably.

"Sterling!" Those fog blue eyes went wide with alarm as Rosemary stepped past him into the foyer and spun around. "You look…"

"I know, I know," he sighed, raking a hand through his knotted hair. He was sparingly dressed in a linen shirt, halfway unbuttoned, and a pair of wrinkled blue trousers sans bracers. He'd not shaved since the morning of the Marigold Ball, and while he'd not confirmed anything with absolute certainty, he strongly suspected that the vague odor hanging in the air was emanating from him. "Please try to keep your hands off of me."

"…horrible."

"I may need a bath and a change of clothes," he allowed.

"I mean, *truly* horrible. Like death."

"All right," he frowned. "I've gotten the idea."

"You've appeared unkempt before. Bloating in your chin and whatnot–"

"Bloating in my chin?"

"–but this is different. You need a doctor. Or maybe a priest."

He snorted at that. "What the devil do I need a priest for?"

"To perform the exorcism," she said solemnly. If not for the be-traying twitch of her lips, he might have thought she was being serious. Then she removed her hat and gloves, placing them on top of a wooden armoire, and her expression sobered. "What's going on? I've not heard from you in a week. I thought…"

"You thought?" he prompted, his own countenance guarded. He couldn't–wouldn't–blame her for thinking the worst of him. That he'd been out gambling, or carousing in one of the dens of pleasures that littered Fleet Ditch, or drinking himself into a stupor at the Gray Pony. Reasonable conclusions to draw, given his history.

"I thought you might have changed your mind. About me. About–about us," she whispered, and the tremble in her voice stripped him raw.

"No. By God, no." Sterling didn't care that he stank. In two strides, he was across the foyer and had her in his arms. Arms that continued to shake even as he wrapped them around her slender frame and drew her firmly against his chest, laying her head over his thundering heart. "I've…I've been ill."

As good a way to put it as any, he supposed.

"You really *do* look ill." As she lifted her head, something flickered in her gaze.

"What?" he asked, abruptly self-conscious of his disheveled ap-pearance. Dear God. When *was* the last time he'd bathed? Or put on a new shirt, for that matter. "What is it?"

"You also look…I'm not sure how to put this…" Her small hand splayed tentatively across his sternum, and he sucked in a breath at the heat radiating from her smooth, silky palm. If that hand slid a tad lower… "Awake. You look awake."

"I've stopped drinking." He winced as soon as the words were past his mouth. He did not mean for it to be an announcement. Being sober was hardly grounds to send out the town criers. But Rosemary didn't scoff or belittle what was–for him–a monumental achievement literally borne of sweat and more than a few tears.

No, not his Rosemary. His Rosemary hadn't a derisive, mocking bone in her body. Yet another reason why he didn't deserve her. But damned if he wasn't going to try his best to earn her. To be a husband she could be proud of. Or at the very least, a husband that didn't fill her with shame.

"That must have been very difficult," she said quietly. A line embedded itself between her winged brows. "I should have liked to support you."

He shook his head at that. "Best you didn't. In case you couldn't tell by the state of me, it wasn't exactly pretty."

"A relationship between two people isn't always meant to be pretty." Her index finger glided along the stitched seam of his shirt until it encountered a glob of what he dearly hoped, for her sake, was food. Unperturbed, she scratched at the stain with her nail. "If you want the good, then it stands to reason you should also be there for the bad. It's like an apple."

"An apple," he repeated, not following.

"If an apple is bruised while growing on the tree and you cut the bruised piece out, soon the entire apple will rot. But if you tend to it where it is, and give it extra care and attention without trying to remove it, then eventually the bruised part shall callus over and the apple will be stronger for it."

"An arborist *and* an animal communicator," he said, amused–and secretly charmed–by her allegory. Lifting a loose curl, he brushed it behind her ear, thumb lingering along the rounded edge of the delicate shell before he allowed his arm to fall. "What topic aren't you well versed in, Romaine?"

"I've had time to read a great many books," she said, peering shyly at him from beneath her lashes. "And anyone can communicate with animals if they just put in a little bit of effort."

Sterling's rueful gaze fell to the squirrel-sized lump in the pocket of her spring green pelisse. "I'm happy to leave all the talking to you."

Rosemary's skirts swished delightfully as she walked further into the foyer, affording him a teasing glimpse at her trim ankles enclosed in silk stockings. She stopped at the bottom of the grand staircase centered in the middle of the room and cast him an inquisitive glance over her shoulder. "Why do you live in Mayfair when you have a larger residence in Grosvenor Square? I went there first, and a footman directed me here."

"It's quieter here," he answered automatically. "No one bothers me, which makes it preferable to the ducal manor." It wasn't a lie, but neither was it the full truth. A truth he'd never shared with anyone, not even Sarah. But then, Rosemary wasn't just anyone, was she? She was the only one to notice that he was missing this past week. The only one that cared enough to come looking for him. The only one that he wanted to trust with his innermost secrets. "Hanover House in London and Hanover Park in Sussex have never felt like mine. They're meant to belong to the Duke of Hanover."

Her head canted in bemusement. "But...but you *are* the Duke of Hanover."

"My brother was the duke," he corrected. There was a single seat in the foyer; a simple wooden bench with decorative spindles and a flat velvet cushion. He sat down heavily and sloughed his hands over his face as all the guilt he'd carried over the years caused his shoulders to slump. Without any whiskey or gin to lighten the burden, the weight was nearly unbearable. "I was never meant to be anything more than the spare. I didn't *want* to be anything more. Sebastian was always the more responsible heir. The serious heir. The heir that everyone turned to when they had a question or a problem that needed solving. He was perfect for the role. It's literally what he was born to be. But then..."

"But then?" Rosemary gently coaxed when Sterling fell silent.

"Then Sebastian died and I inherited a title I never wanted. A title that was never supposed to be mine. Now whenever I walk into Hanover House, all I hear are ghosts. They're so loud," he whispered as he stared bleakly at the floor and clenched his fists in his hair. "They're so bloody loud."

He closed his eyes and didn't see Rosemary when she crossed the foyer and sat beside him, but he felt when her thigh pushed lightly against his. Felt her hand come to rest in the middle of his spine. Felt the soft, soothing circles her palm made as she began to rub his back.

"From what I know, your brother was killed in a duel with Lord Aston," she said quietly. "Why do you blame yourself?"

"Because it was my fault." His teeth clenched and unclenched. "Because if not for me, he never would have taken up that duel. I goaded him into it. I all but put the damned pistol in his hand. Lord Aston pulled the trigger that discharged the bullet that entered his body, but *I* was the one who sent him there to die. Me. Nobody else."

He waited for Rosemary to dispute his claim. Waited for her to tell him that it wasn't his fault. That he couldn't have foreseen what his brother would do. That Sebastian's actions were his own.

It was what Sarah had said, and Kincaid, and Weston.

Over and over again, until he'd grown weary of all the hollow excuses made on his behalf. Because even though somewhere in his head he knew that they were partially right, that he *couldn't* have known Sebastian would take his drunken gibe seriously, in his heart he did not want to be absolved of his guilt.

The guilt was his punishment to carry with him. A daily reminder of what Sebastian had lost and he had gained. It didn't matter that if he had the chance, he would trade his title for his brother without a second's hesitation. The only thing that mattered was that Sebastian was dead, and he was alive, and maybe he *hadn't* pulled the trigger...but he hadn't gotten there in time to stop Lord Aston from doing it, had he?

Bloody hell, but he wanted a whiskey.

Just a sip to take the edge off.

Why the fuck had he stopped drinking again?

"Maybe you are to blame," Rosemary said matter-of-factly.

Sterling's muscles coiled and stiffened beneath her circling hand. Of all the things he'd imagined she would say, of all the platitudes he thought she would give him, that sure as hell wasn't on the list. "Excuse me?"

"Maybe you *are* to blame," she repeated. "Maybe if you hadn't said whatever it was that made your brother want to engage in a duel, he wouldn't have done it and you wouldn't be the Duke of Hanover."

Sterling twisted on the bench to stare at his fiancée in disbelief. "Are you trying to make me feel better? Because I have to say, you're doing a piss poor job of it."

Her hand stilled. "Is that what you want? To feel better? Is that why you've been lost in the bottom of a bottle ever since I met you? Do you even *remember* the first time we met?"

"Course I do," he scoffed. "It was at Hawkridge Manor. During the house party. You were...I was...we were..."

"I was searching for food, as I often am." The corners of her lips lifted in a self-deprecating smile. "I entered the parlor and there you were, stretched out on the sofa. You frightened me half to death, and then you asked for coffee. When I brought it over, you mistook me for Lady Emma Crowley."

"But you look nothing like her," he said, mystified. "She's blonde."

Rosemary nodded. "Precisely."

And that, he supposed, was the point she was trying to make. That his brother's death had driven him to all of his bad habits. That if not for that single tragedy, he'd be a gentleman of fine upstanding moral character. Little did she know he'd been holding a bottle long before he held his brother in his arms as he gasped his final breath.

"I drank before Sebastian died," he said dismissively. "That hasn't changed. You want to see the decency in me, to convince yourself that it's there. Somewhere. Hiding deep inside. But I've always been a ne'er-do-well and a rogue and a scoundrel. *That's* who I am," he bit out. "*That's* who I am meant to be. Not a duke."

"We are who we make ourselves to be. A title is what you were given when your brother died, but it doesn't define you. Only your words and your actions can do that. And maybe you *are* a scoundrel and a rogue and a ne'er-do-well." Removing her hand from his back, she cupped the side of his jaw and brought their faces so close together that he could see the nearly invisible flecks of violet amidst the swirls of blue and gray in her irises. "But you're also a man who loved his brother deeply. You're a man loyal to his friends and family. And you're a man who asked a wallflower to marry you so that her reputation wouldn't be ruined."

He drew a ragged breath. "Rosemary…"

"Maybe you really are to blame for Sebastian's death," she continued. "Or perhaps he would have died the next day walking in front of a carriage. Or the next year in a wave of scarlet fever. We do not know. We *cannot* know. Because when and how those that we love die is not for us to decide. If it were, I'd have my parents with me and Joanna and Evie would have theirs."

How much he wanted to believe her. To release himself from this guilt. To accept that maybe he had said something to Sebastian he shouldn't have, but all that happened after was beyond his control. To acknowledge that he *had* been a good brother. Not perfect. Not anywhere close. But good, and steadfast, and true. To admit that he had punished himself enough. That there was nothing else to gain–and oh so much to lose–by continuing this self-inflected retribution.

"Then what *do* we decide?" he asked.

"How we live," Rosemary answered simply. "We decide how we live."

CHAPTER THIRTEEN

THE INSTANT ROSEMARY had walked through the door and laid her eyes upon Sterling, her anger had faded and her doubts had drained away. She'd never seen anyone, human or animal, in such blatant misery before, and all she'd wanted to do was comfort him. To heal his hurt. To hold his hand. To let him know that whatever agony he'd chosen to endure, he didn't have to travel the path of it alone. She was here now, and she wasn't going anywhere.

Even when he tried to convince her that he wasn't worth saving, she remained resolute in her resolve to stay by his side. Because a relationship between two people wasn't always pretty, and if you wanted the good then you had to be there for the bad.

"For a wallflower who hasn't seen much of the world, Rufina, you're very wise." A half-smile took hold of his mouth as he traced the arch of her cheekbone with a bent knuckle. Their heads remained pressed intimately together, their legs connected ankle to hip, their shoulders touching. Even when they were kissing, they'd never been this close; connected on a level that went beyond the physical…while still leaving plenty of space for Sterling's teasing.

"Rufina?" she said skeptically.

"I may be running out of names," he admitted.

"You could always use mine."

"I could, but what would be the fun in that?" A long, heavy sigh and then he slumped back against the bench, kicking his feet out in front of him as he gazed at the ceiling. "I'm glad that I met you, Rosalind. Even if I thought you were Lady Emma Crowley." A hint of the roguish charm for which he was renowned rose to the surface as he glanced at her out of the corners of his eyes. "You would make a smashing blonde."

Scowling ever-so-slightly, Rosemary touched her hair. "If you'd prefer to marry Lady Emma—"

"God no," Sterling interrupted with a shudder. "Have you ever heard her laugh? The sound of it would make a hyena cringe. Besides, I'm not about to anger that furry-tailed rat in your pocket by reneging on my proposal. He's already brutally attacked me once. I am not about to give him an excuse to go after me again."

"Are you referring to the painless nibble Sir Reginald gave you in the tree?"

"Painless nibble?" he said incredulously. "Is that what we're calling it? You should consider yourself lucky that I'm not a eunuch."

Inadvertently, her gaze flicked to his lap, and she blushed when he boldly patted himself there.

"Not to worry, love. All is in working order."

"I...I wasn't worried." Her blush deepened. "That is, I haven't given that area of, ah, your anatomy much thought one way or another. But I'm glad to hear everything is...everything is, ah, functional."

He leaned in close, brought his mouth to her ear, and purred, "I can assure you it's *very* functional."

As the heat from her face rapidly transferred to other parts of her body, Rosemary resisted the urge to squirm. She'd been more at ease when they were discussing the death of his brother. Grief and guilt. Love and loss. Those were concepts and emotions that she somewhat understood. But passion, lust, and desire? Completely foreign entities, save what she'd already experienced in the arms of the man beside her.

He slowly skimmed the tips of his fingers down her arm and encir-cled her wrist, the callused pad of his thumb hovering above the frantic flutter of her pulse. "Nervous?" he murmured, and she gave a hard jolt when he kissed the side of her neck, his unshaven facial hair rough and prickly against her smooth skin.

"I...I....I did not come here to be seduced," she said in the firmest tone that she could manage given the circumstances.

"Didn't you?" His breath, warm and smelling faintly of coffee grounds, tickled the hairs at her nape as he reversed course and returned to the shell of her ear to run his tongue, hot and wet and wicked, along the outer edge.

"No. I came to see where you've been for the past week and why...why you haven't called upon me," she said weakly, clamping her thighs together as a damp heat trickled between them. She felt both wide awake and incredibly drowsy, a reminder of the time she'd snuck a glass of wine at one of her grandmother's luncheons. After drinking it far too fast, she had spent the rest of the afternoon dozing in the shade of a mulberry tree, her head pleasantly light and tingly.

"Have you received a satisfactory answer?" Easily untying the laces that held her pelisse closed, Sterling slipped his hand inside the cotton-lined garment to massage her breasts while simultaneously drawing her earlobe in his mouth.

"What answer?" she said, her head too muddled to remember what they were talking about. Something in regards to why she was here, and what he'd been doing for the last seven days, and oh–*oh*, that felt *splendid*.

On a mewling sigh she turned into him, draping her arms on either side of his neck when he grasped her waist and lifted her onto his lap. With an alarmed squeak Sir Reginald dove out of her pocket and scurried off in search of higher ground, but Rosemary was too distracted to notice her pet's abrupt departure as Sterling's hands had shifted to cup and squeeze her bottom.

He muttered a curse as he shoved her various skirts and under-garments up past her knees, and they both moaned in pleasure when he settled her directly upon his hard, hot arousal, leaving only a few pieces of linen to separate their pulsing cores which wasn't nearly enough to prevent her from feeling the enormous length and width of his swollen member.

Given her rudimentary knowledge of sexual intercourse–having once caught a cow and a bull in the act, she knew the basics of what went where–Rosemary found herself discomfited by the knowledge that all of *him* would have to fit inside of *her*. A sheer impossibility, given his size. But then he kissed her flush on the mouth, his tongue sliding almost lazily between her lips to lick and taste, and any concerns regarding anatomy were swept away on a torrent of desire.

Her legs automatically tightened around his hips when he reached inside the waistband of her drawers and raked his short, blunt fingernails across the curved globe of her buttock. Before she could decide whether she liked being touched in such an intimate area–she did, most certainly, although she wasn't sure whether it would be sinful to admit it–that devilishly clever hand of his wandered to the front of her unmentionables and he stroked the downy thatch of ebony curls tucked away between soft, pillowy plump thighs.

Probing deeper, he used a single fingertip to rub a slow circle around the small, sensitive nub nestled within the curls, alternating the pressure until she was slick and wanting and ready for…ready for what, she didn't know, but whatever *it* was she craved it like a bird craved the air and a ship craved the sea.

She rose higher on her knees, bracing them against the rigid slats of the bench as he continued to fondle and flick, expertly timing the rolling motions of his wrist with the languid thrusting of his tongue. Her breaths grew harsh and uneven. Her entire body, from the tips of her toes still encased in her walking shoes to the rigid set of her brows, went taut; a bow ready to be set free from its quiver.

Then his finger dipped smoothly inside of her while he bit down on her bottom lip and, with a gasp, her eyes flew open and her back arched as sensation after sensation washed over her in a wave of sensual gratification that left her sprawled in a boneless heap upon Sterling's chest.

"What...what *was* that?" she asked, too weak to even raise her head.

"That is pleasure," he said huskily, brushing a curl off her temple. "Do you enjoy it?"

She nodded wordlessly and his chuckle vibrated against her cheek before he gathered her close.

For a few minutes, they laid together, the wallflower and the rogue, wrapped in contentment and each other's arms with nary a worry in the world. Then, as it tended to do, that world began to come into sharper and sharper focus, bringing with it a myriad of concerns and considerations, not least of which was the bulging arousal pressing against Rosemary's inner thigh.

"Did you...that is...um..." How to put this in a ladylike manner? Not that there was anything exactly *ladylike* about being sprawled across her lover with her dress rucked up past her hips and her belly still quivering from being touched down *there*.

Her lover.

Rosemary liked the sound of that.

She liked it quite a lot, actually.

It made her seem wicked, and sinful, and decadent. Everything that she most decidedly was not...except when she was with Sterling. He'd awoken a spark inside of her, and with every kiss it burned just a little brighter and a little bolder.

She was bolder.

Bold enough to prop her chin on his chest and ask, "Are you satisfied? With, ah, what we did?"

Sterling gazed at her with some interest. "Are you asking if I came?"

Came.

Was that what it was called?

Such a common word, but when he employed the use of that deep, velvety timbre in the back of his throat, it sounded anything *but* common.

She gave a tiny nod.

"Regrettably, no. Not in this instance. As I'm sure you can tell by the phallus-shaped protuberance jabbing you in the leg." He gave a wolfish grin. "That's not to say I didn't thoroughly enjoy myself. But it is probably time I soaked in a cold bath lest this go any further than it should."

"Will a bath help with…this?" She reached between them and passed a light, inquisitive hand across the phallus-shaped protuberance. It was hard as granite and hot as fire, and she was shocked when it seemed to pulse at her touch.

"Well don't do *that*," Sterling groaned. "That just makes it worse."

"I'm sorry." She snatched her hand away as her gaze jerked guiltily back to his. "I didn't mean to hurt it. That is, to hurt you."

"It didn't hurt. It felt good. Too damned good. And you need to go home. Right away." So saying, he sat up with such abruptness that she almost tumbled right off his lap.

Catching herself on the bench by her elbows, she frowned at him as he towered over her. "But–"

"Right away," he repeated and, this time, at least he had the good grace to offer her a hand which she grudgingly accepted. Once he'd hauled her to her feet, he began to assist in the arduous task of rearranging her layers of clothing which consisted of a long corset, corset cover, drawers, chemise, regular petticoat, and flounced petticoat. All that before the dress itself, and the pelisse on top to cap it all off.

"My God." Out of breath by the time they'd finished, Sterling bent forward and braced his hands on his knees. "It's much easier to take off than put on, isn't it? You have to do that *every* day?"

"Sometimes three times a day if there's a social function in the evening." Lips twitching in amusement, Rosemary gave a short whistle to summon Sir Reginald and returned him safely to her pocket once he came scampering back from heaven only knew where. "I've long held the belief that women's fashion has been constructed to occupy as much of our time as possible. If the fairer sex had an equal number of free hours in the day at their disposal as men, we'd have put ourselves in charge of things years ago."

"Undoubtedly," her husband-to-be agreed without hesitation. "That's bloody awful. I'd no idea. Once we're married, you've my full permission to wear as little clothing as you'd like." A gleam entered his eyes. "In fact, I insist on it. No wife of mine is going to waste three hours of her morning getting dressed when she could be out ruling the world."

"Is that so?" Gathering up her reticule and gloves, Rosemary couldn't resist peeking into an adjoining room. What she saw—clothes strewn about, empty plates on the floor, blankets crumpled on the sofa—gave her reason to pause.

It was evident the prior seven days had been anything but easy for Sterling, and she did not want to leave him alone without ensuring that he had everything he required to conquer whatever demons remained to haunt him.

She was hopeful that he had turned a proverbial corner. That the vulnerability he'd shown her was a sign he was ready to let the past rest and move on to a future free of guilt and self-destruction. But she also wasn't going to underestimate the allure of old habits, or the temptation of old sins.

"Maybe I should stay for a while longer. Just to tidy up," she offered. "Do you have food in the kitchen to eat? And fresh water to drink? These glasses are dirty." Her nose wrinkling, she walked into the parlor and began to fill an empty tray with various dishes. It was obvious that Sterling hadn't moved much beyond this room during his self-imposed internment, and just as obvious that he wasn't accustomed to cleaning up after himself. No matter. She may have had the luxury of growing up with a lady's maid, but she wasn't above pitching in where needed.

"Here," she said, carrying the tray over to Sterling.

He stared at the lopsided tower of plates and bowls she'd shoved into his hands as if she had just handed him a mummified head. "What the devil am I to do with these?"

"Take them into the kitchen, then come back for more," she said briskly.

"I'm not sure if you're aware, but this is *precisely* why I have servants. It's one of the few benefits of being a duke. That and women tend to fawn over me in endless droves." He narrowed his eyes at her. "You're not fawning."

"Nor do I have any intention of starting. Shoo," she said, wiggling her fingers at him. "The dishes aren't going to tidy themselves. And once you've done that, I need assistance with this quilt."

Muttering something indecipherable under his breath, Sterling stomped away and Rosemary turned from the door to hide a smile. When he returned—still muttering—she patiently guided him through the proper steps of blanket folding, and then they tackled the carelessly discarded piles of clothes.

After the room was finally tidied, she rocked back on her heels with her hands on her hips and nodded in approval. "There. Doesn't that make you feel better? You've accomplished a task."

Sterling scratched his chin. "I need to pay the maids more."

"Yes, you should."

"It does feel good," he admitted. "To see the before and after, and know that I had a hand in the improvement of it. Not that picking up a few dirty cups and a pair of socks is anything of great significance.

But..."

"It's something," she said, secretly pleased at the glint of pride she saw in the depths of his gaze. A gaze that was, for once, clear of alcohol, cynicism, and pain.

"Indeed. Now, as much as I've enjoyed cleaning my own damned house, it's time for you and your rat to go home, Renita. Unless your grandmother is aware that you've trotted off to the private residence of your wicked fiancé so that you might be brought to sweet release atop a bench in his foyer?" he queried innocently.

"I...I didn't tell her where I was going," Rosemary admitted as a flush crept up into her collarbones. *Naughty duke*, she thought. "My grandmother may be under the impression that I am shopping with a friend at the new department store on Oxford Street."

"I figured as much when you did not arrive with a chaperone in tow," Sterling said dryly. "You've become quite the troublemaker since leaving Hawkridge Manor. I'm not sure if I should associate with you."

"That may be a problem, seeing as we're to be married." Gloved fingers twining together behind her back, she bit her lip as they reentered the foyer. "We *are* to be married, aren't we?"

Positioning himself in front of the door, her fiancé folded his arms. "That's the second time you've brought our engagement into question. Have I done something I'm unaware of to make you doubt my intentions? I'm well versed in my numerous shortcomings, but going back on my word isn't one of them."

"You mean besides asking me to marry you on a whim and then disappearing without a word?" From inside her pocket, Sir Reginald, who was no doubt growing restless, gave a loud chirp. Scooping him up, she placed him on her shoulder where he sat with his black eyes fixed on Sterling and his fluffy tail twitching.

"I did not propose on a whim." Sterling looked at Sir Reginald. "Why is he staring at me like that? I don't like it."

"Then you had every intention of asking me to marry you before Lady Navessa caught us together at the ball?" Rosemary hadn't come here today with the intention of pressing Sterling about *why* he'd asked her to marry him. Whether, she'd just wanted to know *if* they remained engaged. A question he'd already answered. Twice. But doubt was like a thief in the night. It moved rapidly through the shadows, stealing whatever precious sense of security and confidence it was able to get its hands on.

She didn't expect Sterling to be head over heels in love with her. Not yet, anyways. But she needed to know it was a possibility. She needed to be reassured that there was *something* about her that he found alluring enough to want to marry her. Not only because he felt he had to, but because he wanted to.

"I cannot say I specifically went to the Marigold Ball with plans to propose, no." Sterling's gaze remained trained suspiciously on Sir Reginald. "He's plotting my demise. I can tell."

"If you didn't come to the ball with plans to propose to me, then you did, by definition, do it on a whim," she said, almost desperately.

"Then I guess I did." He started to shrug, took note of her expression, and dropped his shoulder. A line chiseled itself into the middle of his forehead. "Is that a problem? You already said yes."

"I know I did, but…"

"But?" said Sterling in a voice that was noticeably colder than it had been just a second ago.

But I need to know that I am more than a convenient means to restore your reputation. But I need to know that had Lady Navessa not come upon us that night, you would still be interested in me. But I need to know that our marriage will be built on more than a whim.

But, but, but.

The words were there, right on the tip of her tongue.

Except when she opened her mouth, they weren't the words that came out.

"But we should probably start planning our wedding earlier rather than later." *Coward*, she told herself. Even Sir Reginald appeared disappointed, if the sound of his chittering was any indication. "We don't even have a date, or a church selected. Evie and Lord Weston are to be married this autumn at the village parish by Hawkridge Manor. She's asked me to be a bridesmaid, and I'd not dare incite her wrath by doing anything before her big day. But perhaps in the spring or summer? That would give us plenty of time to plan, and–"

"We can be married whenever you prefer," Sterling cut in dismissively. "I've never cared about weddings before, and I'm not about to start now. Mindless pomp and circumstance, if you ask me. Tell me where to be, and I'll be there. The rest I will leave up to you and your grandmother and cousins, as I'm sure they'll want some say given how nosy Americans can be. Just don't make the date for Christmas, as that is when my sister is to wed Lord Hamlin."

"Is she?" Rosemary said, startled. "You hadn't mentioned. How exciting."

"Very," he said in a tone that implied he didn't think it was exciting at all. "They're having it at Hanover Park. I haven't decided if I'm going or not."

"Oh, but you *have* to go. It's your sister."

A muscle clenched in his jaw. "We'll see. Regardless, so long as you avoid December 25th, we can be married any day that you like. Wait until summer, or don't. It makes no difference."

"I didn't realize you had such a strong aversion to weddings."

"It's not that I have an aversion. I simply fail to see what all the fuss is about. The wedding night, on the other hand…" His eyebrows wiggled suggestively, her only warning before he leapt forward to wrap his arms around her waist and pull her snug against the hard plane of his chest. "That, I'm *far* more excited about," he murmured, finding and kissing the small sliver of exposed skin above the raised collar of her pelisse.

When her knees wobbled (useless things, knees), she sagged helplessly against him and wrapped her arm around his neck to hold herself upright. Abandoning his perch on her shoulder, Sir Reginald streaked down her other arm and dove headfirst into her pocket. "I thought I was supposed to be l-leaving," she gasped.

"You've already been here this long." He cupped her breasts as his mouth tracked a heated path along the slender column of her neck to her earlobe. "What's a few minutes more…?"

CHAPTER FOURTEEN

A FTER A FEW minutes turned into fifteen, and fifteen into thirty (but who was counting, really?), Rosemary reluctantly pulled herself free of Sterling's embrace and they said their farewells.

"When will we see each other again?" she asked, the wind whipping through her hair as she stepped out onto the front walkway, a wide strip made of limestone framed with rosebushes.

Sterling remained in the door, his tall frame and broad shoulders almost completely obscuring the foyer where he'd made her…what was the word?

Oh.

Her cheeks warmed.

She remembered now.

Even *thinking* it made her blush and she had no earthly idea how she wasn't going to be reduced to a puddle of red on the floor when her grandmother inevitably asked her how she'd found the department store.

"Fancy a ride through Hyde Park at the end of the week before the Royal Gala?" Sterling asked, referring to a private, prestigious event to be held at Marlborough House, the London residence of Prince Albert and his wife, Princess Alexandra of Denmark.

Held biannually, once in autumn and again at the end of spring right before the *ton* fled the city for their country houses, it was a charity auction disguised as a formal ball. Over the years, it had benefited hospitals, orphanages, and the like. In an attempt to repair his public reputation, which had suffered due to a number of not-very-discreet affairs, Prince Albert was hosting this particular gala to raise funds and pique interest in what he'd already deemed the Royal College of Music, an educational enterprise designed to award scholarships and promote talented musicians and composers no matter their title or how much money they possessed.

Invitations were not given but instead purchased, and the price was steep. Rosemary had never attended a Royal Gala before, and she hadn't planned to begin with this one. But when she said as much to Sterling, he merely shook his head.

"If I have to go then so do you," he said, as if that settled the matter. "You can expect two invitations to be delivered by end of day tomorrow."

Rosemary double-blinked. It was going to take some time, she decided, to grow accustomed to the idea that from this day forward nearly any door she wished to step through would be open to her courtesy of her husband's wealth and influence.

"Thank you," she replied, for what else was there to say? Her life was changing rapidly, in more ways than one. Her only hope was that it was all for the better...although given the recent onslaught of unwanted attention thrown her direction, she suspected that those changes, whatever they ended up being, were going to take a lot of getting used to.

"And the ride in Hyde Park?" He propped his shoulder against the doorframe; casual elegance with a touch of disreputable rake. "I'll have my driver ready the landau and you can bring your grandmother if she is agreeable."

"My grandmother," Rosemary said doubtfully.

"I *have* asked her granddaughter to marry me. Seems only fitting I properly introduce myself."

"But didn't you meet her at the house party?" she said, confused.

"A few words, most of which I don't remember."

"Because of…" She mimed tipping a bottle back.

"Being drunk most of the time. Yes, I'm sure that had something to do with it."

"My grandmother can be rather…difficult. Maybe your first meeting as my betrothed should be in a more traditional setting like a parlor or a drawing room." *Where you can run away more easily*, she added silently.

"Not to worry," Sterling said with every confidence. "Women of all ages adore me. The elderly ones especially. I'll have her eating out of the palm of my hand before we've made the first loop."

LADY ELLINWOOD DID not adore him.

But I'm a duke, Sterling felt like saying, for what was the point of the bloody title if he couldn't use it to get him what he wanted when he wanted it? And at the moment, what he desired most of all was an eighty-two-year-old woman's approval.

Approval that was, thus far, less than forthcoming.

Rosemary *had* tried to warn him, he acknowledged.

Difficult, she'd said.

Her grandmother could be "difficult".

A horse that didn't want to accept the bit was difficult.

A friend who didn't want to leave the pub after one too many pints was difficult.

Lady Ellinwood wasn't difficult.

She was a damned ice-breathing dragon disguised as an old woman whose thin lips hadn't budged from their line of disapproval since he'd introduced himself. Several inches shorter than her granddaughter, her diminutive size made her no less intimidating. She was a brittle, dried willow branch that was just as likely to strike you across the face as it was to break in half. Another lifetime and she would have made a fine

Spanish inquisitor.

"Tell me, Your Grace," Lady Ellinwood began in her dry, crackling voice as their carriage passed beneath a row of English oaks whose leaves were beginning to carry a tint of orange as the seasons blurred together. "Do you consider yourself a religious man?"

"Ah…" He looked to Rosemary for assistance. Sitting beside her grandmother, she was as pretty as a spring daffodil in a yellow dress and matching bonnet. By contrast, Lady Ellinwood wore a dark burgundy gown and lace mob cap devoid of ruffles. Seeing them side by side, his cheerful, eternally optimistic fiancée and her glowering grandmother, he was struck by the strength Rosemary must have had to grow and thrive in spite of the dragon-shaped shadow constantly looming over her.

It reminded him of a flower he'd seen once on one of his nights coming home from the pub. Make that early morning, as the sky had been streaked through with shards of red and pink as the sun gradually rose from above the Thames. Weaving a staggering path along the middle of an empty street, he had stopped in his tracks when he came upon a single white daisy.

Daisies weren't an unusual sight in and of themselves. The meadows surrounding Hanover Park were so overwhelmed by the common flower that the farmers considered it a weed. But here, in the midst of crowded shops and townhouses stacked on top of each other and hard-packed dirt and cobblestone as far as the eye could see, any type of plant growing outside of a garden was a rarity.

To this day, Sterling didn't know why he'd bothered to stop at all, let alone crouch down in front of the daisy for a closer look. He was probably still drunk, and not in his sensible mind. But as he'd stared at the delicate white flower courageously sprouting out of a crack in the street where no flower ought to have been able to grow, he just remembered being filled with a sense of awe.

He'd been tempted to pick the flower and bring it to Eloise. But in the end, he had left it alone and bought her a necklace instead. Undoubtedly, the daisy would soon be crushed beneath a boot or a carriage wheel. It was only a matter of time. But he hadn't wanted to be the one responsible for extinguishing a piece of beauty from the world. A piece of beauty that, by all laws of man and nature, never should have existed in the first place.

How fortunate, then, that no one had told the daisy that.

"Your Grace?" Lady Ellinwood pressed, drawing him into the present and reminding him that he'd yet to respond to her question.

"Ah, yes," he said after Rosemary gave a tiny, barely perceptible nod. "Yes, I am religious. Very religious. Practically pious, really."

A bald-faced lie, as he'd barely stepped foot in a church since Sebastian's funeral. But his answer appeared to satisfy Lady Ellinwood, for her perpetual scowl softened ever-so-slightly.

"That is reassuring to hear," she said. "These days, too many young people are turning away from the church. I shall look forward to having you attend Sunday service with us at St. George's in Hanover Square. That *is* where you will be married, I presume, given that is where Rosemary's parents were wed."

Again, Sterling glanced at Rosemary, who shrugged.

"Indeed," he said. "Naturally, that's what we are planning to do. To clarify, are you looking forward to having me attend just *this* Sunday's service, or every Sunday thereafter?"

Lady Ellinwood's watery blue eyes bored into his. "As I am sure you are aware, that depends entirely on you, Your Grace, and how many sins you have committed during the course of your weekly endeavors that will require penance and forgiveness."

He smiled weakly. "Every Sunday, then."

Rosemary snorted.

"Sorry," she said when her grandmother pointed that searing gaze in her direction. "Must have swallowed an insect."

The corners of Lady Ellinwood's mouth pinched. "We have not

yet discussed the matter of my granddaughter's dowry and inheritance. When she was born, my son had the foresight to set aside a reasonable sum for her future husband. A sum which grew considerably upon his death to include monies, gilts, and property, all of which have been held under my stewardship. Upon marriage to a husband that I, as her guardian, deem fit, they shall be released to him in their entirety. Excluding the house in Mayfair where I currently reside and a reasonable monthly allowance to be fairly determined."

The carriage rocked as it struck a bump in the wide gravel pathway that offered a scenic, circular ride around the interior of Hyde Park, but Lady Ellinwood did not weave or wobble or grab for the leather armrest Sterling had a footman install specifically for the benefit of his fiancée's frail, hollow-boned eighty-two-year-old grandmother.

He doubted an explosion of dynamite would bend that iron spine of hers.

"Please do not concern yourself with Miss Stanhope's dowry," he said gallantly. "I've no need of it, and I can assure you that she will not want for anything as my wife. You may do with the monies and properties and gilts as you please. Take a long holiday, or make a large donation to charity. I'd not take something that was not necessary simply for the sake of tradition. Or if there is a property that Miss Stanhope is preferential to, I'd not deny her of it. But it would be hers, not mine. Truly, a dowry is not necessary."

Lady Ellinwood's forehead turned into a map of lines and wrinkles as she arched a gray eyebrow. "Who is to say I have deemed you fit to even *receive* my granddaughter's dowry, Your Grace? Might I note that for a pious man, you are certainly presumptuous."

"Grandmother," Rosemary admonished lightly as Sterling gave considerable thought to launching himself over the side of the landau.

If he jumped now, he would land in a pond. And although he'd never been a strong swimmer, drowning was surely preferable to a slow, agonizing death by dowager.

"What?" Lady Ellinwood demanded. "Am I not to speak my mind because His Grace is of higher rank? You are my granddaughter. My last remaining blood relation and heiress to our family name and fortune. Surely that precedes any formality in regards to title."

"I thought you were pleased that the Duke of Hanover and I are engaged to be married." A flicker of amused exasperation passed over Rosemary's face. "You've certainly hosted enough celebratory luncheons and you've accepted our invitations to the Royal Gala this evening. Invitations, as it so happens, that did *not* appear out of thin air."

"I am pleased," Lady Ellinwood scowled and, this time, it was Sterling who swallowed an insect.

Bloody hell.

If *this* was pleased then he never wanted to see her unhappy.

One glare and he'd probably turn to stone on the spot.

"Are you?" Rosemary asked with unmistakable skepticism.

Their heavy carriage, pulled by a fancy pair of matching bays in gleaming black harness, veered slightly to the left when a curricle whizzed past. The couple squished together on the narrow bench seat gaped openly at the passengers in the landau and immediately began to whisper excitedly before the two vehicles had even cleared each other.

Accustomed to the attention that his presence garnered, Sterling automatically raised his hand in acknowledgment. When he refocused his attention on his fiancée, he found her staring at him with a bemused expression on her face.

"What?" he said, wondering if he'd accidentally committed some slight that would give Lady Ellinwood cause to despise him even more than she already did for reasons not yet unveiled.

"Has it always been like that?" Rosemary asked.

"Like what?"

"People looking at you as if you were the Prince of Wales or the white tiger at the Zoological Society in Regent's Park?"

"How do you know they weren't looking at *you*?" he countered.

"Because no one looks at me."

"They will when you are a duchess."

If not for the presence of Lady Ellinwood, he wouldn't have hesitated to draw Rosemary onto his lap and kiss away the shy, self-deprecating smile that had taken hold of that delightfully plump mouth.

To his surprise, he'd missed her terribly during the last four days they'd been apart.

He never had.

Missed anyone, that is.

At least not anyone living.

If he hadn't needed the additional time to purge his body of its remaining withdrawal symptoms (even now, his hands occasionally shook and a headache came like clockwork every night at half-past six when he would have reached for a bottle), he'd have been standing on her doorstep. Not for any particular reason other than he wanted to be near her. Which was, admittedly, an unexpected side effect of their engagement. This restless, almost feral need to have her. To hold her. To hear the soft catch in her voice when he kissed that little groove between the base of her neck and her shoulder.

But it wasn't just unsated passion that drew him to her.

Plainly put, he enjoyed her company.

Sterling had traveled across Europe. Attended some of the most debaucherously sinful parties known to man. He'd sipped champagne in a hot air balloon and cheered on the great Anatis to victory in the Queen's Box at the Grand National. He'd visited castles. Dined with royalty. Spent a *very* memorable evening attending a private viewing of the Spanish Belly Dancing Troupe. Yet for all of his exploits and all his adventures, he had never been happier, or more content, than when he was with Rosemary.

To date, they'd had some of the most interesting and obscure conversations of his lifetime. She made him think. More than that, she made him pay attention. He couldn't play the fool when he was with her. The affable, amiable duke who didn't care about anything or anyone. Who was quick with a joke, but whose smile never quite reached his eyes.

No one seemed to notice that.

Not Kincaid or Weston or Sarah.

But Rosemary did.

She possessed an instinctive sense for when he was pretending. For when he was saying all the right words and going through all the right motions, but he wasn't there. Not really. She forced him to be present in the moment. To absorb and acknowledge not only the emotions of those around him, but his own innermost thoughts and feelings.

He couldn't hide when he was with Rosemary.

Not from her...and not from himself, either.

But he damned well wished he could hide from Lady Ellinwood.

"My granddaughter raises a valid point, Your Grace." Lady Ellinwood ran her fingers along the top of her cane. Made of whalebone, the handle was worn smooth from years of daily use. "I have raised Rosemary since she was a young girl, and am more aware than most of her shortcomings. The most significant being her inability to ingratiate herself into High Society despite my best efforts to set her up for success."

"What are you saying, Lady Ellinwood?" he asked in a tone pitched dangerously low. By all outward appearances, he was calm and relaxed. His legs crossed at the knee, his spine casually slouched to follow the curvature of the seat, his arms draped out to the side. But on the inside, he was a coiled wolf, ready to launch itself at whoever dared speak ill of his fiancée. Regardless of whether they were an eighty-two-year-old grandmother or not.

He'd tolerated the slights that Lady Ellinwood had directed at him.

Mostly because he deserved far worse. But he wasn't about to sit idly by while she used that vicious viper's tongue on the woman that he loved.

The woman that he loved.

Did he love Rosemary?

In a word, yes.

He did.

"I am merely raising attention to what others are already discussing behind closed doors." Lady Ellinwood lifted her chin and, although she was at least a foot and a half shorter, still somehow managed to stare down her nose at him. "Given your wealth and title, you had the pick of any eligible lady in this country and all those surrounding it. My granddaughter is fair to look upon, I'll grant her that. Fairer yet if she'd stop helping herself to a second plate at dinner."

Rosemary blushed.

A low, rumbling growl rose from the depths of Sterling's throat.

Lady Ellinwood didn't seem to notice.

Or if she did, she failed to care.

"But Rosemary hardly has the qualities of a duchess," the elderly woman continued. "Which begs the question, Your Grace, why you have chosen her to be yours. What do you see in my granddaughter that others do not?"

"What do I see?" His furious gaze shot to Rosemary, who was staring intently at her lap. Not giving a tinker's cuss what Lady Ellinwood thought, he reached across the carriage and covered her hand with his.

Startled, she glanced up and their eyes met; fierce, stormy slate diving into hurt, misty blue.

"I see a woman who is well read and highly intelligent," he began. "I see a woman who is kind to everyone, regardless of whether they are a prince or a pauper, a lady's maid or a lady. I see a woman who is loving to all creatures great and small. A woman who has known loss, but hasn't let it harden her. Who has been ignored and overlooked, but hasn't let it dull her spirit or her optimism." He drew a breath. "But most of all, I see a woman who was brave enough to extend a branch to a man that was drowning. And who was strong enough to pull him to shore."

His gaze cut to Lady Ellinwood. Bolts of lightning flashed in his eyes. "*That's* what I see. Have you any other inane questions, or can we conclude this farce? Your granddaughter and I will be married, with or without your approval. I am not going to beg for it, and neither is she. So you can come to the wedding with a bloody smile on your face or you cannot come at all. It doesn't make a damned bit of difference to me."

"I've no further questions." Instead of being embarrassed, or at the very least chastised, Rosemary's grandmother almost appeared...*pleased*. As if Sterling had said precisely what she'd wanted to hear. "Thank you, Your Grace."

"For what?" he bit out.

"For seeing all of the unique qualities in my granddaughter that I do. Rosemary would not fare well in a marriage where she was expected to put aside her eccentricities and behave in a manner befitting of a traditional duchess. I am pleased to know that with you, she won't have to. You've brought me a great deal of comfort. For that, I thank you."

Rosemary's jaw dropped.

Of a similarly flummoxed state, the best response from Sterling was a hesitant, "You're...welcome?"

Lady Ellinwood delivered a brisk nod. "Now that that matter is settled, please direct your driver to return us home with all haste." Her cheeks drew inwards as she pursed her thin lips. "We've much to prepare for before the Royal Gala. And do advise your driver to take more care with the corners. His handling of a carriage of this size is really quite atrocious. My husband could do a better job at the reins, and he has been dead for nearly thirty years."

Sterling twisted behind him to tap his driver (who was incredibly skilled at his profession) on the shoulder. "You heard Lady Ellinwood, Bentley. Back to Mayfair." He lowered his voice. "An extra ten pounds if you drive like the bloody wheels are on fire."

Bentley tipped his felt bowler. "As you wish, Your Grace."

CHAPTER FIFTEEN

ROSEMARY FLOATED ON air for the rest of the morning and into the afternoon. The things Sterling had said about her…the ways he'd described her…no one had ever seen her as he did. No one had ever made her *feel* as he did. Appreciated for who she was, not what she was lacking.

The clouds carried her all the way up until her lady's maid, Rebecca, a mousy young woman with bulbous eyes and tiny teeth, entered her bedchamber carrying what could only be described as the most atrocious ball gown she had ever seen.

Pink and fluffy, with layers upon layers of bows and ruffles, it was so blindingly ugly that it made the bonnet Sterling had pulled off her head and tossed in the bushes look like a crown befit for Queen Victoria. And Rosemary, who had never–not once–bothered to comment on any of the dresses and various accompanying articles of clothing that her grandmother's modiste had made for her, no matter how frumpy or out of style they were (according to Evie), held up her hand and stopped Rebecca at the door.

"Please don't bring that in here," she said, almost pleadingly.

"I am sorry, Miss Rosemary." In Rebecca's favor, she appeared as if she genuinely meant it. "It just arrived, and Lady Ellinwood requested I bring it up straightaway in case any adjustments need to be made. Do you mind if I set it down on the bed? It's quite heavy."

Yes, Rosemary imagined that 780 bows weighed a lot.

"It's so...*pink*," she said as she and her maid stepped back from the mattress to study the gown as they might a frog that had been laid open for scientific dissection.

"Lady Ellinwood seemed very pleased with it."

"Well, she doesn't have to be the one to wear it," Rosemary muttered.

Normally, she didn't care what she wore.

But there wasn't anything normal about the evening that awaited her.

For one thing, it was the Royal Gala. For another, she was attending as the wife-to-be of one of the most prominent men in all of England. Dozens, if not hundreds, of eyes would be trained upon her from the moment she entered the grand ballroom.

And she was going dressed as a poor flamingo that had inadvertently stumbled into the scrap fabric bin.

If she was only representing herself, it wouldn't have mattered. Oh, people would have undoubtedly stared and snickered. But that wasn't out of the ordinary. Between the books she carried tucked under her arm and the squirrel in her pocket, people were always staring and snickering. In a world of great beauty and dresses that might as well have been walking works of art, she was accustomed to sticking out like a frumpy sore thumb.

But just for one night–for *this* night–she'd wanted her peers to look at her and think to themselves, *"There goes the future Duchess of Hanover. Isn't she lovely?"*

Yes, it was a superficial need.

More of a want, really.

But did that make it wrong?

She fervently wished that Evie was here. If there was anyone talented enough to turn a sow's ear into a silk purse, it was her cousin. But Evie and Joanna were still in Scotland, which meant that she was on her own.

"Do you think we'd be able to remove any of the bows?" she asked. "I've shears in my writing desk."

"Perhaps," said Rebecca, although she sounded doubtful.

"That's all right. I'd probably just end up with a dress covered in holes instead of ribbon." Resigning herself to her fate, Rosemary untied her wrapper and held her arms above her head. "A flamingo it is."

"IT IS NOT *that* bad," Rebecca said some two hours later after she'd helped Rosemary don her undergarments, including a hoop skirt made of flattened steel wire, and the gown itself, which, impossibly, appeared even worse *on* than it had off.

Staring at herself in the full-length dressing mirror propped against the wall, Rosemary exchanged a rueful smile with her reflection.

The dress began with puffed sleeves that sat high on her shoulders and ended just above her elbows. The bodice, generously curved to emphasize her breasts, might have actually been flattering if not for the scalloped trim that most closely resembled a jester's neck ruff. A line of bows ran down the front to the waist. Round as a bell, the skirt was comprised of multiple layers of coral gauze, each slightly longer than the last, which culminated in a hemline made of even more bows. The bustle, padded from the mohair of surely no less than half a dozen angora goats, sat upon her rump like its very own island. It, too, was pink, albeit swathed in a covering of white lace.

"I look like a cake that was swallowed by a flamingo," she said, turning to the side in the hopes that a different vantage point might somehow improve the gown's silhouette.

It didn't.

"Your hair is pretty," Rebecca offered diplomatically. "It's holding the curls beautifully, even without bandoline."

"You've an undeniable talent with the hot tongs." Rosemary's bow-covered shoulders slumped. "I am sorry it's being wasted on me."

"Not at all," her lady's maid protested. "I won't deny that the dress is an...interesting choice, but if anyone was to carry it off, it's you, Miss Rosemary. Your beauty has always come from the inside out, not the outside in. So really, it doesn't matter what you're wearing."

Rosemary met Rebecca's large eyes in the mirror. "Thank you."

"You're more than welcome. Should we go downstairs and see if His Grace is here yet?" she asked, her simmering anticipation palpable.

In addition to the invitations he'd procured for them, Sterling was personally accompanying Rosemary and her grandmother to the ball. It was to be his first official appearance at the house, and all of the staff–including Rebecca–were thrilled at the prospect of having him in their midst. Particularly since most of them had most likely given up on Rosemary ever marrying, let alone marrying a duke.

Her engagement had served to elevate and excite the entire household. Where once they'd served a dowager viscountess and her untitled granddaughter, they were now bringing tea to the future Duchess of Hanover. And the subsequent changes in their behavior, while slight, had still been noticeable.

"I am going to need assistance fitting through the doorway," she said.

Rebecca nodded. "I'll ring for another maid."

Rosemary stretched her arms out to encompass the width of her skirt, then measured that against the door. She turned back to Rebecca and blew a stream of air through pursed lips. "Better make it two more...and a footman for good measure."

"WHAT DO YOU think, Higgins?" Tugging on the diamond cut lapels of his fitted black dress coat, Sterling pivoted away from the mirror to face his valet. And it was probably a trick of the light, but he might have sworn he saw the servant wipe a tear from his eye.

"Splendid, Your Grace." Higgins snapped his heels together and squared his shoulders. "Absolutely splendid."

"In no small part to you and your skills with a straight razor." He ran a hand across his chin. "I feel like a newborn babe."

"If I may, Your Grace…"

"Go on," he invited when Higgins hesitated. Opening the top drawer of his dressing stand, he sifted through a dozen satin ties before settling on a light gray. *To match Rosemary's eyes*, he thought as he looped it around his neck and began to flip the ends over each other to fashion a knot.

"It's just that…in these clothes…with your hair styled back like that…you bear a striking resemblance to your brother, Your Grace."

Sterling's hands stilled. He waited for the familiar wave of grief to crash over him. For the anger and the guilt to nip right at its heels, and a mindless craving for a bottle of gin after that. Instead, all he felt was a dull throbbing. The same a solider with a war wound might experience whenever it rained, or the poor chap closed his eyes and recalled the horrors he'd endured on the battlefield.

The pain was still there.

It would always be there.

But perhaps the trick wasn't trying to get rid of it, or ignoring it, or drinking it into submission. Rather, maybe the trick was to just…exist with it. Acknowledge it. Acknowledge the ache and the hurt and the empty hole that used to be filled. The gnarled, twisted flesh that used to be smooth. The heart that used to be whole. Acknowledge it and keep moving. Keep breathing. Keep *living*.

Especially now that he had someone to live for.

"Thank you, Higgins." He resumed tying. "I am glad to hear that my brother remains in your thoughts. Although I think we can both agree that I'm the far handsomer brother?"

"Yes, Your Grace," Higgins said, reverting to his far more in-character stoicism.

Sterling's eyes narrowed. "You're not just saying that because I pay you more money than any other valet in London, are you? I've taken notes, Higgins. You make a ghastly amount."

"No, Your Grace."

Any further jibing (Sterling did so enjoy ruffling Higgins' feathers) was interrupted when a maid knocked timidly at the door and handed the valet a card before whisking off down the hall. After a cursory glance at the piece of paper, which evoked no more emotion other than a raised brow, Higgins passed the card on to Sterling.

"It appears you have a caller, Your Grace."

"A caller? Don't they know what night it is?" Still, he accepted the card. And liked to believe it was a sign of his strengthening sobriety that his hand didn't shake when he read the name written on it.

"Have our guest escorted into my study, Higgins," he said tightly.

The valet frowned. "But Your Grace, the Royal Gala–"

"I should only be a minute or two. If I'm in there any longer, kindly find a pistol and shoot me with it." He paused. "Actually, don't do that. Don't want to ruin the jacket. Shoot the other fellow instead. Just in the leg or the arm. But not an artery, Higgins. We don't him to bleed out on the carpet. Can you imagine the stain?"

"I can assure you that I have excellent aim, Your Grace."

Sterling sighed. "Of course you do, Higgins."

"I can always have him sent away," the valet offered. "You are due to be at Miss Stanhope's residence in less than half an hour."

"A minute, Higgins," he said grimly. "That's all I will need."

It was what happened *after* that minute was over that worried him the most. Undoubtedly, this was going to be the most significant test of his soberness yet. And on tonight, of all nights. When he'd nothing to do but, oh, he didn't know…escort his fiancée and her fire-breathing grandmother to the biggest social event he'd attended in over a year. Where every eye and monocle in England was going to be trained on him, wondering if he really *was* capable of murder…or if his becoming engaged to a quiet, perfectly mannered (except for the squirrel) wallflower was a sign that the rumors of his misdeeds and poor behavior had been greatly exaggerated.

No pressure.

No pressure at all.

With Kincaid away and Rosemary providing a lovely distraction, he'd almost let himself forget why he'd needed to repair his reputation in the first place. But now that Parliament was in session, time was of the essence. If felony charges were brought against him for Eloise's murder, he'd be marched in front of the House of Lords. And wouldn't *that* be a spectacle.

Given the lack of a body, or any true confirmation that Eloise was even dead, a guilty verdict would be exceedingly hard to come by. But he didn't want to allow his future to be decided by his peers, of all people. God knew they needed a committee just to figure out what wig to put on. Which was why he needed to convince the lot of them that he was a glowing paragon of virtue. Next best thing to a saint, really.

Short of wearing a halo atop his head, he needed to put on the performance of a lifetime at the Royal Gala. No debauchery. No fornication. No drinking. All of his favorite pastimes were, well, things of the past.

Coincidentally, that was precisely where his guest had come to visit him from.

"Lord Fieldstone," he drawled as he strolled into his study and closed the door behind him with a nudge of his heel. "What brings you to darken my door?"

In the six years since Fieldstone had shaken Sterling awake on that tragic morning, the two men, once best mates, had adhered to an unspoken agreement of avoidance.

There was no anger between them.

No grudge.

Rather, they'd stayed apart because neither had wanted to be reminded of what they'd both tried so damned hard to forget.

The smell of smoke in the air.

The sight of blood, red and wet.

The taste of desperation and fear.

When his throat tightened, Sterling blindly swiped a crystal decanter off a nearby shelf. His entire arm trembling, he poured water into a glass and drank it straight to the bottom, then made himself meet Fieldstone's somewhat baffled gaze.

"Spirits don't seem to agree with me anymore. Or maybe they agreed with me too much." His mouth bent in a wry grin. "Either way, I've given them up."

"I wanted to come and offer my congratulations on your engagement." Despite the levity of his words, Fieldstone's countenance was somber, his brown eyes serious. "Miss Stanhope is an unusual choice for a bride. But I can see that her company must suit you, as you haven't looked in such good health since..." Averting his gaze, he trailed off.

In the tense silence that followed, Sterling refilled his glass with more water. "Since Sebastian died, you mean." To his surprise, that particular knife didn't cut nearly as deep as he'd been expecting. "It's all right. You can say it. You were there, the same as I."

"To this day, I wish that we'd gotten there soon enough to stop it."

"So do I," he said simply. "But that's not how it works, is it?"

Fieldstone furrowed his brow.

"What?"

"You really *are* different."

"Ah," Sterling said as understanding dawned. "So that's why you're here. To see if I've truly reformed my wicked ways." Water sloshed over the rim of his glass as he spread his arms apart in a mocking gesture of welcome. "How brave of you to enter the home of a murderer."

"I never thought–"

"Didn't you?" he interrupted with a sardonic cant of his head. "Not to worry. You weren't the only one. The entire *ton* was frothing at the bit to see me stand trial. Some of them still are, I'm sure."

"A lot of the gossip has died down since you became engaged to Miss Stanhope." Fieldstone picked up a small glass figurine of a horse sitting on the middle of a table and ran his thumb across its mane. "I assume that was your intention in selecting her to be your wife."

"My intentions were…varied," Sterling said guardedly.

"I'll admit I never had you picked for the marrying type."

"Neither did I. But Rosemary was–" He stopped short. Scowled into his water.

"Was what?" Fieldstone prompted.

"Unexpected."

"That much is clear." Carefully returning the horse figurine to its place on the table, Fieldstone approached and slapped his hand on Sterling's shoulder. "You really do look better, and I'm glad that you found whatever it was you were searching for."

A brief hesitation, and then Sterling embraced his old friend. "Good to see you again. Let's not wait another six years next time."

"I agree."

Another hearty, very manly squeeze (which was completely different from a hug), and they let go of each other to walk out into the foyer.

"Will you be at the Royal Gala tonight?" asked Sterling.

Slipping into a burgundy frock coat, Fieldstone shook his head. "Couldn't get an invitation this year."

"If only you knew someone who was capable of getting whatever invitation they wanted. Perks of the title and all that."

"It's all right. This was better. Besides, I've a standing appointment at The Black Rose."

The Black Rose was an exclusive, high price club in the middle of the theater district. It had been a regular haunt for both men once upon a time, and where Sterling had first met Eloise after he watched her in a memorable (and completely nude) performance as Cleopatra in a very loosely adapted version of Shakespeare's *Antony and Cleopatra*.

"Go on, then," he said. "Wouldn't want to be late for that."

"You should join me next time. The girls will be pleased to see you."

"Course they would, given what they've had to work with." He delivered a playful punch to his friend's arm. "Unfortunately, I really *am* mostly reformed. And engaged, in case you've already forgotten."

"What does that have to do with…oh," said Fieldstone when he saw Sterling's expression. "You're serious. About Miss Stanhope, that is."

"Why wouldn't I be? I'm marrying her, aren't I?"

"Yes, but I thought…never mind. Clearly, I was wrong. Enjoy the gala. I'll be thinking of you while I've gorgeous women climbing on my lap at The Black Rose."

"God, I hope not." Quietly musing, Sterling waited until his friend had nearly reached the street before he called out, "How did you know?"

"Know what?" Fieldstone shouted back.

"That I was searching for something."

A long pause, and then: "Aren't we all?"

CHAPTER SIXTEEN

"STOP FIDGETING," LADY Ellinwood barked as Rosemary bounced lightly on her heels when she heard the sound of an approaching carriage. "A duchess does not fidget."

"I am not a duchess yet." Belly fluttering with excitement, Rosemary pressed her face to the window as a magnificent black town coach, pulled by a prancing quartet of gray horses all with feather plumes attached to the crown of their bridles, came to a halt outside.

"All the more reason to behave like one." Lady Ellinwood struck her cane on the floor. "Now come away from the window and present yourself accordingly."

With great reluctance, Rosemary moved to her grandmother's side but made sure to position herself so that she still had a view of the town coach. After all, it wasn't every day that a massive carriage arrived to ferry her off to a fancy gala. Despite her pink monstrosity of a gown, she couldn't help but feel a bit like a princess. And she was ready to see her prince.

A footman in formal livery, silver buttons shining in the moonlight, opened the carriage door, and her breath caught on a sharp intake of air when Sterling stepped out.

No.

Not Sterling.

This...*this* was the Duke of Hanover.

Formally attired in an ebony jacket that fit his lean torso and broad, muscular shoulders like a glove, a gray necktie, crisp white shirt, and straight trousers, he was the epitome of a well-dressed gentleman.

In the subtle glow of lamplight, his skin was golden tan, as if he'd just spent an afternoon basking in the sun. His dark hair was swept straight back off his temple and set lightly with pomade in a simple, masculine style that suited him far better than the elaborately coiffed designs being adopted by every dandy in London. He had even shaved, revealing a strong jaw underneath all that scruff.

As if he sensed her watching him, he abruptly lifted his head and stared straight through the glass to where she stood in the middle of the foyer. For a moment, she found herself intimidated by this striking stranger who bore little resemblance to the charming, disheveled rogue she'd agreed to marry. Then he winked at her, and his mouth curved in a grin that was as wolfish as it was familiar, and her unease escaped between her lips on a sigh of relief.

There was her Sterling.

He may have looked like a duke, but underneath all the impeccably tailored clothing he was still the same scoundrel that had stolen her heart.

"Lady Ellinwood," he said, addressing her grandmother first in a deep bow. "If I were twenty years older, I'd be tempted to leave your granddaughter at home and escort you to the gala in her stead. You are positively regal this evening."

"*Hmph*," Lady Ellinwood sniffed, but she didn't quite manage to turn her head to the side fast enough to hide the tiny smile that played across her lips.

"And you, my dear Miss Stanhope," Sterling said as he straightened and cast his gaze upon Rosemary. His eyes widened before his face went perfectly blank; a slate being wiped clean of chalk. "You look…"

"Yes?" she said innocently. Enjoying herself, she spun in a circle to show off every single ribbon, bow, and tuft. "Isn't it the most *gorgeous* gown you've ever seen? Flawless, even."

"Ah..."

"My personal modiste has assured me that my granddaughter's gown is the very height of fashion," Lady Ellinwood said sharply, leaning on her cane. "Do you disagree, Your Grace?"

Rosemary bit the inside of her cheek to hold back a snort of laughter. Traditionally, it was Sterling who gained amusement at the expense of others. How entertaining–and a tad gratifying–to have the shoe placed on the other foot.

Her humor faded when he stepped closer to her and raised her hand to his mouth. He met her gaze across the uneven bump of her knuckles and even through the thin layer of her elbow-length satin glove she felt the possessive warmth of his breath as it fanned across her skin.

"You, Miss Stanhope," he said in a voice that was husky and deep and caused a flash of heat to lick low in her belly, "are the most beautiful creature I have ever had the pleasure of laying my eyes upon."

They were in the foyer with Rosemary's grandmother watching on. But with those words, Sterling stripped her bare. It didn't matter what color her dress was or the number of bows it had (212, per Rebecca's counting). She could have donned a vegetable sack, and through Sterling's gaze...through Sterling's gaze, she would still feel like a princess.

For a young woman who had never quite felt *enough*....beautiful enough, fashionable enough, attractive enough...there was power to be found in feeling pretty. For as much as she told herself that she didn't care what she wore, or what she looked like, or how many of her peers giggled into their fans when she walked past, there was a part of her that *did* care. That *did* want someone to gaze at her and think, *"My goodness, she's lovely–where has she been hiding all this time?"*

To which she'd reply, *"I'm here. I've always been here. Just waiting to be seen for who I am."*

Waiting, as it so happened, for Sterling.

"Shall we?" he murmured. "Wouldn't want to be late for your first Royal Gala."

"I am very nervous," she confessed under her breath after he had assisted her grandmother, and then her, into the carriage. Paneled in rich mahogany with velvet seats and gold tassels, it was easily the most opulent vehicle she'd ever occupied. Smooth as well, she noted, when they set off at a brisk trot with nary a bump or a bobble.

"Don't be." Leaning comfortably into his seat, Sterling sent her another wink from his side of the town coach. "Most everyone is going to be looking at me and those who aren't will be so blinded by the sheer majesty of your ball gown that they'll be struck speechless and you won't have to talk to them."

"It is majestic, isn't it?" Lady Ellinwood interceded. "I will inform my modiste you said as much, Your Grace. She will be honored by such a high compliment."

"Perhaps Mrs. Broomall could even make His Grace a matching jacket," Rosemary suggested. "The pink would truly complement his coloring. Don't you agree, Grandmother?"

"Indeed. An excellent suggestion, my dear," Lady Ellinwood said in a rare show of approval. "I shall visit her on the morrow and request that she set aside some fabric. If there is any left, that is, given that I am certain eager mothers will be knocking on Mrs. Broomall's door come sunrise requesting to be dressed just like the future Duchess of Hanover."

"Oh, drats." Sterling snapped his fingers. "And I was so hoping for that coat."

"Not to worry," Rosemary said cheerfully. "Given that I shouldn't wear this gown again after showcasing it at such a public venue, I'm sure Mrs. Broomall can salvage enough of the fabric to make a formal dress jacket. Trousers, too. Maybe even a waistcoat or a hat! You don't mind bows, do you, Your Grace?"

His resulting glare roused a cheeky smile from her lips and set her nerves at ease just in time for their arrival at Marlborough House.

Set far back behind a towering iron fence and thick green shrubbery, the London residence of Prince Albert and Princess Alexandra was a sandstone replication of a Grecian temple in the classical Greek revival style that had recently taken both Europe and America by storm. Aside from the pillars lining the front, everything was squarely cut with an emphasis on long, straight lines and perfect symmetry.

The manor was three stories high and every window shone from within, illuminating the entire house and its surrounding gardens and terraces in a soft, welcoming glow as lively music spilled through the open front doors and London's elite poured from their carriages to rush up the marble staircase in a convergence of obscene wealth and privilege.

To Rosemary's relief, Mrs. Broomall wasn't the only modiste who had outfitted her client in a bold color. The Royal Gala was the place to see and be seen, and no one wanted to go unnoticed.

There were gowns of blue and yellow, purple and green. Some women had peacock feathers in their hair while others carried mink stoles draped over their shoulders, the poor animal's fur dyed to match their dresses. The men were just as vibrant in jackets of emerald satin lined with gold brocade and powdered wigs that heralded back to a bygone era. When she questioned Sterling about it, he merely shrugged.

"Those must be the composers. Serious lot. Each one fancies themselves to be the next Bach or Beethoven. I'm sure they believe that if they dress the part, the symphonies will ride in on a German unicorn of inspiration."

Her lips twitched. "I see."

Smaller carriages and clusters of guests made way for their town coach as the matching grays pranced straight up to the main entrance, feathered plumes bouncing with every step. Sterling helped her dismount before he ducked back into the coach for Lady Ellinwood, leaving Rosemary temporarily standing by herself; the sole recipient of dozens of curious stares. Awkwardly linking her hands behind her, she managed a small, stiff smile. This was, without a doubt, her worst nightmare. And again, she wondered if she had what it took to be a duchess. To parade herself about like a show pony for the masses. A different ball every night. An endless stream of people to impress. Names to remember. And what about Sir Reginald?

She'd left him at home for the Royal Gala because, well, it was the Royal Gala. But he did so enjoy their outings together. No one minded when a wallflower sat by herself in a corner with a squirrel on her shoulder. She was nothing more than an obscure footnote. But what would they say when she was a duchess?

She jumped when she felt a light pressure at the small of her back.

"What's the matter?" Sterling asked with concern as he removed his hand. "You're as white as a sheet."

"I...I am not sure that I can do this," she said in a low voice as they proceeded through the crowd, stopping occasionally to exchange pleasantries. On Sterling's other side, Lady Ellinwood was in her element.

Having grown up the eldest daughter of an earl before lowering herself to marry a mere viscount, she was accustomed to the attention that came along with rank and title. If Rosemary didn't know any better, she'd almost suspect that her grandmother was sporting a real, honest-to-goodness smile. Which only made her feel worse.

"Do what?" Sterling asked.

But before she could muster a response, they were approached by an older, robust-looking gentleman boasting a salt-and-pepper moustache and his lady wife with chestnut hair threaded lightly with gray and hazel eyes that flicked curiously over Rosemary before going to Sterling.

"Your Grace," said the man in a booming, hearty voice. "I'd heard you would be in attendance. Good to see you, good to see you!"

"Lord Asterly, you old goat." The two men shook hands. "It is my great pleasure to introduce my fiancée, Miss Rosemary Stanhope, and her grandmother, Lady Ellinwood."

Rosemary smiled tentatively. "It's nice to make your acquaintance."

"Indeed," said Lady Ellinwood before she spied a circle of her close friends standing right inside the doorway. Excusing herself, she marched away, her cane striking a loud staccato on the marble stone.

"I must admit," Lord Asterly began in a near shout, "my wife and I have been eager to meet the young woman who got this one to finally propose." He nudged Sterling with his elbow. "Isn't that right, Lady Asterly?"

Lady Asterly patted her husband's arm. "Don't embarrass the young couple, dear."

"Embarrass them?" he blustered. "I'm doing nothing of the sort. I'm *congratulating* them."

"Senility," Sterling remarked mildly. "Terrible disease. Our thoughts and prayers are with you, Lady Asterly."

Her mouth curved. "Thank you, Your Grace."

"Senile?" Lord Asterly huffed. "I'm as healthy as a horse!"

"And deaf as a naked mole rat," his wife mumbled under her breath.

Rosemary's ears perked. Courtesy of her extensive reading, she knew that naked mole rats were, in fact, mostly deaf. Without hair cells to amplify sound, they relied mostly on their sense of touch to navigate their underground burrows. As they were native to the dry, arid regions of East Africa and did not do well in captivity, their existence was not widely known. Until now, she'd never heard anyone reference them before.

"Have you ever seen one?" she asked Lady Asterly eagerly. "A naked mole rat. I just read the most fascinating article in *Gardner's Chronicle* where Charles Darwin compared their social organization to that of ants or wasps, making them the only mammal known to man that relies on an–"

"Eusocial structure for the survival of their species," Lady Asterly finished. "Yes, I found it most informative. But no, I've never seen one in person. I should like to." She looked at Rosemary with renewed interest. "You are remarkably well versed in rodents, Miss Stanhope."

"Don't encourage her," Sterling groaned.

"What on earth is a naked holy rat?" Lord Asterly asked.

"A naked *mole* rat, dear. Nothing to concern yourself with. Why don't we let His Grace and Miss Stanhope make their rounds? I am sure we are not the only ones who wish to express their congratulations." Lady Asterly took her husband's arm, but paused when she walked past Rosemary to say, "Do find me later. I should like to continue our conversation."

"I've known Lord Asterly since I was a boy," Sterling shared as they continued up the steps and through the front entryway into the foyer where guests took the opportunity to mingle and converse amidst themselves before continuing on to the grand ballroom. "He was a close friend of my father's, and my mother and Lady Asterly were fond of each other."

"They seemed delightful." Rosemary's anxiety had faded considerably courtesy of their brief interaction. Maybe some–all right, probably most–of the people surrounding them didn't share anything in common with her. More than a few were probably still questioning why Sterling had proposed in the first place. But perhaps she'd been giving their opinion far too much credit.

For every Navessa, there was a Lady Asterly.

And an Evie and Joanna, besides.

The wallflowers, the dreamers, the bibliophiles–they were out there. In a sea of women trying to fit in, they were the ones who weren't afraid to stick out. To be different. To bring books into ballrooms and speak their minds and be true to themselves, no matter what anyone else thought.

"I'm sure you say that about every person who knows what a naked mole rat is," said Sterling, casting her an amused glance.

"They really are remarkable creatures," she began in earnest. "Did you know they spend the entirety of their lives underground? As a result, they're completely blind in addition to being deaf."

"Poor devils," he grimaced.

"Actually, a recent excavation of an abandoned colony revealed–"

"No," he interrupted, "I'm afraid I have to cut you off there. I've reached my naked mole rat quota for the evening."

"Should you ever like to learn more, you're welcome to my copy of *Gardener's Chronicle*," she said seriously. "I have already underlined the most interesting and informative parts."

"I'll keep that in mind."

After collecting Lady Ellinwood, they advanced into the ballroom where they were officially announced...and after that, the night became a bit of a blur as Rosemary found herself inundated with a swarming barrage of well-wishers who wanted a not-so-discreet look at the untitled and largely unknown wallflower who had managed to snag herself the greatest catch of the Season.

"...when will you be married?"

"...what will you wear?"

"...salmon is such a striking color on you."

"...more of a pink, really."

"...*I* wouldn't dare to wear it."

"...very brave."

After nodding and smiling until her jaw and neck ached, she managed to break free. Unfortunately, Sterling was nowhere to be found. He'd been swept away by a trio of lords before he'd even had the opportunity to ask her to waltz and she hadn't seen him since. Her grandmother was similarly missing and Lady Asterly was dancing, leaving Rosemary to fend for herself.

If this was a normal ball and she was her normal, forgettable self, this was the point in the evening where she'd pull her out her book, find a comfortable chair, and commence reading until Lady Ellinwood decided it was time for them to return home. There was a line of chairs on the far side of the room. And they looked, she noted with a little pang of wistfulness, *very* comfortable. But when a fox was being run to ground by a pack of hounds, it knew better than to hide in plain sight.

Shamelessly ducking behind a passing servant to hide from a fresh battalion of bright-eyed debutantes who wanted to know all the tricks to catching a duke, she waited until they'd rushed past to scurry out onto the nearest terrace.

With all the excitement going on inside the manor, there was hardly anyone outside of it. Save for a group of middle-aged gentlemen blowing cigar smoke into the cool, crisp autumn air, she was alone. A welcome reprieve after what she'd faced in the ballroom. What she would continue to face until the fervor of her engagement had died down. Even then, she and Sterling would always be the recipients of extra attention wherever they went. She had only to glimpse the crowd surrounding the Prince of Wales and his Scandinavian princess to see that.

Not to say that a duke and duchess were *royalty*.

But where the *ton* was concerned, they were far too close for Rosemary's comfort.

She nibbled her bottom lip as her trepidation resurfaced. When Sterling had insisted that she attend the Royal Gala, she'd never imagined it would become the source from which all of her darkest doubts would fester and grow. It was all too much too soon, and she yearned for the quiet solitude of Hawkridge Manor when it was just the two of them.

Things had been simpler then. Easier. Now, secret kisses in the library had been replaced with hasty marriage proposals and instead of a carriage ride into town, they were attending a Royal Gala. Was it any wonder the ground under her feet was spinning faster than she could keep up? Prior to becoming Sterling's fiancée, she was known as the woman with a squirrel in her pocket. In a matter of weeks, she'd gone from the Squirrel Girl to the future Duchess of Hanover.

All things being equal, she preferred the former title.

Her gown rustled as she crossed the terrace and leaned against the balcony to gaze contemplatively at the rose garden below. Had Joanna and Evie been besieged with similar questions and moments of uncertainty after they'd agreed to marry Kincaid and Weston? Probably not. They were both so confident. So sure of themselves and what they wanted.

"Here you are," said Sterling as he stepped out through the glass French doors. "I've been searching everywhere." He nodded a greeting to the men smoking their cigars and then joined Rosemary at the far end of the terrace. "What are we looking at?" he whispered, following her gaze into the roses.

"Nothing." As if things weren't maudlin enough, to her utter embarrassment, she felt little hornets sting the corners of her eyes. Then, without any warning, she began to cry.

"What's this?" Sterling demanded gruffly as he grasped her by the shoulders and folded her into his chest. He was warm, and sturdy, and roguishly perfect. A safe harbor in a storm of silk and satin and snide remarks.

Blowing out a stream of air to steady herself, she tilted her head back and blinked at him through her tears. "I-I don't belong here. I stick out like a sore thumb. My dress..." She shrugged helplessly. "It's awful."

"*I* wasn't going to say anything." Curling his finger, he rested it under her chin, his gray eyes filled with concern. "Then again, none of your dresses are about to win any awards, are they? Boxy rubbish, the lot of them. Just think of the bonfire we'll have when we're married. I am going to have to put Higgins in charge of it, or else we'll set the entire country ablaze."

She gave a watery laugh. Trust Sterling to say the absolute worst thing possible…and somehow make it better. "It's my grandmother's modiste, Mrs. Broomall. Her designs are a tad…antiquated."

"We'll find you another modiste. The best one in all of Europe. Your cousin, Evie, will turn green from jealousy, and won't that be a sight."

"It's not…it's not the gown. Not really."

"No." He tracked a tear as it rolled across her cheek and then dashed it away. "I did not think it was."

How to explain without sounding ungrateful for all that she'd already been given and was about to receive? For most women, becoming a duchess would be a dream come true. They'd be counting down the days to their wedding. Not standing in the dark on a terrace wishing they were home with a cup of tea and the latest edition of *Gardner's Chronicle*.

"Your Grace–" she began, but he cut her short with a wry look.

"I've seen your squirrel, Ravina. I believe we can dispel with the formalities."

"But that's just it, I don't know if we can," she said, hands fluttering in distress as she turned away from him to stare blindly out at the garden. Narrow walking paths dressed in white stone formed a rectangular grid pattern. Each rosebush was of equal size with the same number of blooms. They were beautiful, in a sterile sort of way. But what about the roses that didn't conform? The ones that wanted to grow wild? What happened to those? She had a feeling that she already knew. And that it was the same fate that awaited her if she tried to curb her uniqueness in an attempt to conform to a Society that had never shown any inclination to accept her as she was. "I don't...I don't know if I can be a good duchess."

"That's fine, as I'm a shoddy duke." The tips of his fingers skimmed along the curve of her spine before settling with feathery softness on the small of her back. "In case you haven't noticed."

She frowned at him. "I'm being serious."

"So am I."

How to make him understand?

"You are a duke," she began slowly, carefully. "If I marry you, I will become your duchess. There will be certain expectations placed upon me. Expectations that I am not confident I can meet. In fact, I'm sure that I cannot. I am not...I am not ignorant of the fact that the *ton* finds me peculiar."

"Did someone say something?" Sterling's entire body coiled; a lion ready to spring in defense of his lioness. "Who was it? Tell me their name."

"No one said anything. Not directly to my face, at any rate. But they didn't have to. I know what they think of me. And it's all right. That is, it *was* all right," she amended, "before we became engaged. Don't you see? I don't enjoy these fancy galas. I'm a fish out of water in them, flopping about. And it's not just this one. I'll be a wretched hostess for the house parties we'll have to throw. I am terrible at remembering names, and I always eat too much cake, and I struggle to stay awake for the parlor games."

"Who said we have to throw house parties?" he asked blankly. "Was it Weston? I bet it was Weston, that arse. Don't listen to a word he says. He's only trying to get out of the one he's been saddled with since his father made it his responsibility."

"No. I've not spoken to the Earl of Hawkridge. It's common knowledge that having a house party is simply what's expected of a duke and duchess," she said, gesturing vaguely with her arm. "They have elaborate parties, and attend a different social function every night, and speak at charity events. All while dressing fashionably and being charming and popular."

Sterling shuddered. "That sounds bloody *awful*. Let's not do any of it."

"But…but we'll have to," she said, perplexed by his response. "*I'll* have to. And I am going to be terrible at it. Just awful. I can already tell."

"And?" he asked, arching a brow.

"And…and I thought we should have this discussion now, before things proceed any further."

"By 'things' I assume you to mean our engagement."

When she nodded, he muttered a curse and raked a hand through his hair, mussing the pomade. "For being the most intelligent woman I've ever met, you are remarkably dimwitted."

Her lips parted. "Excuse me?"

He cupped her face between his large hands, his thumbs sweeping away what remained of her tears. His eyes were piercing in their intensity, his temple creased, his mouth a firm, somber line. In all the time they'd known each other, she had never seen him look so serious. "I am not marrying you because of who I want you to become. I am marrying you because of who you already are. I've no interest in a duchess who wants to pack our house full of pompous aristocrats every week. And while I enjoy a good outing now and again, I've sowed my wild oats. There is nothing that a ball or a pub or, God forbid, a charity dinner could possibly offer that would be better than staying home with my wife, if that's what pleases her." His head canted to the side. "Assuming, of course, that we'd both be in some state of undress."

Her face warmed. "But…but you wanted to come here, tonight."

"There will be *some* events that we probably ought to attend. This being one of them, as I'd rather not have Prince Albert thinking any more poorly of me than he already does."

"Why would he think poorly of you?"

Sterling winced. "A few years ago, I may or may not have...erm...kissed his wife."

"YOU KISSED THE PRINCESS OF–"

"Please keep your voice down," he hissed.

"Sorry. It's just that...*you kissed the Princess of Wales?*" Rosemary was not oblivious to Sterling's well-earned reputation as a rake. As she wasn't a jealous person by nature, and he'd shown no indication that he intended to pursue a relationship outside of their marriage bed, his past conquests were not something that she dwelled on very much. But now that she knew one of those conquests was none other than Princess Alexandra, future queen-empress...

"It was dark. There was wine. A complete accident. Could have happened to anyone. And as I said, it was years ago. Practically another lifetime." His brow furrowed. "I believe we've gotten a tad off track. What I am trying to express is that I don't give a damn if you want to attend every soiree from here to Paris. Or if you want to stay home and knit stockings for Sir Reginald. I am marrying you for *you*, Rosemary. To hell with anyone else's expectations. They're not important. *We* are important. The two of us. That's it."

Her name.

He'd said her name.

Tears sprang to her eyes again, but these didn't sting. "You're certain? Because soon, you won't be able to change your mind, and I just want to make sure you know that I'm not...I'm not going to be a conventional sort of duchess."

He kissed the middle of her forehead, then lowered his arms. "I proposed after your pet squirrel bit me on the thigh. I think I've an idea of what I am getting myself into." Behind him, the trio of gentleman snuffed out their cigars and started back in. "Trust me, if I could rid myself of my title, I would. But *you* were the one who told me that a title doesn't define a person."

So she had.

Advice, it appeared, that she'd forgotten to heed for herself. But then that was what anxiety did. When it built and built, like water coming to boil in a kettle, the pressure made it impossible to see anything past the roiling bubbles.

"Should we return inside?" he asked. "Or do you want to remain here?"

"Here. Just a little while longer." Turning around so that her back was to the garden, she tilted her face to the diamonds twinkling in a black velvet cloak. "The stars are pretty tonight, aren't they?"

"Stunning," he replied huskily, except he wasn't looking at the sky. He was staring straight at her...and the smoky glint of desire in his eyes was as bright as the stars.

She wet her lips when the muscles in her belly quivered. "I've–I've always found autumn to be the best season for stargazing."

"Have you?" He prowled to her. There was really no other word for it. No other word to describe the sensual, sinuous ripple of his muscles as he placed an arm on either side of the railing, effectively trapping her between his body at the edge of the balcony. He bent his head, his mouth a hair's breadth from her own. "The moonlight suits you, little hawfinch."

"Are you referring to the bird?" she said, momentarily confused. "Did you know that their beaks are strong enough to–"

On a groan of laughter, he kissed her.

CHAPTER SEVENTEEN

STERLING HAD ALWAYS maintained the opinion that a kiss–while enjoyable–was really nothing more than an interlude to better and far more wicked endeavors.

How wrong he'd been.

About so many different things.

But he was getting to where he needed to be.

Because of Rosemary.

All of it was because of Rosemary.

She'd healed his hurts and chased away his demons. She'd shown him that the future wasn't something to be endured, but something to look forward to. And he was. Looking forward to it, that is. To the life they were going to build together. To the children they'd have someday. A boy and a girl, if he had his way. With his mischievous nature and her gentle, caring spirit.

But first…the kissing.

He slanted his mouth more firmly across hers and slid his tongue between her lips to sample the sweet nectar within. Since giving up alcohol, all of his surroundings–everything he saw, everything he touched, everything he tasted–had come into sharper focus, and passion was no exception. If he'd wanted Rosemary before, he *needed* to have her now. She was an aphrodisiac for his senses…and he was helpless to resist her.

A hard jolt went through his body when her small hands fitted themselves to his chest and began a hesitant exploration of all that laid below. Her gloved fingers traveled down the middle of his sternum and then flitted out to follow the rigid contours of his ribs before encountering the flat, clenched plane of his abdomen.

He wore a waistcoat and a linen shirt, but the heat emanating from her palms made it so that he might as well have been standing on the terrace in the nude. A quick, desperate glance at the French doors to ensure no one was about to come outside and interrupt them, and then he returned his full attention to the fog-eyed siren whose clever, inquisitive hand had just cupped his–

"Bollocks," he cursed on a ragged breath, lifting his head to stare at her in a tortured mixture of desire and disbelief. "I cannot believe I'm about to be the voice of propriety, but we cannot do this here. Anyone could walk out at any moment."

Her hand retreated as an adorably rosy pink blush spread across her cheeks. "Of–of course. You're right. I don't know what came over me."

Sterling did. Since that first impulsive kiss in their library at Hawkridge Manor, they'd been drawn to each other. Two lost souls being pulled in the same direction. Two falling stars plummeting to the earth. It was inevitable that they would eventually come to this place, on this night. To where the anticipation was unbearable…and neither wanted to wait any longer for what was always meant to be.

"That's not to say we couldn't go somewhere else. Somewhere more private. There is a guest cottage on the other side of the manor. A discreet place for the prince to bring his paramours. But given that he is otherwise occupied this evening…" Sterling trailed off, allowing the choice to belong to Rosemary, who did not hesitate.

"Yes," she said. "*Yes.*"

It was all he needed to hear.

Moonlight nipped at their heels as they dashed off to the cottage.

Open, airy, and lit with candles, it smelled faintly of beeswax and lavender. The ornate furniture was tastefully arranged, the walls a pale, creamy yellow. Ivory drapes danced in the breeze from windows left partially ajar, permitting a cool swath of autumn air into the cottage along with the strains of Beethoven's seventh symphony.

Rosemary gasped when Sterling scooped her up into his arms, pink gown and all, and carried her effortlessly over the threshold. He kicked the door closed behind them, somehow managed to turn the lock, and didn't set her down again until they'd reached the master's quarters.

A canopied bed dominated the room. Acres of clean, fresh linens were layered atop the mattress. He set Rosemary on her feet, then turned her away from him to hold on to an oak bedpost while his fingers made quick work of the long line of hooks that ran the length of her spine.

He peeled the dress away, pausing to kiss the delicate vertebrae protruding from the nape of her neck. A few tugs, a gentle pull, and her petticoats fell, leaving her in her drawers and corset. After guiding her out of the pool of fabric, he merely stood and stared, his eyes devouring her with all the hungry possessiveness of a man half-starved who'd just been presented with a banquet to feast upon.

He'd known she was pretty. A sunny daisy growing in a garden of cultured roses. But silhouetted in the glow of candles with her hair tumbling onto her shoulders in loose curls of gleaming mahogany and her face slightly flush, she was...she was ethereal. The most magnificent, beautiful creature he'd ever seen. A fairy queen straight out of glen and glade.

"What?" she asked, covering her breasts as she shifted her weight from one leg to the other. "Is–is something the matter?"

"No," he said hoarsely. "Nothing is the matter. I just...I just don't know what the devil I've done to deserve you."

A shy smile crept across her face.

"Silly duke," she said softly. "You needn't earn what is given freely, and I give myself to you. Heart and body. They are yours. I am yours.

From this night forward into eternity."

He opened his mouth, but was unable to form words past the lump of emotion lodged in the base of his throat. He wanted to tell her how much she meant to him. That she was everything he'd ever wanted but hadn't known how to ask for. That he...that he loved her. That he would always love her. For all of the todays and the tomorrows and the months and years yet to come. But he couldn't speak. For the first time in his life, he was rendered completely and utterly speechless. And so he let his hands say what his tongue could not.

He touched her flesh with reverence while he finished unclothing her, as if she really were a nymph from wood and wild that might spook and vanish at the smallest provocation. When she wore nothing but shimmering firelight, he took her by the hand and guided her to the bed. The mattress creaked beneath his weight as he climbed onto it and stretched out beside her, his head supported by his bent elbow as he used his other hand to trace ever lengthening paths across her ivory skin.

While she watched him with wide, slightly wary eyes, he explored the valleys and the hills of the body she'd gifted him. The generous curves of her breasts. The gentle swale between her last rib and the point of her hip. The soft roundness of her belly. The plumpness of her thighs.

When she asked what he was doing, his answer was simple.

"Memorizing you," he said before he began to retrace the trails he'd forged with his mouth, pressing dozens of light, teasing kisses upon her skin until she was quivering from her head to her toes. Leisurely, he continued his descent, absentmindedly removing his boots, his pants, his waistcoat, and his shirt as he went.

She stopped him right before he reached the downy black curls at the apex of her thighs.

"You–you cannot kiss me *there*," she said, stunned.

Grinning, he lifted his head. "According to whom?"

That gave her pause. "Well I...I'm not sure."

"When you find out, do let me know. In the meantime..." He slid his hands under her legs, fitting his wide palms to her deliciously round derriere and tilting her hips so that he could enjoy her sweet nectar with abandon. She arched her back at the first touch of his mouth, and he welcomed the weight of her heels as her calves wrapped around his shoulders.

For a small eternity, he lingered between her thighs. Licking. Kissing. Breathing in the intoxicating scent of her. The act, in and of itself, wasn't new to him, but it felt new with Rosemary. Everything felt new with Rosemary. He was a blind man opening his eyes for the first time. A painter seeing his first sunset. A composer idly running his fingers across the ivory keys of a newly made piano and thinking, *"What beautiful music we shall make together"*.

When her breaths began to quicken and her legs quivered, he kissed his way back to her neck, bracing his weight on his knees as she gradually became accustomed to the weight of his body enveloping hers.

Her eyes flew open when he nudged at the entrance of all that tight, silky heat. She was slick from his tongue and her own desires, her skin dewy with a light sheen of perspiration, her dusky nipples swollen with arousal.

He'd never seen a woman more ready to be loved.

"Are you certain?" he rasped, his teeth grinding at the effort it was taking to hold himself in the in-between. That devilish space between anticipation and fulfillment. The rounded edge of his cock was as damp and hard as a railroad pike. He'd never experienced anything like it. Every inch of his body pulsed. His heart threatened to pound out of his chest with every loud thump. He felt both clammy and flush, exhilarated and yet somehow nervous.

Beneath him, his little wife-to-be gave a very serious, very Rosemary-like nod. "Yes. I read all about fornication in a journal of research collected during the voyage of the *H.M.S Beagle* to the Galápagos Islands. I know exactly what to expect."

The unexpected admission, so frankly spoken, brought on a husky chuckle. "God, I hope not."

AS IT TURNED out, reading an article on the mating habits of Galápagos tortoises had *not* prepared Rosemary for lovemaking. What she'd read was scientific in nature. Observations and hypothesis, with a diagram for scale. But this…with Sterling…it was heat and emotion and *feeling*. So much feeling.

Every cell was vibrating. Every fine hair was standing on end. Her heart beat madly, pumping blood through her veins to places that trembled and tingled and demanded to be touched. To be filled.

The bold nudge of Sterling's manhood sent an electric shock through her; a bolt of lightning sizzling across a sky of midnight blue. There was a pressure, an intense warmth, and then only pleasure. Waves of it. *Mountains* of it. Tumbling down all around her as his hips established a steady rhythm and his mouth settled on hers and his hand reached between them to stroke and pet and fondle.

When release came, they claimed it together. Each taking a part of the sun as they clung to each other and shuddered. Sterling's back flexed beneath her fingers, the powerful muscles coiling and clenching right before he threw himself to the side and spent his seed (*that* she knew about, courtesy of the tortoises) into the coverlet. While she laid on her back staring dazedly at the silk canopy over their heads, he remained turned away, his breath echoing harshly in the stillness that had filled the void left in the wake of their copulation.

Just as she was beginning to worry that she'd done something wrong, he rolled towards her and wrapped her in his arms, burrowing his face in the crook of her neck as her bottom fit snugly against his loins and his hand came to rest over her heart.

"Was that what you were expecting?" he asked as he caressed her breasts.

"No," she admitted ruefully. "In the twelfth volume of Darwin's

Naturalist's voyage, there was no mention of...ah...what you did with your tongue down...down there–"

"Cunnilingus is the proper term, I believe."

"Yes. That. There was no mention of the tortoises performing–performing cunnilingus on each other."

"Turtles?" Sterling's fingers stopped mid-stroke. "The journal you read was about bloody *turtles?*"

She turned over so that they were facing each other and cushioned her head on a feather-stuffed pillow. "Actually, contrary to popular belief, all tortoises are turtles but not all turtles are tortoises. The difference, you see, is in the shape and design of their shell. A tortoise has a more domed covering, while a turtle–"

"I love you," he said.

"–is more streamlined for...what?" She blinked in rapid succession. "What–what did you say?"

His Adam's apple bobbed as he reached out and brushed a tendril of hair behind her ear. "I said that I love you, Rosemary Stanhope. Even though you have selected quite possibly the worst place and time to give a lecture on turtles. But then, I suppose that's one of the reasons *why* I love you. Your delightful unpredictability. I never know what's going to come out of that beautiful mouth, but I do know that it will never be boring."

"You love me," she said numbly.

He leaned on his forearm and frowned at her. "Rosemary, I'm wild about you. I've been wild about you since we first met. Which, by the way, I *do* remember. Vaguely. Are you really that surprised?"

"No. I mean, yes. I mean...I'm not sure what I mean." An incredulous smile stole across her lips. "Say it again, please."

"I love you." He kissed her forehead, her nose, her mouth. "I. Love. You. I've never said that before to a woman who wasn't my mother or my sister. I just...I think you should know that." His gray eyes delved deep into hers.

In them, she saw a touch of sheepishness, a glimmer of vulnerability, but more than that she saw a man who had fought his way back from the hellish brink...and was ready to embrace all of the light and the goodness and the sheer *joy* that the world had to offer.

He had changed for the better.

They had changed for the better.

She'd smoothed his rough edges and he had sharpened hers. She'd shown him kindness and he had given her courage. She was humbled by the faith he'd placed in her. The trust. The love. It showed in his gaze, and she knew it was reflected in her own even though she'd not yet said the words herself.

"I love you, too." She placed her hand in the middle of his chest where his heart thumped steady and true. "The only man I've ever said that to is Sir Reginald."

The corners of Sterling's lips gave a betraying twitch before his countenance sobered. "I am honored to be in such excellent company. Should we get dressed and return to the gala? The night is young yet, but our good prince isn't exactly known for his fidelity and I'd hate for him to find us in his bed."

Rosemary's muscles whined in quiet protest when she sat up, a testament to the vigorousness of their lovemaking. After disappearing into the adjoining water closet, Sterling returned with a damp cloth which he used to tenderly clean the sore, sensitive skin between her thighs. There was a small streak of blood; a sign of another change. She was now a woman that had been loved by a man. *Was* loved by him, both in bed and out of it.

"A hot bath will do wonders," he said, kissing her navel before he rose to his feet and helped her dress.

As they left the cottage, neither Rosemary nor Sterling noticed the flowers that had been trampled outside the front window. Nor did they see the tears that had christened the dark, loamy soil beneath. Tears born of sorrow, bitterness...and pure, unadulterated rage.

CHAPTER EIGHTEEN

ROSEMARY HAD HER nose in a book when she heard a maid open the front door and admit someone into the house. It was nearly a week since the Royal Gala and Sterling had come to visit her every day since, but generally never this early.

With Lady Ellinwood as a watchful chaperone (much to Sterling's grumbling displeasure), they'd taken long walks through Kensington Gardens, gone to see the white tiger at the Zoological Society, and attended a play at the Gaiety Theater. But to the best of her knowledge, they hadn't anything planned today until later in the afternoon when he was taking her to watch a rowing race from the shores of the Serpentine. And her grandmother was out, which meant *she* wasn't expecting a visitor.

Curious, Rosemary set her book aside after taking care to mark her place with a frayed hair ribbon. She made her way into the foyer where, much to her surprise and delight, she discovered Evie, newly returned from Scotland if her cranberry-colored traveling habit was any indication, and Weston, dashingly formidable in all black.

"I was hoping you'd be in!" Evie said brightly. "We just got back ourselves early this morning after traveling most of the night. Exhausting, really, but at least you can sleep on the train."

"Have you brought more fabric samples to show me?" Rosemary asked, only partly teasing.

Evie glanced at Weston. "Actually…there won't be any need for those."

"You picked a color for the bridesmaid dresses?" she said with no small measure of relief. "Was it the mauve you showed us last time, or the…um…ivory?" Truth be told, Rosemary hadn't the faintest idea how to distinguish between the seemingly endless number of samples. She could tell blue from green and red from pink, but pearl and alabaster looked the same to her. According to her cousin, however, they were as different as night and day.

"Not exactly." Again Evie looked at her husband, who gave the tiniest of nods. She clasped her hands together under her chin. "We are already married."

"You're…what?" Rosemary said blankly.

"Married. We eloped. To Gretna Green. That's where we've been."

"But I thought you were traveling to Campbell Castle?"

Rosemary's geographical knowledge of Scotland wasn't as strong as it should have been, but even she knew that Glenavon, where Lachlan and Brynne lived, and Gretna Green, a little village right over the border, were on complete opposite ends of the country.

"We were on our way, but I became too ill to continue." Morning sunlight stealing in between the gaps in the heavy drapes that Lady Ellinwood favored illuminated Evie's brilliant smile as she placed her hand low on her belly. "It appears my increased appetite these past few weeks was not from nerves."

Rosemary's stunned gaze bounced from her cousin to the Earl of Hawkridge. Thus far, all of her interactions with Evie's fiancé–make that husband–had given her the impression that Weston was a stern, somber individual who reserved his lighter side for those he loved the most. But at that moment, he couldn't have looked happier or more proud.

"Do you mean to say that you're…"

"*Expecting*," Evie trilled. "I am going to be a mother, of all things."

"And I am going to be a father." Extending his arm, Weston wrapped it around Evie's waist and pulled her snugly against his chest. "You should rest. You've been on your feet for almost an hour."

Evie rolled her eyes at Rosemary. "He's been like this since we returned to London. It is going to be a *very* long seven months. But I know what you're thinking, and not to worry. Once the baby is here, I've been promised an enormous ball to celebrate our wedding."

It wasn't even close to what Rosemary had been thinking, but she wasn't about to disagree with a pregnant woman or her overprotective husband. "I am so glad to hear that."

"It actually works out splendidly, as I'll have something to keep me busy during my lying in. Naturally, it will call for an entirely new color palette for the dresses." She waved her hand in the air. "But I can figure all that out later. The *best* news is–"

"Our future child wasn't the best news?" Weston asked, lifting a brow.

"Women have babies every day. And while *our* baby will undoubtedly be the best of the bunch as long as she doesn't inherit your stubborn nature, what's even more exciting is that now Rosemary and Hanover can be married in our place!" She beamed from ear to ear. "Isn't that *wonderful* news?"

"Ah…" Rosemary didn't know what to say. She wanted to marry Sterling. Especially after their night in the cottage. But so soon? She'd just adjusted to being a fiancée! A role that she wanted to have time to enjoy before she leapt straight into being a wife and a duchess. "That's a lovely offer. Truly. But–"

"You needn't lift a single finger," Evie interrupted airily. "I already have everything planned. The food, the decorations, the invitation list. Which you can change as you see fit. Although I'm sure Hanover and Weston have similar acquaintances, so it shouldn't need to be changed that much. The music is accounted for. A solo harpist for the ceremony at the church, and then a full orchestra for the reception. It *will* need to be at Hawkridge Manor as construction has begun on the pavilions–"

"Pavilions?" Rosemary said weakly. "As in more than one?"

"–but surely that won't be an issue. I've ordered cases of champagne in advance that should be arriving any week. The doves are nearly ready. Apparently, there is one that isn't staying with the others when they're released, but the farmer assures me they'll all be expertly trained by the wedding so you needn't worry." She paused, but only to take a breath. "I have the *perfect* modiste, Mademoiselle Claudette. It's a tad late to start a gown for you from scratch, but if we keep the square cut neckline and adjust the length of the sleeves–"

"You're frightening your poor cousin half to death," Weston cut in. "Maybe give her time to decide if she *wants* to be married in six weeks before you bludgeon her over the head with all the details. And in case you've forgotten, a wedding generally requires two people."

"Bludgeoning?" Evie huffed. She looked at Rosemary, who shifted her weight uncomfortably from her left foot to her right. "I'm not *bludgeoning*. Am I?"

"Um…yes?" she said hesitantly. "I mean no. I mean…maybe?"

"See?" said Evie, poking her husband in the ribs with her elbow. "Maybe."

"Maybe is what nice people say when they don't want to hurt your feelings as you are bludgeoning them," he said mildly. "Besides, the last I checked, a wedding requires a bride *and* a groom. For all you know, Sterling has his heart set on getting married in the spring."

"What *he* wants doesn't matter. This is all about Rosemary. But I do suppose it *is* a lot to absorb on such short notice," she allowed. "Why don't we take our leave and let you sleep on it, then we can begin planning in the morning. Have you ever been to the outdoor tea room at the Staffordshire Hotel?"

Rosemary shook her head.

"Excellent. Neither have I, but Brynne says they have the most divine muffins anywhere in the city. The American kind, not those plain, chewy circles of dry bread that you lot call a muffin." Evie's nose wrinkled. "I'll have a table reserved for the four of us, as Brynne and Joanna should be returning tonight. They continued on to Glenavon while we remained in Gretna Green for some celebratory...erm..."

"Bird watching," Weston supplied, straight-faced.

"Yes," Evie said with a wink. "Bird watching."

"Oh. *Oh*," Rosemary repeated, her cheeks heating. "What—what time tomorrow?"

"Half past ten?"

"That should be fine." She didn't yet know what she was going to tell her grandmother. While Sterling had won Lady Ellinwood's approval, that same acceptance had decidedly *not* been extended to Evie or Joanna. Courtesy of her cousin's impromptu venture to Scotland, they hadn't needed to address the proverbial elephants in the room. But if they waited much longer, the elephants were going to show up wearing matching bridesmaid dresses.

"Until tomorrow, then." The cousins shared a brief hug and then Evie flitted out the door with Weston right on her heels.

The earl was going to make a good father.

Far better, Rosemary suspected, than his own had been.

She wasn't privy to all the details that comprised the cold relationship between the Marquess of Dorchester and his twin children. But when you were quiet, and read books, people tended to talk as if you were no more present than a piece of furniture. Which meant she'd overheard many a conversation over the years, and more than a few of those conversations had centered on Brynne, Weston, and their father.

She knew that they'd been raised by a small army of nannies and governesses. That the marquess had been an absent figure in their lives, preferring to travel to remote areas of Europe rather than remain in England and raise his own children.

How fortunate for Evie and her baby that the cycle of icy dismissiveness would break with Weston. It was obvious, just by the way he'd gazed at her as she touched her stomach, that their future child was going to be blessed with two loving, attentive parents...in addition to a quartet of adoring aunties.

But his wasn't the only cycle that needed breaking.

When Lady Ellinwood returned home, Rosemary was there to greet her with tea and a cucumber sandwich sans crust, just like her grandmother liked. She'd even gone so far as to add a green olive, spearing it through the middle with a sewing needle to hold the olive onto the bread. It was, she knew, her grandmother's favorite food...and a blatant attempt at bribery.

"What's all this?" Lady Ellinwood said sharply as she took to her preferred chair in the drawing room and set her cane aside.

"I thought you might be hungry after your morning of shopping. Did you not find what you were looking for?" Rosemary asked, noting the lack of packages that would ordinarily follow her grandmother through the door after an outing on Bond Street.

"I was searching for a blue scarf to match my gloves with the white stitching."

"And?" Pouring them both cups of tea, she set her grandmother's on a small circular table beside her chair along with the sandwich and sat directly across from her on a hard, flat sofa that had undoubtedly been placed opposite Lady Ellinwood's winged armchair because it *was* hard and flat, and thus would automatically place anyone who visited her at a disadvantage.

"And I didn't find one. What is this about, Rosemary?" Leaving her food untouched, even the olive, Lady Ellinwood assessed her granddaughter with the critical eye of a hawk. "Has the Duke of Hanover called off the engagement? Is that what you need to tell me? Because if it is, best come out with it now and we can set about finding you a replacement suitor before too much damage is done."

"What? No! The duke hasn't called off our engagement." Rosemary set her cup down with a clatter. "Why would you think that?"

Her grandmother lifted a bony shoulder. "One never knows about these things."

"Well *I* know. Sterling wouldn't do that. He…" *Loves me. Cannot live without me. Is counting the days until we're married.* Except he hadn't said any of those things, had he? No matter. She didn't need the words. Not when she knew how he felt. "He cares deeply about me."

"Then you're expecting," Lady Ellinwood said matter-of-factly after a surreptitious glance at Rosemary's belly. "I suspected as much, given how pudgy you've become lately. No matter. We'll move up the wedding and say the babe came early. It's done all of the time. Why, just look at Lady Ives. As if we're to believe she miraculously birthed a healthy four-month-old baby. Ludicrous."

The pictures, Rosemary told herself.

Remember the pictures.

Of all the people that her grandmother had loved and whose subsequent loss had made her this way. Bitter, and cynical, and callused over like a heel that had been crammed into an ill-fitting boot. It hurt at first, to wear a shoe that didn't fit. But if you ignored the pain and wiped up the blood then eventually the blisters would harden and the skin would thicken and you wouldn't feel anything anymore.

Or…or you could just take off the boot.

"No, Grandmother, I am not expecting. But Evie is."

"Evie?" Lady Ellinwood said, and it was impossible to tell if her lack of recognition was real or feigned.

"Evelyn Thorncroft. Lady Evelyn Weston now, I guess, given that she and the earl were wed. *She* is to have a baby."

"How nice for her," Lady Ellinwood said curtly. "Is there anything else you wanted to discuss, Rosemary? It has been a long morning and it will be a longer afternoon. I'd like to rest before we depart for the boat races."

"That is what I wanted to discuss." Rosemary inwardly braced herself for the storm that was to come. She could already taste it in the air. See it in her grandmother's stiff, unyielding posture. "I understand that you do not have a favorable opinion of my American cousins. But they've done nothing to deserve your malice except to welcome me with open arms. If you gave them a chance…if you got to *know* them–"

"I have absolutely no interest in getting to know my sister's illegitimate granddaughter or her sister. And neither should you." Lady Ellinwood picked up her cane. "This conversation is over, Rosemary."

"But I *do* know them," she persisted. "I know that they do not deserve whatever preconceived notions you may have of them. Whatever happened to drive you and your sister away from each other, Joanna and Evie were not a part of it, Grandmother. They weren't even born yet. Their *mother* wasn't born yet."

"Anne Thorncroft." Lady Ellinwood's mouth twisted around the name as if she'd uttered a curse. "Proof that the apple doesn't fall far from the tree. And as far as I'm concerned, her daughters are made of the same rotten fruit. You are *not* to see them, Rosemary. If you have been sneaking about behind my back, which I suspect you have, you are to cease all communication at once. Is that clear?"

"No!" Rosemary burst out as she rose from the sofa. "No, it *isn't* clear. Why don't you want me to see them? To have a relationship with them? They are my cousins. My family."

Lady Ellinwood struck the floor with her cane. "*I* am your family."

"Yes, you are. That is not in dispute. But why–"

"*Because they will leave you.*"

The silence that followed such a dire proclamation was raw and filled with hurt. Eyes wide, Rosemary sank slowly back into her seat while her grandmother took a moment to compose herself.

"Mabel left me." Lady Ellinwood's voice was uncharacteristically soft, and small, and Rosemary's chest ached to hear the hint of bewilderment in it. "She fancied herself in love with a dashing American businessman. I asked her to stay. I begged her. I didn't want to be alone."

"But your parents—"

"Our parents were not kind. When our father drank..." Her lips trembled as she pressed them together. "Mabel and I looked after each other. When one of us slept, the other would listen for the creak of footsteps on the stairs. But then she left. She left me, and there was no one to listen."

"I am so sorry." Her eyes swimming with tears, Rosemary rushed across the room to kneel beside her grandmother. She gathered her hands. Hands that suddenly felt old and frail. The hands of a woman that had endured more than any woman should have to. "No wonder you were upset with her when she went to America."

"There was a part of me that was happy Mabel got out. That she escaped what I couldn't." Lady Ellinwood was gazing at a picture on the wall, but it was evident by the vacancy in her stare that she was looking far into the past. "But the other part of me was bitter and angry. When she finally returned to London, she had a daughter nearly full grown and I had a son. Your father. But too much time had gone by, and the bridge between us had grown too long. We did not leave things on good terms. I never...I never spoke to her again."

It was strange, to imagine all of the different lives that Lady Ellinwood had lived before she became a grandmother. Rosemary only knew her as one person. Which was how everyone tended to think of those who were old. And they forgot about who they'd been before. When they were a daughter, and a sister, and a wife, and a mother.

As she gently held her grandmother's hand, Rosemary's heart wrenched. It was easier and simpler to paint someone with a single stroke of a brush. Easier still if that brush was filled with paint that coated everything beneath it in a layer of thick, oozing black.

It was easy to dismiss a crotchety old woman as mean.

A lecherous duke as a drunken scoundrel.

A shy, unique debutante as a boring wallflower.

What was far more difficult, what required actual effort and a deep emotional investment, was to scratch off the paint once it had dried. To peel back layer after layer to see what had caused it to darken and harden in the first place.

"I cannot imagine the losses you've endured. If it makes *my* heart feel heavy just to think of them, I cannot imagine what it does to yours." She considered telling her grandmother about the pictures she'd found, then decided against it. When an open wound was exposed maybe it was better not to poke and prod, but to let it close up and heal. "What I do know, however, is that more pain has never helped anything or anyone. I have seen my cousins. Multiple times. It was disobedient of me, but it wasn't wrong. Because Evie and Joanna are family, Grandmother. They're *our* family, and all you have left of your sister."

"The dark-haired one looks like her." Lady Ellinwood drew a deep, shuddering breath that crackled in her lungs. But she didn't let go of her granddaughter's hand. "She looks just like Mabel. When I first saw her at Hawkridge Manor I thought…I thought I was seeing a ghost."

"That must have been unsettling."

"It was." She closed her eyes as a lone tear, the only one Rosemary had ever seen her shed, trickled down her papery thin cheek. "But you are right, my dear. They are our blood, our family, and all that remains of my Mabel. I couldn't take it upon myself to make amends with her when she was alive, and I shall carry that regret to my grave. But perhaps…perhaps I need not make the same mistake with my grand-nieces."

"Evie has invited me to have breakfast with her and Joanna and Lady Brynne tomorrow morning at the Staffordshire Hotel," Rosemary revealed. "With your permission, I'd like to go. You could even join us, if you'd like. I hear their muffins are very good."

"You may attend breakfast," Lady Ellinwood said with a grand inclination of her head. "I will require another day or two to collect my thoughts. However, given that my grand-nieces *are* uncultured Americans, I am sure they would benefit from my wisdom and tutelage as soon as possible. You can tell them that they may call upon me later this week, and we shall begin their education on correct manners and proper etiquette."

There was the grandmother Rosemary knew and loved.

Biting the inside of her cheek, she turned her head to hide her smile. "I'll be sure to let them know."

"Excellent." Brushing aside her granddaughter's hand, Lady Ellinwood reached for her cane. "If there is nothing else, I will retire upstairs. It has been a long day, and I am tired."

It wasn't yet noon, but Rosemary knew exactly what she meant.

"Thank you," she said, kissing her grandmother's cheek before she quit the room.

"For what?" Lady Ellinwood sniffed, any previous signs of vulnerability having vanished into a puff of proverbial smoke the instant she stood up. If not for the dampness Rosemary had felt against her lips when she pressed them to her grandmother's skin, she might have been fooled into thinking she'd imagined their entire conversation. Such was Lady Ellinwood's ability to cloak herself in armor. Armor that she'd needed throughout her life to protect her from any manner of ills.

"For always being there for me," said Rosemary, "even though those you loved were not there for you." A thought occurred. So clear and obvious, she wondered how she couldn't have seen it earlier. "Is that why you've been less than enthusiastic about my engagement, even though you were the one who encouraged it in the first place? Just because Sterling and I are getting married does not mean I am going to leave you, Grandmother. Things will be different. I won't live here anymore, it's true. And I'll have a husband. Maybe even children of my own, one day. But I will always love you. I will always be there for you. That is never going to change. Even if you wish to be, you'll never get rid of me. No matter what the future brings."

Lady Ellinwood was quiet for a long moment. Then she struck her cane on the floor with an authoritative *tap, tap*. "Be careful you do not have too many muffins tomorrow. You must be more cognizant of your waistline." The rigid brackets surrounding her mouth softened imperceptibly. "You are a gracious child, Rosemary. Next to raising your father, watching you grow has been my greatest privilege."

It wasn't an outright admission of love. But it was the closest Lady Ellinwood had ever come to revealing that she cared. And some-times...sometimes close enough was the best that you could hope for.

CHAPTER NINETEEN

ONCE THE PRIVATE London residence of the Duke of Staffordshire, whose descendants had subsequently squandered his fortune and sold off all the family property in an attempt to save themselves a one-way trip to debtor's prison, the Staffordshire Hotel was a grand old dame with ivy crawling up the painted blue brick and window boxes overflowing with dahlias, pansies, and purple shoots of heather.

Rosemary's shoes sank into lush carpeting as she entered the grand foyer. She gave her name to a host dressed head to toe in royal red, and was promptly taken past an open dining hall and out through a double set of glass doors to the outdoor tea room.

Half a dozen circular tables, covered in white satin cloths and sterling silver cutlery, surrounded a trickling stone fountain. Nearly every seat was taken by a variety of patrons, mostly female, but it didn't take Rosemary more than a second to spy Joanna's telltale red hair amidst the more subdued colors.

She hurried over and was immediately greeted with a flurry of hellos from her cousins and Lady Brynne Campbell, a tall, slender blonde whose natural beauty and reserved elegance Rosemary had always found a tad intimidating.

Fortunately, there was nothing the least bit daunting about the warm hug Brynne gave her, and before her first cup of tea had been poured, she was already completely at ease.

"…still cannot believe I missed the Royal Gala," Evie complained after she'd made Rosemary recount exactly what Princess Alexandra had worn for the third time. "Weston never said a word about it. He claims to have forgotten, but I know better."

"It's a stuffy, prestigious affair," said Brynne. "Everyone is on their best behavior, hoping to impress the royal family. Personally, I've always found it dull. I was glad to have been able to skip it this year." Her lips quirked. "In twelve months, we may find ourselves similarly engaged."

"Easy for you to say. You've been before." But Evie did look slightly appeased as she spread strawberry jam across one of the Staffordshire Hotel's infamous muffins. "There is always the next one."

"Won't you be a tad busy?" Joanna asked with a purposeful glance at her sister's stomach.

Evie smiled sweetly. "That's what aunties are for."

"Speaking of aunties, *this* arrived today." Procuring a rather battered-looking envelope stamped with a series of postmarks, Joanna laid it on the middle of the table. "It's from–"

"Claire!" Evie cried as she snatched the envelope up and pried off the wax seal. Yanking out a letter comprising two pages, front and back, she read it quickly, her eyes lighting when she reached the end. "Oh my goodness."

"What is it?" Joanna said, trying–and failing–to grab the letter from Evie's grasp. "You do realize I could have opened it when it first arrived. I wanted us to read it *together*."

Evie waved the pages in the air. "Claire and Grandmother. They're coming to London."

"But that's wonderful news!" Brynne exclaimed.

"Another cousin," Rosemary said, beaming. She was eager to meet Evie and Joanna's younger sister, who had stayed behind in Somerville to care for their elderly grandmother. By all accounts, she and Claire had many things in common. They were the same age, both enjoyed reading, and loved animals.

But Joanna appeared concerned. "Grandmother cannot endure a trip of that magnitude. We need to write her back at once and tell her not to come. That we're already planning a lengthy visit next spring, and we'll see her then."

"Too late," Evie announced. "In the letter, it says that they plan to depart by the end of the week. Which means–"

"They're already on their way." Joanna sighed, then reached for the butter. "Well, we've always known who we inherited our stubbornness from."

"Claire will take good care of Grandmother. They'll be fine. Even more importantly–"

"What could be more important than their safety?" Joanna interrupted.

"–they should arrive just in time for the wedding!"

In unison, Evie, Joanna, and Brynne all turned their attention to Rosemary who froze in the act of slicing open her second muffin.

"This is my last one," she said defensively.

Brynne smiled. "Have as many as you like. Evie shared her idea with us. About you and Sterling marrying at Hawkridge Manor at the end of the month. I think it would be lovely. All of the preparations have already been made. It would be a shame to waste all that hard work. And the countryside is positively stunning in autumn."

"I know." After a wistful glance at her muffin, Rosemary nudged the plate aside and set her arms on the table. "It's just that...it's so *soon*. We've only been engaged a few weeks."

"Love doesn't adhere to timelines," Evie said with a careless flick of her wrist.

"You do love Sterling, don't you?" Brynne asked, studying her intently.

"I do," Rosemary said without hesitation. "I truly do. We...we fit together."

Joanna's auburn brows wiggled suggestively. "I'll bet you do."

Evie poked her sister with her elbow. "Don't embarrass our cousin. Look at the poor thing. Red as a tomato in Grandmother's garden."

"I can share from personal experience that a short engagement has *several* benefits," Brynne revealed tacitly. "One of which I'm sure you'll find quite pleasurable."

"Umm...we...ah, that is to say..." As the splotchy heat in her cheeks migrated down into her neck and chest, Rosemary sunk low in her chair. "We already did that part. At–at the Royal Gala."

"Where?" Joanna asked, blue eyes wide with curiosity.

"The Prince of Wales' private g-guest cottage," she squeaked.

"You really *are* a minx!" Evie declared, raising her fork in the air. "It's always the quiet ones."

"Lachlan and I had our first time at the Queen's Head Inn after our elopement," Brynne's smile took on a dreamy quality. "It was wonderful. Like a fairytale come true."

"Until you threatened to shoot him in his manly bits," Joanna pointed out.

"Yes, well, no one ever said marriage was *perfect*. But you work your way through it. And the difficult times make the happy ones all the more joyful." Reaching across the table, Brynne patted Rosemary's hand. "You're going to be a beautiful bride, regardless of whether you marry Sterling now or next summer. The wedding isn't what makes a relationship. It's the before and after that does that. The days you get along, and the days you don't."

"The days you want to throw your husband off a cliff," Evie put in cheerfully.

"And the days you love him so much that it's almost unbearable." Joanna gave an encouraging nod. "Brynne is right. You are going to be a beautiful bride. And we'll be here for you, every step of the way.

You're our family. When you marry Sterling, he'll be our family, too."

Rosemary took a deep breath, then looked at Evie. "How many pavilions did you say there were?"

CHAPTER TWENTY

T HE DAY OF the wedding dawned cool and crisp. As they did every year, the leaves had changed colors seemingly overnight, offering a breathtaking backdrop of orange and red and a blue sky so bright and so clear it was as if it had been taken straight from one of Brynne's paintings.

Rosemary and Lady Ellinwood had come to Hawkridge Manor five days prior, giving them the opportunity to settle in before the guests–nearly fifty in total–began to arrive. Happily, Claire and Ruth Thorncroft had made it to England just in time and were part of that guest list. Consumed with last minute preparations and Evie's daunting to-do list, Rosemary hadn't had much of a chance to sit down and converse with her cousin or Mrs. Thorncroft, but what little interactions they'd been able to have thus far had been nothing short of wonderful. Not a great surprise, given how well she had gotten on with Joanna and Evie.

What *was* a surprise was the immediate friendship that had kindled between Lady Ellinwood and Mrs. Thorncroft. The two elderly matriarchs were nigh on inseparable, and it was heartwarming for Rosemary to see her grandmother so happy after so many years of bitterness.

It also gave her one less thing to be concerned about, as she had worried what Lady Ellinwood would do when she married Sterling and moved in with him. He had (grudgingly) invited her grandmother to come live with them at his townhouse in Mayfair which was where they'd chosen to spend the winter, but Lady Ellinwood had been adamant that she remain in her own home.

Now, as fate would have it, she'd be living there with Mrs. Thorncroft, who had already announced that she intended to remain on this side of the Atlantic until after her first great-grandchild was born. Claire, seeking some independence, would stay with Evie and Weston at Hawkridge Manor. Come Christmas, everyone would once again gather at the estate to celebrate the holiday together.

Joanna and Kincaid.

Evie and Weston.

Brynne and Lachlan.

Lady Ellinwood and Mrs. Thorncroft.

Claire.

And the newly married Duke and Duchess of Hanover.

So many lives intertwined. So many destinies changed for the better. Rosemary was honored to be a part of it. A part of the story. A part of the love and the trust and the faith that bound them all together.

They'd crossed a literal *ocean* to be here, in this moment. They'd set aside their fears. They'd opened their hearts. And they'd fallen in love. With the men of their dreams, with each other, and with themselves.

As she stood in her bedchamber waiting for notice that the carriage had arrived to ferry her off to the village church, Rosemary was pleased to note that she had never felt this sure of herself. Never been so comfortable in her own skin. Never been filled with such conviction that no matter what obstacles came to stand in her way, she'd have the strength and the ability to topple each and every one.

"How far we've come, Sir Reginald," she whispered, slipping a hazelnut into the covered basket she carried on her right arm. Anyone looking at it would assume it held her most cherished possessions. Satin gloves from her mother, or perhaps an embroidered handkerchief from a beloved aunt. Only those who knew her best would guess that the basket actually *did* contain a cherished possession–or in this case, a cherished pet.

Carrying a squirrel down the aisle instead of flowers was unconventional at best. But then, Sterling had already made it clear that her peculiarity was one of the things he loved best about her.

As she thought of the handsome duke that awaited her at the church, butterflies danced in her belly. She was glad they were getting married. As Brynne had said, a short engagement did have several benefits. And the wedding night was certainly one of them.

In just a few hours, she would be wrapped in Sterling's arms in the private guest house that Evie and Weston had generously allowed them to have for the duration of their stay at Hawkridge Manor. There was no place on earth she'd rather be. No person she'd rather be with. If only she could figure out a way to jump straight over the wedding ceremony and the formal breakfast to be followed by an evening ball, she'd be happy as...well, she'd be as happy as Sir Reginald with a hazelnut!

A knock at the door caused her to turn in anticipation as the butterflies took flight. This was it! The carriage was ready. The pews were filled. Sterling was waiting.

Except he wasn't.

Because when she opened the door, there he was standing on the other side of it.

"You cannot be here," she gasped even as he sauntered past her into the room. A quick peek down the hallway to ensure no one had seen him enter, and she both turned the knob and locked it. "It's bad luck for the groom to see the bride before the ceremony. You have to leave before Evie finds out."

"I'm not afraid of her," Sterling scoffed, folding his arms.

She waited patiently.

"All right, maybe I'm a *little* afraid. But who wouldn't be? Your cousin is marching about out there like General Charles Cornwallis. Kings would do well to remove themselves from her path."

"Wasn't Cornwallis defeated by George Washington at Yorktown?"

"Precisely why I'm hiding in here. And so that I can do this, of course." Two strides, and he was kissing her. A soft, caring, frustratingly brief kiss that left her yearning for their wedding night more than ever. He pressed his mouth to the middle of her temple, then rocked back onto his heels. "Not a bow or a ruffle in sight. I suppose we have the brunette devil downstairs to thank for that."

"This dress was supposed to be Evie's," Rosemary admitted, stroking a hand across the pale blue skirt. Snug across the arms and bodice, it fell away at the waist into a cascading spill of silk and chiffon. The gown was intended to be worn with a full crinoline and padded bustle, but she'd opted for a simpler, more comfortable version.

"I like it better on you." His teeth flashed in a wolfish grin. "I'll like taking it off even more. Do you think anyone will notice if we don't go to the church?"

"Only five dozen or so," she said ruefully.

"Head up, my little hawfinch." He nudged her chin with his finger. "You'll have me all to yourself soon enough."

Little hawfinch.

He'd taken to calling her that since the Royal Gala. She vastly preferred it to Rebecca, Renee, and all the other litany of names he used to tease her with. Especially when he had shared the special meaning it held for him.

"I love you," she said.

"How strange. I snuck up here, risking life and limb, to tell you exactly the same thing." He kissed her again. Lifted her hand and brought it to his lips. "I love you, Rosemary. I wanted to say that before–is Sir Reginald in your basket?"

Biting the inside of her cheek, she quickly tucked her arm behind her. "What basket?"

"The one you put behind your back with a squirrel in it."

"Oh, *that* basket."

"Yes. That basket." The corners of his eyes crinkled. "Just make sure he doesn't bite anyone."

"Sir Reginald would never," she said, aghast that Sterling would suggest otherwise.

"He bit *me*."

"As I said before, that was a misunderstanding. Now go," she ordered, pointing at the door. "Before Evie really does find you in here and puts both of us in the stocks."

"Misunderstanding my arse," Sterling grumbled with a glare at the basket. "He knows what he did."

But with a final kiss, he did leave and, soon after, Rebecca came rushing in to tell Rosemary that the carriage was ready.

THE WEDDING CEREMONY was a blurred stream of colors and music and emotions. Sitting in the front pew, Evie and Claire wept openly, while Joanna and Brynne watched on with pride. From the other side of the aisle, even Lady Ellinwood could be seen dashing away a tear, although when questioned later she blamed the dust.

Rosemary couldn't recall the vows she had spoken by the time she left the church in a shower of rice and well wishes, but she knew that she would never forget the way Sterling had gazed at her as they stood facing each other.

It was the same way the songbirds looked at the sunrise after a night spent in the dark. Or a horse looked at its warm stall after a day of hard work. Or parched, thirsty flowers looked up at the rain as the first drops fell.

It was comfort. It was home. It was love.

Sterling boosted her into the decorated carriage that would take them back to Hawkridge Manor and didn't miss an opportunity to squeeze her bottom. Falling into the seat on a helpless laugh, she was already kissing him before the door had closed. A kiss that rapidly turned into something decidedly more heated which made them late for their own receiving breakfast...much to her chagrin and her husband's wicked amusement.

They dined outside beneath the pavilions where Evie had truly outdone herself. White linens blew lightly in the breeze, sunny bouquets of sunflowers adorned every table, and a quartet of violinists played on a raised stage littered with fallen leaves.

When breakfast was over, everyone retired to their rooms to rest and change for the evening ball. After ensuring that her grandmother was comfortably resting, Rosemary sought her own chamber where she fell upon the mattress with a sigh and a happy smile. Sir Reginald jumped up on the windowsill beside the bed, the remnants of a hazelnut clutched possessively in his tiny paws, and kept watch while she read the most recent edition of *Gardner's Chronicle*.

"Listen to this," she said excitedly as she sat up on her elbow. "It says that Darwin is proposing a fourth theory of evolution. Something he is calling natural selection. After concluding his study of iguanas during his most recent journey to the Galápagos Islands, he found that–"

She was interrupted by a knock at the door.

Assuming it was Sterling returned from the celebratory cigar he'd taken with Weston, Kincaid, and Lachlan, she swung her legs over the edge of the bed and bounced to her feet just as the door opened.

"I was wondering when...*you're not Sterling.*" Ice seeped into her veins when a stranger entered her room. A stranger that she vaguely recognized from the church. Or maybe the Royal Gala? Whoever they were, wherever she'd first seen them, they did not look well. In the dappled afternoon sunlight their eyes held a metallic, shiny sort of glint. Their face was beaded with sweat. Their breathing was short and uneven.

"No, I'm not," the stranger said in a deceptively calm, pleasant tone. "But you are going to come with me nevertheless. You're not going to scream. You're not going to make any noise at all. We're going to have some time alone, you and I. Just the two of us. Nod if you understand."

Rosemary looked at the pistol aimed straight at her heart.

And then she nodded.

CHAPTER TWENTY-ONE

S TILL GRINNING FROM the good-natured ribbing he'd received from
his friends, Sterling bounded up the main staircase two steps at a
time. He wanted to see Rosemary before the ball. No, he corrected
himself silently, he wanted to see his *wife*.

He was a married man now.

Something he'd sworn he would never become.

And he was over the bloody moon about it.

What he'd felt when he'd first laid his eyes upon Rosemary at the
end of the aisle…shrouded in soft light, surrounded by their closest
friends and family and forty of Evie's guests…the words did not exist.
Or if they did, he had never heard of them. With every purposeful step
Rosemary had taken towards him, his heart had seemed to grow, and
grow, until it was fit to burst by the time she put her dainty hand in
his.

He continued to be staggered by the trust she had placed in him.
To love her. To care for her. To protect her. *Him*. Sterling. A once-
dissolute wastrel who'd been ready to burn it all to the ground until he
crossed paths with a shy, awkward wallflower who had fulfilled every
dream he never knew that he had.

He passed a vase of yellow roses in the hallway. Then he doubled
back to grab the longest one and wipe the stem dry on his jacket
before he proceeded to Rosemary's room. Their belongings would be

moved to the guest house during the ball. These few hours were the last ones they'd ever spend living apart.

The door was slightly ajar. Which he did not note as odd until he nudged it open…and was subsequently attacked by a chattering ball of red fur.

"Bollocks!" he cursed, dropping the rose as he tried to grab Sir Reginald. With tiny nails as sharp as miniature daggers, the distraught squirrel streaked up one side of his body and down the other. "Rosemary, call off your bloody guard rat before he bites off something you'd rather I have tonight."

But there was no response.

Because the room was empty.

"Rosemary?" The chill from her absence sank straight into his bones. And he knew, even without Sir Reginald screeching in his ear, that something was terribly wrong.

In an instant, he found himself brought back to the morning that he'd lost his brother. To the field, damp with dew, where Sebastian had bled out in his arms. He experienced the same choking fear. The same surge of helplessness. The same blinding rage that someone he cared about, someone he loved, had been taken from him.

Goddamnit.

Why hadn't he taken Kincaid seriously?

The detective had warned him that an unknown threat was still out there, but he hadn't listened. Hadn't *wanted* to listen. For how much hell could one person possibly endure?

He'd put his father in the ground.

His mother.

His brother.

He wasn't going to put Rosemary there.

He refused.

"Up you go, on my shoulder," he ordered Sir Reginald. "We'll find her together."

The squirrel clung to his collar as he bolted out of the room and back down the hallway to his room where he found Higgins laying out his attire for the ball.

"Your Grace," said the valet, visibly startled. "I apologize. I wasn't expecting you this—"

"Rosemary's gone. Someone has taken her. I want you to work with the Earl of Hawkridge's butler and go door to door. Find every guest, every servant, every fucking mouse if you have to, and send them into the ballroom, then make sure no one leaves."

Years of training ensured that Higgins did not quaver or question.

"Yes, Your Grace." He snapped to attention. "Right away, Your Grace."

Sterling found Weston, Kincaid, and Lachlan in the study where he'd left them surrounded by a haze of expensive cigar smoke. A glance at his expression and all conversation ceased at once.

"What's happened?" Kincaid said tersely.

"Aye, and why do ye have a rat on yer shoulder?" Lachlan asked in his rolling brogue.

"I think Rosemary has been kidnapped." Just saying the words out loud caused his heart to race and his palms to turn clammy. "I went to her room just now and she wasn't there, but Sir Reginald was. She'd never go anywhere without him. Not without seeing that he was properly cared for first."

"That might not be a reason to panic." Ever the cool voice of reason, Weston held up his hands. "She could be anywhere. In the parlor or the drawing room or the stables. Maybe even the pond, as Evie said she was taking Posy on a walk."

Kincaid stepped forward. "Then we'll split up and search both the inside of the manor and the grounds, then meet in the main entryway when we are done. I'll make sure the other guests are secluded in one area so that we are able to keep track of everyone."

"My valet is already doing that," said Sterling.

"Good." All business, the private detective gave a curt nod. "That's a start."

It was a start…but not an ending as their search revealed no sign of Rosemary anywhere. With every minute that ticked by, Sterling became more and more agitated. He was crawling inside his own skin with no way out and no way to find the woman that meant *everything* to him.

Rosemary was the very air that he breathed.

And he was already starting to suffocate.

They'd gathered back in the foyer. Kincaid had sent a footman to find the guest list, a small, leather-bound journal every person had been asked to sign upon entering the manor. It was to be a memento of a remarkable day. A special keepsake to look back on with fondness during the anniversaries that would follow.

When the servant returned with it, Sterling yanked the book out of his hands and began to flip through the pages with such force that several tore completely in half and fluttered to the ground.

Beside him, Evie and Joanna exchanged a worried look.

"Maybe we should–" Evie began, but he silenced her with a fierce glare.

"I need to concentrate," he snarled. "The bastard who took Rosemary is in here. I know they are. They have to be."

Another significant glance, and the American sisters wisely retreated to where their husbands stood guard in front of the door lest someone enter with news of Rosemary's whereabouts…or anyone attempted to leave. Lachlan, Brynne, Sarah, and Lord Hamlin (the only other people in attendance that Sterling trusted unequivocally) were blocking similar entrances across the rest of the manor. Everyone else had been sequestered in the grand ballroom where they remained under the careful watch of Higgins, Mrs. Thorncroft, Claire, and Lady Ellinwood, the latter of whom had already threatened to beat anyone that dared try to leave with her cane.

"What do you think?" Evie whispered to Weston.

"I think if your cousin has been kidnapped, the perpetrator wasn't foolish enough to write their name down," he replied in an equally subdued tone.

"Maybe," said Kincaid. "Maybe not. If this is the end, they might want Sterling to find out who they are. Especially if that knowledge will make him suffer all the more."

Joanna paled. "The end?" she said, grabbing his arm. "What do you mean, the *end*?"

"The end to the game they've been playing," he said grimly.

"I know who did this. I know who took her." Sterling drilled his finger into a name on the very last page. It was written sloppily and misspelled, an indication that it was written by whatever servant had been placed in charge of collecting signatures and not the actual person themself.

"Who?" Joanna and Evie asked in unison.

"Lord Aston and his wife." He waved the guest book in the air. "Were they invited?"

"The Marquess of Aston?" Weston's brow furrowed. "No, not that I recall. Evie?"

"Lord Aston? The same one you told me was responsible for..." Evie's gaze darted to Sterling, then lowered. "No. I wouldn't. I *didn't*. He should not be here."

"What do you think?" Sterling demanded of Kincaid.

"I cannot speculate as to his motivation, but the shared history is there. Your brother, the duel, and all the aftermath that followed. If he wasn't invited for the wedding, then he has no conceivable reason to be at Hawkridge..."

"Other than to harm me by hurting the woman that I love," Sterling finished harshly.

"If Lord Aston has taken Rosemary, then where has he taken her?" Joanna asked, speaking aloud the question that no one seemed capable of answering.

"All of the horses and carriages are accounted for," Weston supplied. "If he were hiding somewhere on the grounds, Drufus would have found him by now and alerted us."

Drufus was Brynne's beloved hound; a monster on four paws.

"Surely someone would have remembered seeing Rosemary if she came downstairs," said Evie. "She's the bride. The belle of the ball. No one is going to overlook her today."

Joanna frowned. "Then if she is not down here, and she's not upstairs–"

"The servants' wing," Kincaid said. "We gave it a cursory search, but–"

Sterling was already sprinting up the stairs with Sir Reginald holding on for dear life. He hit the second level at a dead run, sprinted the entire length of the hallway, and turned left to access the narrow stairway that led to the third story where the servants slept.

Here, the corridor was dimly lit with flickering wall sconces and wooden floors that creaked. Most of the doors were open, allowing him easy access into the small, neat rooms where the staff slept. All of them were the same: double beds, a set of drawers, a white porcelain wash basin.

And all of them were empty.

A dark pit of despair formed in his stomach as he searched the last and final bedroom to no avail. At the far end of the hallway, he heard the others reach the top of the stairs and begin to look as well, but it was no use. Rosemary wasn't here. She wasn't anywhere. She was just...gone. Disappeared into thin air without leaving so much as a trace.

Except that wasn't true, was it?

Because she'd left Sir Reginald.

Without warning, the squirrel leapt off his shoulder and skittered across the room to a door that Sterling hadn't noticed. A door that someone–Lord Aston–had pushed a tall armoire in front of. When Sir Reginald wiggled underneath the piece of furniture and began to scratch furiously at the door, Sterling's heart lodged itself in his throat.

"Rosemary? Rosemary!" With a single mighty shove, he sent the armoire crashing to the ground. The door was locked. He broke that as well. Damn near ripped the entire thing off its hinges. And found his wife cowering on the floor amidst a pile of crates, a rag stuffed in her mouth and her hands tied with string behind her back.

"*Rosemary.*" On a muffled groan of relief, he dropped to his knees and gathered her against his chest. There were tears in her eyes, and when he yanked the cloth out from between her teeth she cried out in pain. The sound nearly broke him. "I'm sorry. I'm sorry. I'm sorry," he repeated, over and over, as he stroked her hair, her back, her arms. Every part of her that he could reach.

"I–I was so scared," she said between choked breaths. "It was so dark. But I knew you'd find me. I knew it. I–*Sterling, watch out!*"

Her scream caused him to cover her with his body. They both fell backwards into the closet as the bullet that was intended for his skull struck the doorframe instead.

Wood splintered. After making certain that Rosemary hadn't been injured, Sterling told her to stay down before he whirled around and charged at their assailant with his shoulder lowered.

Right before he collided, he registered who had attacked them. The shock of it made him hesitate, which gave Lady Aston the split second she needed to aim her pistol and fire it a second time.

This bullet took a shallow slice of Sterling's thigh with it before it plowed into the wall. He barely acknowledged the pain through the red haze that descended over his vision. One strike of his fist on Lady Aston's forearm and the weapon she held went flying across the room. Were she a man, he would have done more. Were she a man, he would be hard-pressed not to wrap his hands around her neck. As it was, he towered over her, trembling with barely restrained fury.

"Why?" he said, unable to conjure a single plausible reason as to why she would want to do him and those he loved any harm. *"Why?"*

Lady Aston was a petite woman. The top of her head barely reached the middle of his chest. But she merely tipped her chin and met his gaze with nary a hint of remorse and more than a touch of madness. "Because Sebastian was going to marry me. He was going to marry me before he died in that silly duel that *you* drove him into."

Old, familiar guilt struck him with all the force of a bullet. Causing far more pain than the one that had just glanced off his leg. "But…but *you* accepted Lord Aston's proposal. You chose to marry him."

"To make Sebastian jealous," Lady Aston shrieked, stomping her foot like a child in the midst of a tantrum. "The engagement was supposed to make him come to his senses and stop wasting time! If not for you, I could have been a duchess. A duchess!"

She continued to scream and carry on even when Weston and Kincaid appeared to drag her away. Eventually, the sounds of her mad bellows began to fade, and then ceased altogether as she was presumably taken to another wing of the house.

"She is ill, Sterling," Rosemary said quietly, and he flinched when she linked her fingers through his. "I imagine she has been ill for a very long time. You must not blame yourself."

As his old demons gnashed their teeth and sharpened their claws, he clenched his jaw and turned his head away. "Who else is there to blame? She's right. I did drive Sebastian to that duel. Had he lived–"

"Had he lived, there is no telling what might have happened. But he didn't, and this is what we're left with." She moved in front of him. "Look at me, Sterling. *Look.*"

Bleakly, he met her gaze. And saw a thousand shining stars in the depths of all that blue-gray.

"Lady Aston is not a lesson in what might have been avoided, but an example of what can happen to a person's soul if they let bitterness and anger drown out all of their light and love. But you chose light,

Sterling. You chose love. You chose *me*." She stretched up her hand and cupped his cheek. "So choose me now. Choose us. Choose the future that's still waiting."

"I do," he said hoarsely, leaning into her palm as his demons receded into the shadows. "I always will. You saved me, little hawfinch. For that and for a thousand other reasons, I love you. Beyond reason. Beyond eternity. Beyond anything on this earth, real or imagined."

"I love you, too, Sterling." Her lips curved in a tremulous smile. "Might we go somewhere else? We need to see that your wound is tended to. And I've had my fill of small, cramped spaces for the day."

EVIE AND WESTON sent everyone home with apologies. They did not give a reason. It was not theirs to give. And while speculation ran rampant, it was obvious the Duke and Duchess of Hanover were wildly in love, and thus most assumed they merely wanted to get to the business of their wedding night.

Kincaid questioned the Marquess and Marchioness of Aston at great length. Both Sterling and Rosemary agreed it best that they not be there. The newlyweds were ready to live in the present; so long as they were no longer in any danger, they were happy to let go of the past.

Still, Kincaid–with Joanna's help–gave them a brief summary on his findings.

It appeared that Rosemary was right. Lady Aston had not been well for a number of years. In fact, her husband revealed she'd been in and out of a discreet medical facility intended for those incapable of caring for themselves due to issues of the mind. Over the last few weeks, he claimed she'd seemed better. Lucid and calm. *So* lucid and calm that he'd agreed to bring her to the wedding after she had presented him with (forged) invitations.

In trying to paint himself as an innocent party, he said that at first he'd tried to keep her at home. And when he finally did agree to take her to the wedding, it was only because she had vowed to him that she wanted to use it as an opportunity to make amends for the awful things she'd done. Including having Sterling's sister kidnapped and paying his mistress an appalling amount of money to stage her own death.

The marquess did an excellent job of painting himself as just another victim of his wife's nefarious actions. Right up until he accidentally revealed, upon further questioning, that he was the one who had blocked the door with an armoire after Lady Aston kidnapped Rosemary.

Love, he'd tearfully admitted when Joanna had demanded why he had gone along with his wife's evil scheme. He had helped her because he loved her. And he'd chosen not to see her madness for what it was because of the very same reason. Which put him in the unique position of being both a villain *and* a victim. A weak man who had followed his heart straight into ruin without any consideration for the pain that his actions–or lack thereof – would create.

It was decided that the safest place for Lady Aston was the same facility that Lord Aston had recently taken her out of (against her doctor's orders, as it turned out). He'd convinced himself that she was better because that was what *he* needed her to be. But it was readily apparent that barring a miracle, Lady Aston was going to require medical care and supervision for the rest of her life. A mind wasn't a bone to be set and, sadly, hers was twisted beyond recognition. While it couldn't be healed, perhaps, with time, it could be helped. While ensuring those she had hurt would be safe as well.

Kincaid considered bringing Lord Aston back to London and turning him over a magistrate to face charges as an accomplice in his wife's crimes. Ultimately, however, it was decided that a public trial would only create more scandal and unnecessary heartache. Instead, the marquess agreed to leave England entirely. Banishment was a harsh, but fitting punishment for a man whose entire self-worth was defined by what others thought of him. Being forced to live without the constant admiration of his peers was a prison in and of itself.

As for Rosemary and Sterling, they *did* finally get to enjoy their much anticipated wedding night. Again. And again….and again.

The next morning, they woke to a damp, drizzly day which left them with no inclination to leave their bed. Propping herself up on a mountain of pillows, Rosemary cracked a yawn (neither of them had gotten much sleep) and giggled when Sir Reginald leapt up onto the bed and promptly made himself a comfortable nest in between the two newlyweds.

"He's in my spot," Sterling said, eyeing the squirrel with narrowed eyes.

She scratched Sir Reginald between his ears. "He doesn't think so."

Grumbling, Sterling crossed his arms. "How long do these things live?"

"According to recent scientific findings summarized in *Gardner's Chronicle*, with the right care and in an environment free from predators, squirrels have the potential to live…forever, really." Only the twinkle in Rosemary's gaze indicated she was jesting.

But Sterling found no amusement in her words. Just a deep, profound gratitude.

"The rat saved your life," he said gruffly. "Forever sounds good to me."

EPILOGUE

"I STOPPED IN to visit Evie the other day," Rosemary began. As they did every morning since returning from their honeymoon on the coast of France where they had played in the ocean like children during the day and committed a blush-inducing number of wicked sensual acts by night, she and Sterling were having breakfast together.

It was a wonderful way to start the day. Some mornings they spoke at great length. Other mornings they were quiet, content to bask in each other's company while they drank their coffee or read the paper or simply gazed out the window at the falling rain. Most of all, it was a time to be appreciative for everything that they had. The most important of which was each other.

For as long as she lived, Rosemary would never forget the terror she'd felt when she was locked in that closet. Unable to see. Unable to move. How frightened she had been! But in hindsight, after the initial shock of the entire ordeal had faded, she came to realize that her fear hadn't stemmed from dying. Rather, she'd been afraid of losing Sterling. Of losing *this*.

This beautiful life that they had created.

That they *were* creating.

One morning at a time.

Nudging his plate aside, Sterling rested his elbows on the table.

"How is the mother-to-be?"

"My feet are as fat as potatoes," Evie had moaned as she'd laid in the parlor with a damp rag draped across her temple. *"My belly is the size of a watermelon. I run out of breath walking up the steps, and I cannot go twenty minutes before rushing into the water closet. Carrying a baby is awful. Whoever says otherwise is not to be trusted."*

Rosemary bit the inside of her cheek. "In excellent health and good spirits. Glowing, really."

"Is that so?" Sterling said with a great deal of skepticism. "Because Weston mentioned that she tried to kill him with a fire poker when he offered to bring her a glass of water."

"I, ah, believe the fire poker slipped."

"Yes, but why was she holding one in the first place?"

"To kill Weston," Rosemary sighed. "But in Evie's defense, she has terrible aim."

"That's not a defense, it's an admission of guilt."

"I believe she may be finding childbearing more difficult than she anticipated."

Sterling snorted. "I'd certainly not want to do it."

"How fortunate, then, that you won't have to," Rosemary said with equal amounts of exasperation and amusement. "Evie did ask me a question that I found interesting, however. Especially since I didn't have an answer to give her."

"Was it how many times you can achieve climax in under ten minutes?" Sterling said seriously. "Because I've been giving that a great deal of thought since the last time we–"

"No," she hissed, her cheeks blooming with color. And even though she knew they were alone in the front parlor, she couldn't help but take a surreptitious glance around the room. "And not that it is pertinent to this conversation in any way, shape, or form, but I believe the number you're searching for is three. Surely no more than that."

Sterling nodded in satisfaction. "Challenge accepted."

"Scoundrel," she murmured into her cup as she took a sip of coffee.

"Absolutely." Lifting his fork, he absentmindedly reached onto her plate and stabbed a roasted potato. "What was the question?"

"Evie wanted to know where we plan to maintain our primary residence after the winter is over. Here, in London, or at Hanover Park. Knowing your feelings about that place, I wasn't sure what to tell her. I'd just as soon stay in Mayfair. It's close to my grandmother and not too far from Joanna and Kincaid. But…"

"But you like the country," he said, studying her closely.

"I do." She set her coffee on the table. "So does Sir Reginald. And when we have children someday, I'd like them to have room to run and play and explore. A place for them to call home. For all of us to call home."

"Then I may have the perfect solution. I know a man. Thomas Edison. Friendly chap. He's an inventor of sorts. Something to do with telegraphy. Seems he's found a way to send two simultaneous telegraph messages on the same wire, if you can believe it. Anyway, apparently he's quite successful in America and wants to make a name for himself abroad, starting here in England."

"He sounds fascinating. How did you two meet?" Rosemary asked curiously, as an inventor wasn't exactly the sort of person that her husband was generally known to associate with.

Sterling helped himself to another potato. "I accidentally attended a lecture he gave at Breton Hall a few years ago, and we've maintained a general correspondence ever since. I happened to receive a letter from him yesterday, and have been contemplating what my response will be. What *our* response will be."

"How does someone accidentally attend a lecture?" She picked up her own fork and pointed the tines at him. "And what's wrong with your potatoes?"

"Nothing," he said cheerfully. "I just like the way your nose crinkles when I steal yours. I went to Breton Hall because I was told there would be dancing ladies. A false lead, if you can believe it. By the time I figured out what was happening, Edison was already speaking, and as I'd made sure to have a front row seat…"

"You couldn't sneak out," she surmised.

"I had to sit there and *learn* something. It was awful. Not to say Edison was awful. He's actually a very dynamic lecturer. I only fell asleep once the whole time, and just for a few minutes. If you asked my professors at Eton, I think that's a record."

Her lips twitched at the corners. "What does all this have to do with where we are going to live?"

"Ah, right." Sterling straightened in his chair. "As I said, Edison would like to come to England. To make the trip worth it, he plans on staying for six months. Maybe longer. But he has a young wife, and children, and doesn't want to be away from them for that long. I thought we might offer him and his family the manor in Grosvenor Square. If the *ton* were under the impression that the Duke and Duchess of Hanover are his benefactors–"

"–then they'd take him seriously, and want to invest their money in his inventions," Rosemary finished.

Her husband grinned. "Precisely. I also thought, given that my aversion to Hanover Park is not likely to change, we might sell off the entire estate."

Sell it?

She'd never been to Sterling's ancestral home. Had never seen so much as a painting of the grounds. And she understood why he didn't want it. Why some ghosts loomed too large to ever be completely vanquished. But it was still his family home. The place where he and his brother, and father, and grandfather, and great-grandfather had all been born.

"I fear that may be a decision you'll come to regret," she said gently. "And once gone, it might prove impossible to get it back."

"I've considered that as well."

Her brows drew together. "You've been considering a great deal, haven't you?"

"I almost lost you, Rosemary." When his voice hoarsened, he shoved his chair away from the table and came to kneel beside her, his hand resting on her thigh and his gray eyes gazing beseechingly into hers. "If that experience taught me anything, it's that life is short and precious and you cannot waste time dwelling on anything that does not bring you happiness. Hanover Park does not bring me happiness. It won't bring *us* happiness, to live in a place that feels like it belongs to someone else. Which is why I want to let the entailment expire and sell it...for the grand sum of one hundred pounds to Sarah and that poor fool she has wrapped around her little finger. They're already living there. Lord Hamlin is a good, solid man. He'll be a good caretaker. Better than I've been, at any rate. This way, it will remain in the family, and one day pass on to Sebastian's future nephew or niece. I think..." Sterling cleared his throat. "I think he would like that."

"I think he would love it." Brushing an ebony curl out of the way, she kissed his temple. "Then we'll remain here. And visit Hawkridge Manor should we need a dose of country air. I'm sure Evie and Weston would be happy to receive us."

Sterling tipped his head back. "Not *exactly*."

"What, then? Need I remind you that we've just about run out of houses." Her mouth curved. "If we give or sell this one away, we might be forced to move in with my grandmother and Mrs. Thorn-croft."

"Don't jest like that," he said, grimacing. "It's bad for my digestion. Besides, I've a particular fondness for this house. If you'll recall, it's the first place I brought you to orgasm. That alone is reason enough to keep it. No, I thought we might build new."

"Build new," she repeated, bemused. "What does that mean?"

"It means buying virgin land and building something that's never been there before. A house, an entire estate, without ghosts or tragic stories of the past or a history that isn't our own. Someplace where we can make our own past and create our own future." He covered her hand with his. "Together."

"And Sir Reginald," she said earnestly.

Sterling sighed. "Heaven forbid we forget the rat."

"For the *last* time–"

He kissed her. Slowly. Sensually. Until she'd all but slid off her chair and onto his lap, her entire body quivering with unspoken desire as need pooled in her belly. One touch was all it took to ignite the flames of desire that simmered between them. That had always simmered, even when she was a stuttering wallflower and he was a dissolute scoundrel.

In some ways, they were still those people. Petals on a flower that remained even as it blossomed into something brighter, something bigger, something unimaginably beautiful.

There were going to be times, she was almost certain, when the flower would wilt, or the soil would become too dry, or the leaves would fall. It was going to take patience, and care, and gentle tending to ensure that the flower bloomed year after year. But the reward was worth the work. Especially when the reward was a charming duke who loved every inch of her, inside and out.

"–Sir Reginald is not a rat," she finished weakly when the kiss finally ended. Her lashes fluttered to find Sterling gazing at her with such tenderness that it made her eyes sting. Blinking away happy tears, she poked him on the shoulder. "He belongs to the *Sciuridae* family, as you well know."

"A rat with a furry tail is still a rat." Sterling playfully tapped her nose when her cheeks began with puff with indignation. "But I suppose we can bring him along. In the meantime..." Lowering his head, he pressed his mouth to the sensitive spot right behind her ear and murmured, "Let's get started on that challenge, shall we?"

THE END

About the Author

Jillian Eaton grew up in Maine and now lives in Pennsylvania on a farmette with her husband and their three boys. They share the farm with a cattle dog, an old draft mule, a thoroughbred, and a mini-donkey—all rescues. When she isn't writing, Jillian enjoys spending time with her animals, gardening, reading, and going on long walks with her family.